STRAY DOG WINTER

A NOVEL BY DAVID FRANCIS

STRAY DOG WINTER

A NOVEL BY DAVID FRANCIS

MACADAM CAGE

MacAdam/Cage
155 Sansome Street, Suite 550
San Francisco, CA 94104
www.MacAdamCage.com

Library of Congress Cataloging-in-Publication Data
Francis, David, 1958-
  Stray dog winter / David Francis.
      p. cm.
ISBN 978-1-59692-315-7
I. Title.
PR9619.4.F73S77 2008
823'.92–dc22

                                          2008030001

Selection from Untitled Poem by Anna Akhmatova from *THE STRAY
DOG CABARET: A BOOK OF RUSSIAN POEMS* translated by Paul
Schmidt, © 2007 by the Estate of Paul Schmidt, used by permission of
New York Review Books(NYREV, Inc.).

Selection from *Winter Skies* by Boris Paternak, translated by Eugene M.
Kayden. All attempts have been made to locate the owner of copyright
material. If you have any information in that regard please contact the
publisher directly.

Printed in the United States of America
1 2 3 4 5 6 7 8 9 10

Graphic design by Dorothy Carico Smith

IN MEMORY OF MARY BRIGHT

☆

Why is this age worse than all the others? Perhaps
in this: it has touched the point of putrefaction,
Touched it in a rush of pain and sorrow,
But cannot make it whole.

In the west the familiar light still shines
And the spires of the cities glow in the sun.
But here a dark figure is marking the houses
and calling the ravens, and the ravens come.

Anna Akhmatova, from *The Stray Dog Cabaret*

February 1984

He arrived in winter on a sleeper from Prague and the sound of the train went *boogedy boogedy—what do you want, Darcy Bright? Darcy Bright, what do you want?* He pressed his open hand against the shivering window and the edges of the sky seemed unnaturally close. A figure trudging alone in a snow-beaded field with a scythe. A scarved woman behind a wooden fence shaded her face as if there were sunlight. A row of sheets hung flat behind her, mute as teeth, and a pair of what looked like silver foxes capered in the snow. Darcy pulled up his Pentax and snapped a quick shot, feeling foreign, unaccountable. I could paint that, he thought, then he noticed the food-seller watching from the dark and noisy space between compartments. Darcy lowered the camera, smiled. *The meaningless incidents present the most danger*, that's what Dostoyevsky said. Fodor's *Moscow & Leningrad* just said *don't take photos of anything strategic.*

He pulled his faux-fur Kenzo coat about himself and leaned back against the cold metal railing, trying to appear unconcerned. He was accustomed to being noticed, his skin paper-thin, his sculpted lips. He was too pretty for this train. Men often wondered, at first glance, if he were a man, while others knew intuitively and still they stared. But men here stared for different reasons; afraid of themselves, suspicious of everyone. The weight of it sat in their faces.

It was morning and Darcy was somewhere outside Kiev, wondering at being in an alien place so quickly, three weeks since the crackle of Fin's first telephone call. Amid the echoes she'd told him how Moscow felt weird and great, but she was lonely. He'd thought of her as many things but never that, not lonely.

The train shunted through a town. Prefab tenements shaped like horseshoes, smoke gushing up from a towering Ukrainian chimney merged with a tattletale sky. Darcy took a pull from his Polish cigarette and felt the warm smoke curl inside him, imagined his throat staining dark. He slid the icy window down and flicked his half-done Popularne onto the tracks. One cigarette and a hot nudge of wind could burn a million acres where he came from, but the ground was frozen here.

Fin had left Melbourne unexpectedly in late September, just over four months earlier. A commission to paint the industrial landscapes of Moscow, announced as though people often did that. But Darcy was the one with the painterly hand; she'd only done abstracts and that political installation she'd called *The Burning of the Witch-Hunt Manuals*. Books in an incinerator. Some at the opening seemed incensed, but she'd tried to convince them it was just about *The Malleus Maleficarum*. It was a book, she'd said, but Darcy'd never heard of it.

The corridor rattled around him. A horse-drawn hay cart waited at a muddy level crossing, the horse unfazed, its nose just feet from the train. Darcy opened the window a slit for relief from the smell of onions and the breath of an Albanian who boarded in Warsaw in the middle of the night and kept putting on more socks beneath his sandals then guarding his bag on the seat. He'd shown Darcy where he'd travelled from, rimy fingers on a tiny scrunched-up map. A country south of Yugoslavia.

From the corridor, Darcy now snapped a picture through the bobbing doorway, the Albanian from his knees down, the wrinkled bottoms of his pants. Darcy imagined a photo essay—'Cold War Feet'—then felt a chill and cinched his coat, aware of the leather money belt girthed against his groin: a calfskin cover with a pocket for passport and cash. It had arrived at his flat in St Kilda, delivered with the tickets inside: Qantas to London, Lufthansa from Heathrow to Prague. Fin had kept phoning him, asked if he'd received his birthday present, but she knew he wasn't born in December. There was no card.

Why the money belt? he'd asked.

Just bring it with you, she'd told him through the echo, an insistence in her voice.

Don't have me packing treats, he'd said. It was their nickname for hallucinogens. But there was no special sleeve in it, no space for anything secret.

Trust me, she'd told him. He'd always been leery of those two words, but if he didn't trust her he didn't trust anyone. He explained how he'd just been accepted for the fine arts course at Sydney Uni, the graduate program beginning in March, but she'd persuaded him to defer, seduced him as usual. Come paint here, she'd said, I need you…we'll have fun. Then she'd hung up. And Darcy knew he would go as much as he knew he shouldn't; he'd been plotting his escape since he was nine and there in his hands was a free ticket out, to a place without the new gay cancer, with barely a capitalist, barely an Australian. A place you weren't supposed to go, where there would be unfamiliar vistas to paint; *tramontane*, was that the word? And anyway, for Fin he would have gone anywhere.

The train slipped into a tunnel and Darcy glimpsed himself in the window, his epicene features chequered by the blur of stones that passed in the dark. Don't be paranoid or even inconspicuous, she'd said. It only works against you. Spike your hair and be yourself.

His hair had grown in fair already, no dark streaks from where she'd dyed it; his pierced nostril healed over since she'd been gone. She'd taken him to Brunswick Street to have his nose pierced while they were still at Monash Uni, the day she announced she'd changed her name to Dobrolyubova, by statutory declaration, so their names were suddenly different. The surname of some dead Russian intellectual she'd told him, while Darcy was who he'd always been. But now, on this train panting north through the white-flurried snow, he couldn't wait to be back in her orbit; that sense of entitlement that came with their parallel youth and allure, how they looked oddly alike, and how, together, they moved through the world with a false imperviousness, gliding on tracks of their own.

She'd advised him to carry something obvious for the guards to confiscate. It's good to be naïve, she'd said. At the Soviet border an inspector tore up Darcy's *Newsweek* with Reagan on the cover, but they also took his Turgenev, *Sketches from a Hunter's Album*. It had made him more nervous than he'd imagined. He thought they'd be pleased he was reading a Russian, but English was as foreign to that inspector as the Cyrillic signs thrumming by on the railway platforms were to Darcy. Small stone houses, side by side. It could have been a hundred years earlier. Darcy didn't need Turgenev—he was seeing it live.

The food-seller in his pinstriped waistcoat wedged the trolley against a door. On his cart stood Polish vodka, chunks of cheese and crackers in plastic, something like Saltines. A shot of vodka held a certain promise, but he'd given up drinking after Fin had left. It had been easier than expected. It was encounters with strangers that rattled him still, compelled him. In Prague men mostly watched the ground, living behind their eyes, but as he'd waited alone on a bench in the railway station, a strong-jawed Slavic boy in uniform caught his eye square on, so knowingly, and Darcy found himself following. Darcy who'd promised Fin he'd abstain, who'd promised himself, but the uniform had triggered him somehow, its crispness, and all he could manage was to keep the money belt hidden as the young man rested his military cap on the cistern and kneeled. Darcy pressed his fingers into the thick wheaten hair, abandoned himself to the crud-covered ceiling, imagined it as a porcelain sky.

The sound of a siren at a crossing. The Albanian buying soup from the food-seller's cart and, unhurried, sipping it direct from the bowl, his face rutted as a quarry. But for his fez, it could have been the face of an Australian farmer. A silver ring embedded on his swollen wedding finger. Darcy pictured a stark Albanian life, eking out an existence there, problems that seemed an epoch from his own.

The vendor pushed the trolley past with an expression that bore the blankness of obedience. Darcy's underarms ached in the cold, his nerve endings raw. And this was supposed to be one of the mildest Soviet winters on record.

Fin had advised him to get out of Melbourne quietly and he'd left without telling a soul, not even his mother.

That part was easy—he rarely told anyone much—but now the train guard, not the food-seller, observed him from between compartments, balancing where the carriages shifted on their couplings; the guard who still held Darcy's passport because there'd been no transit stamp for Poland. Who knew Poland would appear in the night between Prague and Moscow? Fin had never mentioned this. It made him wonder if she knew what she was doing. Tell them you're staying with me, she'd said, let them think I'm your girlfriend. They'd always been lovers of a kind, their spirit collusive, incestuous. The way she'd cleaved their family apart had somehow sewn the two of them inexorably closer. And still the train guard, unkempt and woolly in the fashion of Trotsky, stared.

Darcy breathed out a misty flute of air and stepped back inside the compartment. He prayed for Fin's bright face at the station, enveloped in fur, her red karakul coat a flame in the crowd.

Mount Eliza, Autumn 1972

Darcy heard tyres on the gravel the afternoon Fin first arrived in Mount Eliza; a taxi edging up the drive. He watched through the sitting-room window, from between the high-backed chairs, as a girl emerged in an African print dress. Darcy recognised the woman she was with from photos—Aunt Merran, his mother's younger sister, the one who'd gone back to live on the orange grove near Montecito, somewhere in California, where Darcy's mother grew up.

Out on the drive, where the gumnuts fell on the gravel and you could smell the eucalyptus, Aunt Merran gave Darcy's father a quick peck on the cheek, but his father didn't move his face towards it. The girl observed Darcy in the window, a frozen moment, his feet stuck to the carpet. She looked like him, but her ears were pierced with glinting silver studs—like a gypsy, his mother would have said, but luckily she wasn't home, just the girl presenting his father with a small wooden carving from the pocket of her dress. A gift received awkwardly, his father glancing back at the window, his free hand around the back of his neck as he saw Darcy watching, squinting through the glare.

Aunt Merran kissed the girl's hair and jumped back in the taxi before his father could stop her. She waved through the back window as the girl stood stunned and then came to life, chasing the car to the gate. Darcy's handsome flummoxed father hurried behind her as the taxi turned onto Baden Powell Drive. His father's arm about the girl and then he was kneeling, consoling her, his big hands on her small shoulders like calipers, holding her there.

Aunt Merran's taxi was gone, back to Humphries Road, towards Frankston and the suburbs, a knapsack left in the gravel like a small dead animal. While his father comforted the girl near the gate, Darcy crept out and collected it. The smell was stale and sweet. A pair of sandshoes, washed so the dust had yellowed them, a sweatshirt that had *Banana Slugs* written across it in yellow and a T-shirt that said *Big Sur*. In the front pocket was a blue American passport with an eagle in the coat of arms. Los Angeles Passport Agency and a photo of the girl with her hair loose. Finola Bright, the same last name as Darcy's. Born 13 June 1960. A year before him. She was eleven and he was ten. He blinked to himself as the fact of it crystallised in him. Their mothers were sisters. Their father was the same.

As Darcy looked up, he saw the girl's narrow shape at the end of the drive beside his crouching father. The sun was getting red as it lowered in the gum trees behind them. A secret had been delivered.

Moscow, Sunday evening

The platform of the Byelorussian Station was under a cavernous Quonset hut, bleak and foreign, not the elaborate halls Darcy'd seen in photos, no *Stalin's underground cathedrals*. Standing on the cold train steps, waiting for his passport from the guard, he nervously scanned the sea of shapeless coats for Fin's, anticipating her luminous face.

Fin's hair had been redder than usual when he'd seen her last, but the only red here was in frosted banners that hung from the porticos, stiff in the breeze. People's heads were well-covered, purple lips and pallid faces crowned in fur hats, enveloped by scarves and turned-up collars. It was colder than Prague, if that were possible. He'd read that if you cried in the streets in a Moscow winter your eyes might well freeze over. Where was she?

He put on his Ray-Bans to shield the sting and hitched his backpack over his arms; the money belt dug into his hip like an injury. The bearded train guard handed the Albanian a passport but offered Darcy nothing. With flat open gloves, Darcy gestured politely in the shape of a book. My passport? he asked. His was Australian for God's sake, an innocuous country.

The guard just scowled, not understanding, then picked up Darcy's duffel from the platform and hefted it. Special treatment, thought Darcy, unsure if he should be relieved. He pulled his woollen beanie down and followed,

the glacial cement seeping through the soles of his Blund-
stones like chilblains, the air infected by a heavy smell of
diesel and an icy staleness, distorted announcements
screeching through loudspeakers. He rubber-necked for
Fin as they shoved past a counter selling grease-papered
sausages, lines of steaming people queuing for tickets to
places whose names he couldn't read, then the guard held
open an iron door and motioned him inside. A sudden
claustrophobic heat, an office with a sepia photo of Lenin
hanging half in shadow, bearded chin jutting like a shovel.
The guard dumped Darcy's duffel on the floor and lazily
saluted a puffy-necked inspector, handed Darcy's passport
over. The guard retreated out the door and Darcy glared
after him, betrayed, folded his arms with mock impatience
and searched for traces of Fin through the window.

The inspector, spit gleaming between his grey teeth,
picked at the edge of the passport photo. Darcy's hair cut
shorter in the picture, still streaked back then, but his eyes
were surely the same, keen and unmistakable, the femi-
nine aspect to his features. He pulled his Ray-Bans off and
met the guard's expression as if unintimidated, a sinking
awareness of how the photo was only glued on; typically
Australian, he thought. An instinct to run welled up as
the inspector read from a slip of morse-coded paper.
Examining the photo, he sucked his teeth as if wondering
what sort of creature would streak his sandy hair black.
He looked up with bloodshot eyes and launched into a
throaty lecture in what Darcy sensed was an attempt at
French.

J'attends mon amie, Darcy interrupted, an attempt of
his own, but he realised charm would get him nowhere.
He pulled Fin's address from his coat pocket and placed it

on the desk. *Dobrolyubova, 13-211 Ulitsa Kazakov, Moscow.* The guard shaped the letters carefully, copying them onto the morse-coded paper, and Darcy felt the depth of his foreignness, the absence of language like dry ice sticking to his tongue.

Welcome to Moscow, the words from behind him like manna, and with them a rush of cold air. And there she was, signature red lipstick against pearl-white skin, eyes glistening beneath their hooded lids. In the nick of time, as if she did it half on purpose. The inspector gazed up, took her in, her features slightly elfin, slightly shark-like, her eyes as green as Darcy's were blue. She glowered at Darcy as if to say: *what the fuck?* A brown fur hat with a grass-green brim and a leather patchwork sheepskin coat he hadn't seen before. Better late than not at all, he whispered, his voice a shadow of itself. She ungloved and spread a slender hand on the edge of the inspector's desk. She spoke to him fluently, tilting her head. A gesture she and Darcy had in common—or had he picked it up from her? The timbre of her voice lower in Russian, sultrier, perhaps not just from smoking, but studied, unfaltering. Just three years of Russian at Monash and barely five months here. A gift for languages he didn't have.

The inspector improved his posture, responded, and Fin translated. A message sent ahead by the train conductor: photos taken. She cocked her head again, but this time she was imitating, gripping the fur ends of her scarf. He wants to examine your camera, she said.

Darcy reluctantly unzipped the pocket of his backpack and fished out his Pentax leaf-shutter sports model, three hundred dollars from Tom the Cheap in Dandenong. I took a shot of a woman in a field, he said.

She must have been strategic, said Fin, extending a hand. Her nails were painted a foresty brown.

She handed the camera over to the inspector, smoothed him along with quiet conversation, the guttural language seemed to lilt from her lips, while he fiddled with the camera until the back clicked open, a shining roll of undeveloped pictures released onto the arm of his chair. Darcy mourned shots of Albanian feet, foxes frolicking in snow through the smoky train window, the endless steppe. Fin turned to Darcy with a cool, false calm, retying her scarf. We can go, she said.

He still has my passport.

She eyed Darcy intently. Later, she said, teeth gritted, then flashed a sharp, pained smile. I need my passport, he said, stubborn now, but she grabbed his arm. We'll come back.

Fin waved to her new inspector friend as he watched her from his office doorway, still holding Darcy's camera. Her seduction had currency here. The Albanian stood nearby, his socks bulging through the straps of his sandals. Darcy paused to acknowledge him but Fin took his arm. Don't say anything, she whispered, the warmth of her breath in his ear.

Out in the cold, among the crowd of commuters and blaring announcements, they hugged each other hard. The familiar musk of her Prince Matchabelli, her cold sepulchral cheek. As she held her narrow frame to his, Darcy felt his loneliness transcended; in her strength and frailness he knew why he'd come.

☆

The night fell quickly, swathed in fog. The taxi driver hunched low against the door, eating as he drove. It smelled like herring. Fin produced a pack of Gauloises and patted the box, offered Darcy one. After all, it's Europe, she said. Sort of. Darcy cupped his hands over her flame, uncertain if it was a reward or consolation. Her lighter was covered in hammers and sickles, and she smoked with a small black cigarette holder, a new affectation. She rotated the slim silver ring in her nostril.

I can't believe you let him keep my passport.

Don't be too chatty, she said. She motioned with her chin at the driver, but Darcy sensed it as an excuse. I needed a transit visa for Poland, he added, then he saw the driver's eyes brush across the rear-view mirror and fell silent. He looked out at the bluish sprays from occasional street lamps, the red tentacles of the tail-lights.

You'll need to be careful, said Fin, her lips left slightly parted as she returned the cigarette to them.

You were the one who told me it was good to seem naïve.

Not *that* naïve, she said, smiling.

Darcy stared out at the grim-looking people, eyes down as they crossed at the lights. I was only taking photos of the countryside, he said.

I know, she said. I'm just glad you're here. She placed her fleece-lined fingers over his ski gloves but his hand felt unsteady. He'd always assumed he was expert at being out of his element, he'd always been that, but he'd never been this far away.

This is my home, said Fin, as though gleaning an aspect of his thought. Sometimes it seemed they didn't need to speak at all. She gazed out as if the darkness held some private fascination. She seemed different here, somehow uneasy; she usually found everything funny. Darcy was used to sharing adventures with her, the secrets only she knew, but now he decided he wouldn't mention his encounter in the station in Prague, how he'd felt jangled by it, the glazed collusion in the soldier boy's eyes, how easily it had skewered him. But that had been Prague and this was Moscow. He promised himself again.

It's great you're here, said Fin, giving him a weary but grateful smile. He wondered why she'd said it twice. As the taxi turned to cross the river, Darcy caught their twin reflections mirrored in the window, two sides of a coin. Almost thirteen years since he'd first seen her on the drive in Mount Eliza. When she was young her hair had been untidy and long, so fair it was almost white, blonder than his. Now it was cropped, orange hints of it poking from beneath her fur hat. Her freckles had faded to silk. A slight masculinity in the set of her mouth, a firmness. He was tempted to reach over and touch her face.

The bridge seemed foolishly wide and foreboding, statues of heroes. Fog hung in layers through a light that shed like a scrim on the river, the ice glistened black like shards of coal. See the Kremlin, said Fin, turning.

Behind them, he made out the vague misted beams from towers. The driver coughed into a handkerchief, skirted a street sign fallen onto the road. The fabric of the city is fraying, said Fin, as though she'd lived here since the time of Stalin. The way her eyes held the distance without squinting.

Do you have a man here? he asked.

In lieu of an answer she drew deeply from her cigarette and blew two quick smoke rings in Darcy's direction, pointed to the distant gates of Gorky Park. On a clear night you can see the lights of the Ferris wheel above the trees, she said.

They turned into a street that was narrower than the grand boulevards, and darker, rimmed by low-rise apartments: Ulitsa Kazakov. The taxi parked outside a red brick building with curved art deco corners. Old-fashioned, iron-framed guillotine windows. Three storeys high with an identical block beside it: her brave new world. Is it a special place for foreigners? asked Darcy.

If I'd wanted to live with Australians I'd have stayed there, she said. They didn't quite think of themselves as Australian, their mothers from California, but that didn't make Fin or Darcy feel American either. They came from a country of their own. It had two inhabitants.

Fin negotiated the fare while Darcy unloaded. It seemed the driver wanted extra for carrying bags he hadn't handled. Fin gave him a note and dismissed him in an off-hand way that reminded Darcy of his mother.

As the taxi receded through the slush, the mist iced Darcy's face, dampening his cigarette, and then the street was quiet save for the whining of lorries from a main road, the buzz of the overhead wires. Fin was silent too as they followed a side path to a raised courtyard littered with snow, up some stairs that whistled with cold. He'd never imagined this kind of cold.

In the corridor, the burgundy carpet was black along the edges from damp, the smell of cabbage boiling, urine-stained walls. A man stood at the end where there wasn't a light. I expected a babushka at a desk, said Darcy.

Fin unlocked a deadbolt and top lock; the door had two utility handles. A large broken sign was nailed in her entry hall, oxidised Cyrillic letters. That's cool, said Darcy.

From a demolition.

The apartment was stuffy, the smell of burnt oil and vegetables. He plonked down his pack and duffel. An ancient Bakelite radio played softly on an end table beside a worn velvet couch draped in a swirled blue sheet. He hoped he wasn't sleeping there.

You can't turn down the central heating, said Fin. She didn't switch on the lights.

Through the window a woman stood in a kitchen in the building opposite, not thirty feet away. She didn't look up as Fin forced the window slightly open. I call her Svet-lana, said Fin.

Why aren't there curtains? asked Darcy.

They get taken down.

By whom?

It's hard to know.

He followed her into a bedroom without windows. A poster from the 1980 Olympics, five rings like halos above an image of Brezhnev. He looks like Gargie, said Darcy, except for the eyebrows. Fin didn't answer. She never acknowledged his grandmother as her own, but it wasn't just that. She was preoccupied. She closed the bedroom door behind them, then turned on the bedside lamp.

Above the bed hung long black peasant dresses on wooden hangers, empty cigarette boxes pinned on their fronts among white-painted quotes from Tolstoy. I thought you were painting smokestacks, said Darcy.

Fin unwound her scarf, watched him with eyes that almost seemed blue in the light. I thought you might help me with that.

Whatever you like, he said hopefully. I came to be

with you. He lay his gloves on the end of the bed as if claiming a place. It would be cool to make art here, he said. He foresaw the shapes of chemical factories and power stations, grain elevators thrusting into the skies.

Fin's pillows were stained; she must have dyed her hair and slept with it wet. Blood on the pillows, he said. Nice. A T-shirt lay on the covers—the logo read *Keep Holland Beautiful: Get Tattooed*. He wondered how it was she'd been to Holland.

Show me your tattoo, he said; he imagined a rose engraved on her ankle or a red star on her shoulderblade. But she wasn't in a playful mood.

It was a gift, she said.

He wasn't sure if she meant the trip, the tattoo or the T-shirt. She pointed at his waist, extending a brown ungloved fingernail. I have to return your girdle, she whispered. It belongs to a friend. She hadn't taken off her coat or hat.

Darcy felt a stab of suspicion. It was my belated birthday present, he said. You have to return it *now*?

She nodded, her finger pressed to her lips with such intensity it unnerved him. She wasn't fooling. He unbuckled the money belt, fishing his bundle of roubles from the front. Coins left from Prague, his ANZ Visa card and international driver's licence. He dangled the plain leather belt by the strap and for a moment it hung in the air between them. Maybe there was a sleeve sewn in the back of it, he couldn't tell; maybe he'd been her pack mule after all. She grabbed it and hitched it under her coat as if she was used to attaching the fastener. Stay here, she said. She grabbed her scarf and gloves and left, bolting the front door behind her.

Mount Eliza, Autumn 1972

When Darcy's mother appeared in the Vauxhall at the end of the drive, Darcy dropped the knapsack. His father stood by the girl, motionless, as if in a painting, while Darcy's mother stared, putting pieces together. She saw what she saw and then she was shouting. Darcy dropped the girl's bag and hid where he always hid, inside his dead grandmother's little blue car, a bubble-shaped Austin of England parked behind the shed.

He heard the Vauxhall door slam, the kitchen flywire, the fridge opening, the flywire again. She'd have her Gilbey's and tonic in her hand. She'd sit in her folding beach chair around the side where the incinerator smoked against the chestnut tree, and drink. And her mind would be working so hard you could almost see it in the veins that reddened her forehead.

Darcy could still see the girl, she was down in the gravel now, wouldn't budge, even as Darcy's father tried to drag her up to the house. In the end his father just left her there and walked up alone. He didn't look at Darcy in the Austin, just veered off to Darcy's mother and her drink.

Darcy leaned back in the seat, a moment of silence. He imagined them there, beside the burning leftovers, his father mumbling admissions, and then she was yelling again. Darcy furiously practised the gears, his legs straining to reach the pedals, doubling the clutch like his father did on the Humphries Road hill. Another round of shouts and he closed his eyes tight, the way he did to avoid the sound of her *battle fatigue*. That's what she called it.

When he opened his eyes, the girl was standing at the passenger door, watching. She held the knapsack to her chest, her face set. They heard glass breaking, and she turned towards the sound. In the sharpness of her profile and her hooded eyes, Darcy saw both his mother and his aunt, but mostly he saw himself. And then he realised she was waiting for him to open the door and he wondered if that's what she was used to.

She got in warily, sat on the vinyl seat and rummaged around in her knapsack as if making sure everything was still there. Darcy looked out across the drive. The sun was now shimmering through the flowering gums, setting down molten somewhere over Davies Bay. What's it like where you come from? he asked. He'd tried to picture it from photos in the *National Geographic*; the presidents carved into rocks, the bridges extending over the bays.

She looked at him askance. The sunsets are better, she said. Her accent was different from his, like from television. She touched the knob on the glove compartment.

That's private, said Darcy. He hid things in there: the Risen Jesus pamphlet and the Book of Mormon from the missionary, Jesus in the Americas, his grandmother's travelling clock.

So's my bag, said the girl.

He didn't dare look at her, played with the worn leather cover on the gear stick. I just wanted to know who you were, he said.

Satisfied?

Darcy tried to catch reverse but he could never quite get it up and over. You're my sister, he said.

Kind of, she said.

I never heard of you. He played with the plastic dinosaur that dangled from the key chain. You'll have to sleep inside, he said. On the foldaway. He figured he'd spend the night out here in the back seat, under the picnic blanket. He might need to sleep in the car forever; his mother was screeching like a parrot.

I'm not staying, said the girl, looking down the drive. She just dropped me off for a visit. But Darcy could see how the girl braced her eyes and cheeks to hold back tears. Then Darcy's father appeared with his sheepish face and a drink.

Is he your father? asked the girl.

Darcy nodded as if it was obvious. Who do you think he is?

When his father got to the car they were silent. His father's mid-section through the passenger window, his *penal colony* Darcy's mother called it, the cause of all the problems.

The girl opened the door and took the glass suspiciously, gulped it down then let the glass drop on the bricks so it shattered. She knew about *accidentally on purpose* as if she'd learned from Darcy's mother.

Darcy's father said nothing, knelt down and picked up the shards of glass, feeling on the ground to find them. He stood with the splinters of glass cupped in his hands. Naughty, he said, heading back towards the incinerator.

It was only cordial, said Darcy.

The girl ignored him at first, reached into the back seat and pulled Darcy's picnic blanket through, wrapped herself inside it like a big woollen scarf. My mother says he's a bastard anyway, she said. She glared out from the blanket, and even though she'd just arrived she made Darcy feel disloyal.

He got out and went to the Vauxhall, picked up the grocery bag his mother had abandoned, along with her mohair picnic blanket, brought them back to the Austin. He tore the silver top of the milk bottle free and passed the bottle to the girl, then he ripped open the ginger nut biscuits.

Another episode of shrieking from the side of the house.

What do you do here? asked the girl.

Sometimes I drive, said Darcy nonchalantly. He now let off the parking brake and they rolled a few inches. I don't have a licence for night-time, he added.

The girl looked over at him like he was an idiot and it made him feel young. The fact was, since the day he ran into the ti-trees on Baden Powell Drive he'd been banned from driving. Since the day he met the missionary.

He peeled a mandarin, threw the pith out the window, and handed a decent section to the girl. As she ate it, she leaned against the door and closed her eyes and Darcy wished he hadn't said the thing about the licence. Outside the daylight was fading, the silhouette of his father on the phone through the living-room window, making his calls.

She'll be back, said the girl, her eyes opening for a second, but they glistened in the dark and Darcy knew Aunt Merran was gone. He slipped between the seats to the back and lay down, covered himself with the mohair, listened to the girl in the front, her occasional whimpers, his mother's sporadic shouts, a bottle smashed against the incinerator. He knew everything would be different this time, for everyone, not just for him. The missionary was his secret and he held it close, but this girl was his father's. Darcy was glad to be near her but he guessed she wouldn't be here for long—he knew his mother, and he knew secrets were best when they were secret.

He woke to the rustle of the flowering gums, the scent of the eucalypts, his father opening the passenger door. Fin, his father said softly, but the girl was still sleeping. The sound of her nickname made Darcy want to say it too, but his father lifted her, still blanketed, out into the morning and Darcy sensed she was already being taken away. His mother in the sitting-room window glowering, guarding the house now, eyes on the girl called Fin.

The girl struggled awake, ripped herself free like she shouldn't be touched. What are you doing? she asked Darcy's father as he put her down. He never did anything right.

I got you in at Toorak College, he said. As a boarder. I'm taking you. He guided her gently into the kombi.

Darcy grabbed her knapsack from the front seat and followed, handed it up to her. She glared down at Darcy as he closed the door, and then the kombi was rattling down the drive.

Ulitsa Kazakov, Late Sunday

The Moscow night was still and quiet save for a TV somewhere. No neighbours talking nor any sign of the woman
through the uncurtained glass across the way, just silent
flurries of snow. A black phone that wasn't connected. He
sorted through Fin's tapes—Joy Division, Boomtown
Rats—flipped on the portable tape deck and lay on her
bed in his underpants listening to the Divinyls' 'Boys in
Town.' The ceiling above him stained and peeling, pasted
with roses and butterflies, and pictures from Soviet mag-
azines. Antiquated blenders and appliances, dresses and
hairdos. The raspy verse that ended with *get me out of here*.
He tried not to believe in signs but the words had him
wishing he still had his passport strapped against him.

There was no evidence of what she'd been commis-
sioned to paint. Books lined a shelf in the headboard: *The
Wretched of the Earth*, *The Soviet Achievement*, *Nagorno-
Karabakh and Other Nationalities*. He picked out Lenin's
What Is to Be Done? Phrases underlined: *The task of our
Social Democracy is to subvert spontaneity*. That didn't
sound like the Fin he knew. Maybe she had become a
commo instead of just being left wing and chic. No
wonder she'd lost her sense of humour. He flipped the
pages. *Only those devoid of principle are capable of change.*
Maybe that made sense; he wasn't sure.

He nuzzled the familiar slightly stale bed-smell,

smoky sheets that hadn't been washed for his arrival. He reached for a narrow volume called *The Meaning of Love* by Vladimir Solovyov, a philosopher he'd never heard of. It had a chapter entitled 'Love in humans is not akin to propagation.' A possible vindication, he thought. He nestled his hand under the elastic of his boxers and conjured the soldier at the railway station in Prague, the falseness of that as intimacy, rutting hurried as primitives, then the euphoric recall of his recent visit to Sydney for New Year's Eve stole over him.

He never even saw the Harbour Bridge illuminated with fireworks or homing pigeons released from the wings of the Opera House. The alternative had slipped over him as easy as skin. The car almost drove itself to Centennial Park, the paradise of his despair. Men marauded there in silent ritual, triceps tattooed, the shadows of a chain-link fence. Down in the Brambles there was Kleenex in the dirt. He skirted the edges like a fringe-dweller, the way he'd done before, following a man with clamps on his nipples, thin as a snake with arms. Darcy hadn't seen the new virus up close. He imagined it twisting through veins as he watched the young man suction liquid with an eyedropper from a small brown bottle, squirt it into his mouth, then offer Darcy a sample. Darcy accepted with a cautious insatiability, as if to celebrate the end of life as he'd known it. A taste like wheat in his teeth, infusing him and making the darkness seem light. He thought of his mother, drunk and alone in Mount Eliza, watching the living-room clock as the New Year struck, looking for Darcy in the crowd on TV, but she'd lost him this time.

As the fireworks lit up the distant midnight, it was the dawn of 1984, the Orwellian era, but not as he'd expected.

The poofter-bashers came through the trees like fluid, with *Clockwork Orange* nightsticks, and Darcy glimpsed his thin sick friend folded up in the paspalum, being beaten. Darcy ran blind through the park in a sort of paranoid fulfilment, strung on a line like a dress in the wind, there but far away. Even as he was escaping, tearing through branches in the dark, he knew if he stayed in Sydney he'd be back there again. Like a dog that returns to its vomit.

Darcy woke with a start to bolts being opened, Fin's peasant dresses hanging above him and the radio turned up in the other room. She came in and switched off the bedroom light. Jesus, he said, you scared me.

Sorry. She lit a candle on the ledge beside the bed. Darcy looked at his watch; she'd been gone an hour.

Did you find food in the fridge? she asked. The candlelight wavered a shape on the wall as she took off her coat and clothes, went into the bathroom.

I was too tired to look.

The hushed sound of her peeing, brushing her teeth, cleaning off her make-up. She emerged without lipstick or eye shadow, slightly older-looking but lovely, ready for bed.

How did it go? he asked.

I'll tell you about it in the morning. She lay on the bed and kissed him gently on the mouth. I hope I didn't seem angry at the station, she said. I was just worried. I'll get your passport back.

You should have told me if I was carrying something, he said.

She put her finger to his lips this time. I know. She turned her back to him, the nape of her neck pale where her hair had once covered it. He touched a small tattoo at the knobbly top of her spine: a red swallow, its wings spread and flying upwards. A sailor's tattoo. She blew out the candle and moved closer to him in the dark. He traced the tattoo's shape with his finger, the curve of the wings. If he'd ever wanted to be with a woman it would have been her. The apple shampoo scent in her hair, the muted whistle with each of her breaths reminded him of things. He hugged her gently from behind, his arm draped over her ribs.

When were you first with a man? she asked.

Darcy stared into the soft white nape of her neck, pretended he was asleep.

Mount Eliza, Summer 1969

Darcy's mother lay in bed reading Morris West and smoking, flicked ash into her hand then let it fall onto a crossword magazine. She was nicer in the mornings. Get me a drink will you Darcy?

He didn't wear clothes in the summer when it was only the two of them, just his lace-up school shoes. He was only nine. He poured his mother a gin and tonic from the bottom of the desk in her bedroom, like he always did. Make it stiff, she said, then laughed as if at a joke.

His father had driven up to Melbourne in the kombi, delivering farm-fresh eggs to housewives in the city. He stayed for cups of coffee while their husbands were at work. He went every Tuesday, the day Darcy's mother kept her son at home for company.

He put in a slice of lemon and balanced her drink on her trophy tray. She liked a fresh glass for her first drink of the morning, didn't mind that the tonic was warm, as she propped herself up on a pillow and pushed back her hair. Feel free to wear some clothes, she said to him.

It's too hot. He looked out into the garden with his hands on his hips, the cotoneaster bush standing by itself. I'm going to drive the car, he said.

The Austin's battery had been taken out when his grandmother was still alive so she couldn't get it started; she'd had accidents on Humphries Road, trouble on the hills. After she died they put the battery back in and parked it behind the shed. The first time Darcy drove it, he sat on a pouf so he could see over the dashboard. His mother got out of bed and stood at the window in her nightie, laughed out loud as he hit the side of the shed. He propped up the broken dahlias and bashed the tin out with a hammer before his father came home. You should have seen your face, his mother called from the window. The canvas awning above her looked like a big ripped hat.

He left her in the bedroom and put her cereal bowl with the dirty dishes on the kitchen bench, and as he did the top of a man's head went by the window. There's someone here, he called to his mother. He covered himself with a tea towel and opened the screen door. The man's hair was chestnut and his suit an even redder brown, his tie had leaves all over it. Is it the Jesuits? his mother called out. Darcy wasn't sure. The man had a fine silver necklace with a blue cross hanging from it.

Jesus Christ of Latter-day Saints, he said to Darcy nervously, and smiled. His nails were clean and even, not bitten like Darcy's father's or smoke-stained. He had a tattoo on the back of his hand.

Darcy turned as he called back so his mother could hear. It's Jesus of the Saturday Saints.

Don't let him in, she shouted.

The man didn't move to come inside but stood at the bottom step. He had a ring on his thumb. We don't have any money, Darcy told him.

I'm not selling anything, he said. He was from somewhere else, an accent like on television, a bit like Darcy's mother's, America or Canada. His tattoo was a coil of barbed wire, and when he saw Darcy looking he pulled up the cuff of his jacket to show him. It's a crown of thorns, he said. Do you know what that is?

It's from Jesus, said Darcy.

The man turned his hand over and opened his fingers —there was a rose tattooed on his palm, it looked like a real one. The Rose of Sharon, he said. His eyes were deep and brown, kinder than Darcy was used to.

Are you wearing any clothes? his mother shouted. Darcy could hear her getting out of bed.

Shoes, he shouted. But I'm covered.

She was coming up the hall. The man looked as though he knew what would happen as she brushed Darcy aside. We don't need Jesus, she said, closing the door without even looking at the man. For Christ's sake put some clothes on, she said to Darcy.

Through the sitting-room window Darcy watched the man walk down the drive. He took off his jacket and rested it on his arm, looked back but didn't see Darcy there. His mother came in with a fresh drink from the bottle she hid behind the plastic bags. It was time for ice but no tonic.

He had a tattoo, Darcy told her.

Really, she said. Tight pants.

I think he was American. Like you.

They watched him disappear from view, hidden by the trees.

Not my kind of American.

What kind of American are you?

Miserable.

Darcy went to his desk in the corner and drew the coil of wire on the missionary's hand in his sketchbook while his mother gazed out the window as if she were looking for something that wasn't quite there. They were silent for what seemed like a long time. Darcy never knew whether to be quiet or to talk about things.

He had a rose in his hand, he said.

No he didn't, she said, as though she was the one who had talked to him.

Darcy didn't like it when she wouldn't believe him but he kept his head down. The coil that he drew looked like a snake, the spikes like the bands on a python. She came over to see what he was doing and he wanted to shield it with his fingers but he knew not to. You should eat something, he said to change the subject. It was better if she ate.

Don't talk about lunch unless you're cooking it, she said. She looked at Darcy's picture. What is that?

A crown of thorns, he said. He knew he should have said a snake, or a circle of climbing roses.

There are other ways to annoy me than believing in Jesus, she said. She put the cold glass against his ear.

Dad believes in Jesus, he said.

Your father's not very bright, she said. She moved away as if distracted, leaned against the piano. Why don't you sing something? she said. Or you could tap? It was always like this around lunchtime.

Tuesday's my driving day, he said.

The red vinyl seat was hot against his bare skin, the mothball smell of his grandmother. He turned the key and pulled the choke to start it in gear so he didn't have to reach for the pedals. As it jolted forward, he turned to avoid the compost heap. His mother wasn't at the window so he steered across the dandelions and down the driveway, past the wattle stump and onto Baden Powell Drive. He'd never driven out on the road but he was compelled to see where the man in tight pants had gone, compelled in a way he didn't understand. He steered down the hill so he didn't need the accelerator but the car got loud and went too fast. He pushed the choke to stall it and ran into the ti-trees, jolting to a stop in the leaves not far from the Easterbrooks' gate. The blinker was ticking, a branch pressed against the windscreen, smearing the bird dirt. Darcy wished he'd put some clothes on.

You okay? It was the missionary, kneeling at the window; Darcy hadn't seen him coming. He cupped himself with his hands like he'd caught a small bird.

I won't hurt you, said the missionary, but Darcy cupped his hands tighter, watched the leaves on the missionary's tie and the cross on his chain as it balanced in the window. The speedometer rested at twenty mph as if they were going somewhere.

The missionary took out his wallet and showed Darcy a photo of a young red-haired boy, standing by a hollow tree with a Bible in his hands. That's me, he said. In Indiana.

The boy was about Darcy's age, short American hair. Darcy thought of the right to *bare* arms because that's what his mother said they had in America, though Darcy didn't know what it meant. He looked down at his own bare arms, his small white hands. He wondered if Indiana was close to California, where his mother was born, but he had a sense that it wasn't.

I have something else, the missionary said. He reached in and put a miniature Bible on the seat beside Darcy.

My mother says the Bible's dangerous, he said.

It's beautiful, said the missionary. He touched Darcy's ear with his long pale fingers—softly, as if afraid to hurt him. The missionary's face looked big in the window but

Darcy liked the look in his dark brown eyes; they were glassy, as though he might cry.

Can you drive me home now? asked Darcy.

The missionary smiled to himself and nodded. Darcy moved over the gearstick to the passenger side, careful not to sit on the Bible. He opened it up and covered himself with it before the missionary got in. It sat on him like a small leather hat, the pages cool against his skin. The missionary started the car easily, put his arm along behind Darcy and turned his head to reverse back onto the road. Darcy felt safer when the car was moving. He watched the coil tattooed on the back of the missionary's hand, the pale fingers around the steering wheel. His skin looked soft like he didn't grow up on a farm. He turned into Darcy's driveway and stopped.

You're a good driver, said Darcy.

You're a strange boy.

Darcy sensed he meant it nicely.

I should leave you here, the missionary said, so your mother won't see us. He smiled, a gap between his two front teeth. He put on the parking brake and patted Darcy on the Bible. The church is going to be built on Two Bays Road, he said. Darcy nodded and watched him walk away, down the drive and onto the street. His mother was right; his pants were tight for a man.

Darcy stayed in the Austin. He looked for the Song of Solomon but it wasn't that kind of Bible. It had a picture called 'Jesus Christ visits the Americas'. Jesus was surrounded by Indians. Darcy hid the book in the car, behind the Melways street directory in the glove box.

His mother still wasn't at the window so he sneaked in the door, got to his room and took off his shoes. He put on his flares with the flap-over front, his short-sleeved navy shirt and cream cravat. He always dressed nicely when he put on clothes. The silk of the cravat felt soft against his neck as he looked at himself in the mirror. It was what he'd wear to church. He saw his mother behind him at the bedroom door; she'd been creeping. Her nipples showed through her nightgown.

Were you out on the road with nothing on? she asked. She'd brushed her hair but it didn't look good, her skin was like pastry.

He knew he'd have to be careful with her, it was already afternoon. I'm dressed now, he said.

I'm not stupid, she said.

He waited for her to move into the room, for her open hand against his ear; the cold glass had been a warning. I had trouble with the car, he said.

You shouldn't be driving, she told him. Instead of the slap she held him to her, her arms crossed over his back, her breath and lipstick in his hair. He was afraid of the smell of her nightgown, her salty, pretzel hands, sweat from her palms.

I saw him drop you off, she said.

Ulitsa Kazakov, Monday morning

Darcy squinted at Fin's lime green travel clock. It was 10 am. The sound of Russian voices in the other room, but this time he knew it was only the radio. The bedroom door was open and the apartment ice-cold; the heater had gone from full steam to freezing. Fin? He waited. Nothing.

He got up.

Snow spilled down outside the sitting-room window and the pipes that ran along the wall were barely warm. No Svetlana in the kitchen opposite. He checked on the orange laminated counter that separated the kitchen from her living area. No note, no breakfast.

He dragged a poloneck and a windcheater from his duffel bag, pulled his black cords over his thermals. White letters painted on one of the hanging black dresses, a looping script: *The mysteries of the clitoris*. Had that been there last night? He folded her Polaroid camera into itself, silver with inlaid wood, angles of a small architectural building, and slid it into his daypack. He grabbed some cheese-sticks from the fridge and an apple, ventured into the corridor. She'd left him no keys but at least she hadn't locked him in.

He tested the door; he was now locked out.

Triangular stains on the walls the shapes of sconces, but no hall-watcher lurking at the dark end. He ate as he moved down the stairs and found the main entrance, the one they'd circumvented last night. Steel-rimmed swinging doors, glassed and unattended, an empty desk and chair. Why hadn't she left a note?

Outside everything seemed bleak and deciduous, even the buildings were bare, the street covered in dove-grey snow, an arctic beauty. Darcy'd never seen a city so bathed in snow, was surprised by its silence—squat figures in fur walked with their heads down past the bleached alabaster structures. He decided to head back to the Byelorussian Station and try to retrieve his passport, see about his Pentax. Maybe that's where she was. But as he examined his plastic foldout map it seemed too far to walk and the wind was like an icepick. He'd hail a taxi.

Out on the slush-covered boulevard a trolley bus passed, whining on its overhead wires; if only he knew where it was going. He turned to get his bearings. The distant Ferris wheel rose above the leafless trees in Gorky Park as promised, a couple of bundled-up bodies suspended in air, small as frozen peas. In spring it might have held a certain beauty but the cold had crept deep into his feet already, through the sheepskin lining of his combat boots. He wasn't bred for this, his skin and his blood were too thin, and the station suddenly seemed too difficult.

Across the street the low swinging gates of a local park that wasn't Gorky, empty but for an elderly *baba* pushing at snow with a wooden scraper, a keeper of paths in the frost-bitten wind. He could take a picture of her in the avenue of bare elm branches that umbrellaed the pathway. Surely that wasn't strategic. But as he reached for the camera a man glanced back at him nervously. Darcy wondered if this could be his shadower, but he led a narrow dog in a quilted tartan blanket, a whippet or miniature greyhound, the type Darcy imagined being walked by a gay man in New York, not a KGB agent. The man glanced back again. Striking aquiline features, dark for here, late thirties, slender-lipped and earnest in his horn-rimmed specs. Darcy heard Fin's words: *Be careful, the places you go.* He heard his own promise but the intrigue already flitted about his consciousness, luring him like a finger seeking its hook inside his mouth, and he'd barely stepped out the door. He tried focusing elsewhere but the man loitered near a bench, averting his eyes, then he stared furtively. Intellectual, Jewish perhaps, thought Darcy, if you could still be Jewish here. He remembered the *Spartacus Gay Guide* only listed 'outside the Bolshoi in summer' under 'Cruising in Moscow', and warned against it. But it was winter now and this wasn't the Bolshoi. The man removed his fur hat and Darcy received it as a signal. His hair was silver-flecked and wavy, a few strands flew up like a crest in the wind and the pleading in his eyes spoke a need that Darcy recognised, mirrored. Too cold to be hatless and waiting unless you wanted something badly.

The shivering whippet sat on the path like a statue, its head into the wind as if it were a dog at sea. Darcy waited for the man to make a next move but he seemed stricken with uncertainty, so Darcy, emboldened by nothing but a rush in his brain, turned off the track into a thicket of prickly evergreens. He realised he wasn't so cold anymore as he pulled off a glove and held it under his arm and the man began fumbling, tying the windswept dog to the bench. He began to pick his way through the icy branches but as Darcy unzipped himself a figure approached, obscured by foliage. With neither a word nor a smile the Russian was panicking, backing away through the trees.

Darcy shook his head—it was only the babushka, she couldn't see them—but the man was already scaling a low metal barrier. Hands deep in pockets, he leaned into the wind and half ran towards the road. He'd forgotten his dog.

The *baba*, buried in her coat and scarves, sat down on the bench where the dog was tied. The woman looked over at Darcy as he appeared from the trees, narrowed her sunken eyes into their creases. Seduced and abandoned, said Darcy, then he remembered Fin's other warning. *Don't trust anyone here.*

The dog's tail curled under its crouching loins, its pelt a brindled silver. It greeted Darcy cautiously as he felt the ridges of its spine through the blanket. He pulled out the camera and unfolded it, took a close-up of the dog's fine face, one ear forward, one back, then a second, better one, with its head slightly cocked and both ears pricked. It had no tag on its collar—Darcy wasn't even sure if they did that here.

He flapped the Polaroids dry and the woman looked over, confused but unmoved. She had a postcard face, so he took a photo of her too, felt a certain guilt about his for-eigner's presumption. At least she wasn't a bridge or a reservoir; still she shot him a look of distaste that chilled him.

With the whippet on its lead by his side Darcy felt less foreign, as if this could have been his city. Together, they walked through the snow-fleeced park to the wrought-iron arch at the main entrance. A woman in a woollen balaclava was opening the flap on an old yellow van. She uncovered a row of red sausages on buns. Darcy reached for his wallet but the dog lifted a paw, its leg as fine as a knitting needle, and began to whine, snatching at the leash and pulling. Darcy felt conspicuous. He caught sight of

the delicate man in the distance, returning, and Darcy
unclipped the lead, let the whippet loose before it barked.
It rippled across the frosted ground, galloping low like a
racing dog, and the man leaned down to greet it. Darcy
gazed at them, suddenly alone, the fine leather dog leash
in his hand.

Mount Eliza, Summer 1969

Darcy's mother was doing her best; she had her shiny housecoat on, buttoned up over her nightie, her hair tied back in a ponytail. Her hands looked thin coming out of the sleeves to serve dinner, but she didn't eat. She sipped her brandy and dry; she switched to brown drinks after dark. Darcy's father had returned from the egg run, he'd showered and slicked back his hair. Did you have a good day? his mother asked. Spreading your eggs around? But his father never looked at her. He lifted a chop and chewed it. Darcy didn't tell him there was something wrong with the chops, that she'd fried them before they were thawed. Darcy pushed his food about his square plate; the instant mashed potato looked lumpier than usual.

His mother held an unlit cigarette and observed Darcy's father as if daring him to eat. We had a visitor, she said. Didn't we, Darce?

Darcy felt his stomach churn. He didn't think she'd mention it; she was always good at secrets.

His mother sipped her drink. Jesus in tight pants, she said.

Darcy's face was being searched by his father to see if he should believe her but Darcy looked away from him, down at the radiogram. He was just a missionary, said Darcy.

Not just a missionary, his mother said, raising her chest as if offended. A Mormon. She turned to Darcy's father. He took your son for a drive.

Darcy's empty fork froze in his hand and then his mother reached and gently took it from his fingers. She smiled to herself. Didn't he, Darce? Under the table Darcy felt her bare toe stroking his calf, a quiet back-and-for-thing.

You let him go off with a stranger? his father asked.

What could I do, she said, here on my own?

The feel of her toe on his leg gave Darcy an eerie feeling. He wished he could disappear, the way his father did after dinner on nights like these, off in the kombi.

He didn't have clothes on, his mother said.

Who? asked Darcy's father, suddenly flustered.

Darcy shifted his legs from her touch. I covered myself, he said.

What with? his mother asked, surprised.

A Bible, said Darcy. He looked at his father. It had a picture of Jesus in America.

His mother guffawed. I never saw Jesus when I was there, she said. I suppose he'll be coming here next.

Darcy's father stood, irritated; he hated being teased about Jesus. He took his unfinished plate to the kitchen and started washing up. Darcy lay down on the rug and put his ear to the faintly crackling radio.

Go help your father, his mother said, but Darcy listened to the distant static as if it were life on a capsule in orbit, felt himself begin to sway. Then there was a kick in his ribs. Where's the Bible? she asked, suddenly conspiratorial.

Darcy pretended he couldn't hear so she kicked him again, her bare foot against his back. For God's sake leave him alone, his father said, returning for Darcy's plate.

It's just a love kick, she said. She put her silver cigarette lighter against her cheek. If you were a Mormon, she said to Darcy's father, you could have multiple wives.

I wonder if you'd be one of them, he said. He took the plate and the placemats back to the kitchen.

Darcy's mother lit one of her Virginia Slims. Bring me the Bible, she said, or I'll tell him everything.

Darcy got up, flustered, wondering what she meant by *everything*. He went out in his socks, let the flyscreen bang shut because he knew how much she hated that. Like a car crash, she called it, but her ears were always roaring anyway, something called tinnitus. His father thought she imagined it but she said it's the same, whether you imagine it or not.

In the Austin, Darcy opened the glove box. The small light flickered inside it as he took out the Bible from under the Melways. Inside the cover it said *The Book of Mormon*. The picture of Jesus in white, standing on a rock, the Indians in feathered headdresses. Darcy wondered if the missionary would visit again.

Through the lit kitchen window he saw his father hang the frying pan on the hook by the sink and put his hands on his hips, staring out into the dark. Darcy could see the creases in his father's cheeks that he knew were supposed to be from all the smiling, but his father didn't smile. Darcy suspected he only came home because he had to, and he wondered if his mother had once been different, when they met on the beach near the Mornington pier, or before she left America.

Darcy's father closed the flyscreen quietly behind him, and Darcy slid through into the back seat as his father got in the driver's side, sat with his hands on the wheel. Did anything bad happen today? he asked without turning around.

No, said Darcy, not moving.

Can I see the book? his father asked.

Darcy passed it around the edge of the seat and his father examined it in the dark. Jesus Christ in the Americas, he said, I never knew about that. He put the book down and ran through the gears and Darcy sat up to watch him, then he left it in neutral and looked at Darcy in the rear-view mirror. What are we going to do? he asked.

Darcy wished his father were talking about the American Jesus but as his mother opened the door and slipped her empties quietly into the box by the rubbish he knew he wasn't.

Are you going to leave? whispered Darcy.

His father shook his head slowly.

Ulitsa Kazakov, Monday afternoon

When Darcy returned to the apartment it was unlocked. A vague bituminous odour came up from the central heating and the place was hot again. He tried to forget where he'd been, his already broken promise, and yet all he'd really done was take care of an animal briefly. He hung the leather leash on a coat hook as if it belonged.

Fin was perched on a stool near the edge of the frosted window, her face swathed in a cream satin scarf. Innocent as a young Muslim woman, but fairer. Where were you? she asked. She was working on a small canvas that leaned against an old wooden easel, outlining a shape in crayon.

Isn't that what I should be asking?

She told him she had gone back to the railway station but the office was closed. I'll sort it out tomorrow, she said. She seemed to regard it as a formality. Crouching further forward, she spat on her thumb and rubbed it against the canvas to make the crayon resemble paint.

Are you sure you want me here? asked Darcy.

Fin stood up, concerned, and came to him. No evidence of anything under her smock, just the shadow of her breasts and the faint elastic of her underpants. He was never attracted to anyone pale but her. She held him to her gently. I'm sorry, she said.

He tried to relax into her but the questions still niggled at him. Tell me about the money belt.

Don't worry, she said, no drugs or explosives, but she freed herself and gazed past the canvas out into the grey afternoon, and Darcy remembered how they'd left the station so hurriedly. Whatever he'd brought in with him had been more valuable to her than his passport or camera. As he knelt to see what she'd drawn, an abstract mountain shrouded in pink, he felt disappointment taking seed in him. He'd been her carrier pigeon.

I just want to know what's going on, he said, but she was copying a Polaroid pinned to the wing of the easel. A bleached-out picture of a woman's chest, a large single breast on one side and a florid scar on the other, the stitches wide and primitive, a miniature rope. The freshness of the scar and the rough-hewn needlework were disquieting. She wasn't drawing a mountain.

Soviet mastectomy, she said. She tore paper from the end of another crayon. She'd mixed red and purple for the mottled burgundy scar. Am I onto something? she asked almost timidly. Abstract Feminism? She smudged the edges with the remains of crayon on her thumbs.

Darcy looked back at the photo, more lurid and disconcerting than anything she could recreate. The photo speaks for itself, he said. He stood up. Why don't you paint what you're supposed to?

She looked at him seriously, her pupils a piercing green against the scarf. They want a big canvas of the Museum of Science and Achievement. It's a whole field of buildings and fountains and statues, she said. Soviet Realism. The exhibition's next Sunday. Her knuckles seemed knotty and anxious. I need you, little brother, she said.

Darcy looked at her canvas and felt a tightness in his skin, a disingenuousness in the way she'd called him that.

Or perhaps it was just her admitting her work wasn't painterly; she was a moulder of things, an installationist. She'd studied Russian and psychology, not art. He remembered her abstracts back at Monash, the incinerated witch-hunt books. I don't understand how you got this gig in the first place, he said. Didn't you have to submit a portfolio?

She glanced at him and then examined the paint on her hands, red on her brown nail polish. I sent Polaroids of your Melbourne paintings, she said.

Darcy sat on the arm of the couch, felt the tightness rise up through his neck. The charcoal and oils of art-deco warehouses in Footscray, the curves of the red-brick walls off Dynan Road as you wound through the back way to the showgrounds. They got him the scholarship to Sydney. He pressed his fingernails hard against his chin. You could have asked me.

She cautiously pushed a snake of white from a tube and mixed it with turps into a pale, viscous grey. You might have said no, she said. I needed to get myself here.

But for what?

I can't tell you, she said. Not here. She surveyed the ceiling as if the cornices were listening. I just need your help with the painting. She reached for his Fodor's guidebook from the arm of the sofa, flipped to a photo of the strange museum.

Darcy stared at a spread of neoclassical buildings strewn with ice-crusted lakes and frozen fountains, no smokestacks or chimneys. I need to know about the money belt.

Darce, please don't harp on it, she whispered.

I hate it when you call me that. In the photo a shining

obelisk projected high above the buildings into a low white sky. As if the only reason she'd wanted him here was to paint this.

Don't be a detective, she said, just focus on what you're good at, but he wondered what she'd become good at. He looked out into the dark afternoon. No sunset here, just grey then an orbiting blackness. If you'll come clean, he said, I'll paint the museum for you. I'll need photos and decent brushes and paints.

A light came on outside. Again, the woman in the kitchen opposite, standing at her sink. Fin got up, took the torn sheet she used to clean brushes and twisted it over a window hinge to block the view, but as she pulled it the sheet caught the corner of the canvas. Her painting fell slowly against the side of the couch. Darcy didn't jump to save it, just crouched to peel the canvas back. The ridges of the scar had smudged flat against the velvet couch like a birthmark, the nipple smeared; remnants of paint on the fabric. A landscape now. You don't have breast cancer? he asked.

No, she said.

But she had something. He took a chrome Crayola from her paintbox and angrily scrubbed an abstract new moon shape onto the canvas, from the ground up into the sky. The crayon impressed lines in the wet oils like fingerpainting. He added rough black squares for buildings, fronted them with silver Corinthian columns. He tried to ignore Fin as she wiped paint from the couch then rubbed her hands in turpentine, cleaning each finger separately, but he knew she had what she wanted: him beginning to work. She lit a cigarette and leaned against the window sash in her scarf and paint-stained smock, watching.

Darcy daubed the crayons with turps instead of saliva,

made it paint-like, then etched more boxes with random columns, everything out of proportion. He could feel her lips gathering to pull on her cigarette, calculating. The mastectomy scar he morphed into a railway track, the surviving nipple a fountain. Frustrated by his own naivety, he tore wrappers from other Crayolas and scribbled hard in white, added oversized petals to the base of the fountain, a jagged black lake beside the swooning obelisk, everything rushed and random, more her style than his. The waxy nub of the black was near the end of its colour as her roughshod picture became his.

Fin examined her Polaroid. Where did you get that? he asked but she didn't answer. She went to stab her cigarette out on the glass of the half-covered window, but changed her mind, and he wondered if she'd purloined the photo from some office, like she'd slipped copies of the portfolio photos from his desk in St Kilda to get herself here. Now she had him as well. He'd breathed life into her canvas, turned a breast into structures. He rubbed at the pigment on his hands and looked at her in the scarf, her face the shape of a leaf. You're different here, he said.

How do you mean?

You're just not the same. He stood and pushed a coloured finger onto the ridge between her eyes, branded her with a bindi. You even look different.

She lifted her cigarette to her mouth, blew a smoke ring that wandered between them. Some of us are capable of change, she said.

Mount Eliza, Summer 1969

Darcy sat alone on the railing outside school when everyone else had gone home. His mother had forgotten him. He imagined her drunk on the chaise, the late afternoon sun coming in beneath the awning and her cigarette burning down in her half-asleep fingers, the ashtray on her chest. He started walking down Wooralla Drive towards the Nepean Highway. It was hot so he took off his flannel shirt, tied it loosely about his waist.

He followed the trail that ran through the scrub alongside the highway but stopped when he saw the missionary on a bike, approaching. The missionary slowed, put his foot down in the dirt, and they stared at each other, Darcy with the sun in his face. The missionary smiled curiously but Darcy didn't smile back. He held his satchel to his bare chest and watched with a dry mouth as the missionary slid the bike beneath a clump of oleanders and disappeared from the verge, down into the gully.

Darcy walked up, the tyre of the bike just visible in the bushes. He felt a queasiness he didn't understand as he held a branch for balance, picked his way down through Scotch broom and bees, the sound of the cars on the highway behind him. He was drawn to the edge of a clearing sheltered by flowering wattles. The missionary, waiting, dappled in both light and shade, one hand in the pocket of his khaki pants. A hand gently moving, and Darcy watched it.

You're a beautiful child of God, the missionary said to him softly, coming nearer. The sweat on the missionary's sunburnt neck trickling down into his open collar. No one had ever called Darcy beautiful; they'd just teased him in mean ways about being pretty. Darcy looked up as he felt the missionary's fingers run over his chin then quietly slip the strap of the satchel from his narrow uncovered shoulders, over his head. Then Darcy looked down as the missionary gently untied the shirt from his waist, spread it out carefully on the ground.

You could take your pants off, the missionary said, if you wanted.

Darcy didn't say anything but the missionary knelt and was unzipping Darcy's fly and at first Darcy moved away but the missionary extended his arms. I will take care of you, he said, and Darcy believed him, found himself slipping from his school shoes without untying the laces, pulling them off by the heels the way he did before bed. He felt self-conscious now, out here in his underpants, but the missionary laid Darcy's trousers out with his shirt, Darcy's shape on the grass. It will be comfortable, he said.

As Darcy lay down he felt rigid, like a marionette, laying his arms along the spread-out sleeves. He looked up through the quivering wattles, their leaves like waving caterpillars. Then the trees were half hidden with the weight of the missionary, his stubble against Darcy's chin, his soft breath kissing about his neck and ears, and Darcy heard the missionary's whispers and thought they could be prayers. *When I drink from your river, oh Lord…*and the hum of cars seemed far away, Darcy's mother on the chaise and his father in town, but none of that mattered with the missionary's breath and the words that he swallowed, the

Rose of Sharon in the missionary's palm gently covering Darcy's lips. Darcy stared up through a smothering panic, past the missionary's sorrow-filled eyes, through the glinting caterpillar leaves, his own body shuddering, and for a moment he felt connected to the sky.

Bolshoi Theatre, Monday night

The Bolshoi looked spectacular at night, the columns lit yellow against the inky winter sky, a statue shadowed above the portico, a chariot. That's Apollo, said Fin as they mounted shallow steps in a wind that licked the night, Fin in her woven grey-rabbit coat. They lined up in the colonnaded atrium among dour locals to collect their tickets, seats to Chekhov arranged through the embassy. This was more how Darcy had imagined his arrival.

It's *The Lady with the Dog*, said Fin, handing Darcy the tickets then shedding her coat. She gathered her wrap around her shoulders, shiny like butterfly wings, and the air around them hinted at her tuberose scent. Do you know it? she asked. It's from a short story.

Darcy remembered it vaguely from European Lit, but he'd not finished it. He'd also started *Anna on the Neck* but never worked out if it was the neck of a river or Anna's own neck.

Communists love ballet, Fin said as they walked amid the din and expectation, the echo of heels on the grey and white marble tiles. She pulled at her elbow-length gloves and Darcy carried her coat. It must have taken forty rabbits. Her clothes were from opportunity shops but she wore them as if they were *haute couture*. She had on a quilted velvet dress, high-heeled boots with a zip up the front. Her fresh-dyed hair was sienna and slick, plastered to her temples in little swoops, her lips red against her striking porcelain face.

Darcy wore a fifties black tuxedo that fit like a glove; second-hand in Prague for thirty Australian dollars. He liked the narrow pants legs and the polyester was so flammable it was warm. You look like a lipstick lesbian, said Fin, without the lipstick. But Darcy didn't mind feeling slightly androgynous. The local evening wear seemed heinous to him by comparison, although there was one glamorous woman, statuesque in a fitted indigo suit, something exclusive. That's Chernenko's daughter, I think, said Fin, as if a star had been spotted. Her father might be the next General Secretary.

Darcy remembered Chernenko from newspaper photos, full-faced and glaucous; the woman looked like a different species. Most of the other Russian women wore dark scarves, the men clasping ushankas as if afraid they'd be stolen from the coat check, treating their hats like a Melbourne woman might treat a fur.

Darcy followed Fin into the auditorium, past elderly ushers who didn't seem interested. They could have sat anywhere. Five balconies ranged up above the orchestra level like a pile of shining ashtrays. It's very red and gold, said Darcy.

Ro-co-co, said Fin, three separate words. And it felt almost as if they were back to their old selves, now they were out in public. Most patrons sat up in the higher levels or way back in the orchestra cheap seats. The elegant woman was already up in a box with a group of grey-suited men. Apparatchiks, said Fin. She pointed at the chandelier, told Darcy it was famous, two tonnes of crystal floating above them.

Why are we the only ones under it? he asked. He imagined carnage: a crystal indoor Hindenburg, their bodies impaled on the red velvet seats. Fin read a program that looked made from paper bags. I wish they had one in English, said Darcy. She'd already lost interest in translating anything. He remembered plagiarising a paper of criticism on Chekhov: *the language is colourless, devoid of verve or understanding.* The Hungarian tutor thought his response original and radical. Darcy missed his time with Fin at uni, even though they studied different things and were in different years. They'd meet for lunch in the Small Caf and talk politics, smoke among the young bisexual communists, artists and stoners, the radical Mauritian he had a crush on—they all thought Darcy and Fin might be lovers. They acted like they were, didn't tell their real story, hung out in a kind of sly cahoots, studying together in the library, making their versions of art. Darcy felt safer with her then. He looked up at the gilded Bolshoi ceiling, the way the light brushed over it; this wasn't Monash. Instruments squawked in the pit, flutes and violins being tuned. Is Anna Pavlova dancing? he asked.

She died in 1931, said Fin. It's Lyudmila Semenyaka. Fin seemed to think that was good. Next Thursday there's a tribute to the classical heritage of the peoples of Czechoslovakia, Hungary and Poland, she said. Marvellous.

Darcy wondered if *Bolshoi* and *Bolshevik* were related but he didn't ask. He knew there were patterns and connections he couldn't yet see; he wished he'd read more Chekhov, and found out what Fin was really up to before he got on a plane.

The bell jangled loudly and the lights went down. It's about a man who searches only for passion but accidentally finds love, Fin whispered. She gave Darcy a peck on the cheek but he knew it was more for the Bolshoi than him, the place so grand and deteriorated, the crowd so frowzy. Darcy felt oddly off-kilter.

The curtain folded up into itself and a woman flitted across the stage wearing a shining white tutu. Her movement was lovely. A flourish of strings, then a male dancer. Fin slipped a pair of small binoculars from her heart-shaped clutch and Darcy looked at her in the dark, her pale freckles barely visible but her concentration fierce, the binoculars pressed to her eyes. Passion and love. He supposed there were differences, that there could be one without the other.

A fake satin seashore rippled over the stage and the ballerina twirled among its folds. He borrowed the binoculars, focused them on the male lead who reappeared from the trees. Lust was different from passion, he thought as the dancer was drowned in a flood of ballerinas. Darcy focused on Chernenko's daughter, already dozing up in her shell-shaped box. He felt redeemed somehow. It would be a long ballet for a short story but Fin was engrossed. Her leg rested easily up against Darcy's and he felt the casual magnetism still there. He pressed his feet on the back of the seat in front of him, his toes still cold in his Albert Schweitzer boots. A new ballerina entered, wearing black, carrying a parasol. Is that the lady or the dog? he whispered, shifting in his seat. Someone along their row went *shhhh* and a masculine Slavic woman turned with her lorgnette. Next there'd be a troika on stage and cotton tufts of falling snow.

Darcy stood and moved past the knees, trying to be discreet, then walked up the aisle and through the echoing

foyer. Hardly anyone was out there now, just the remnants
of their smoke and some ushers. A row of silver-framed
ballet posters—a swan with flying ballerinas, a painting of
a sylphlike dancer in harem pants and turban, playing in
Scheherazade perhaps. Darcy found his way downstairs
into the tiled darkness.

It stank like a pissoir because that's what it was. An
inexplicable comfort, a stall, but the toilet was too filthy to
sit on, no seat just a foul tin bowl. In the next stall a
brown-suited man stood balanced with his feet on the flat
metal rim of the seat, glancing anxiously over the rusted
divider. His door was open, his old Russian erection half-
hard. As Darcy went and stood at the urinal, he gave him
a cheerless smile, a moment of graceless communion.

A cistern ran but it was otherwise silent. Darcy wondered why he was here, inexorably, with himself in his
hand; he didn't need to pee. There would be no boys from
the ballet, not even an understudy, just the cowering comrade with the shame in his eyes. In a shining strip of metal
in front of Darcy, the shadowy shape of his own face, narrow
and distorted, waiting for…what? A young Baryshnikov?
He'd be upstairs dancing or in a dressing room, or
watching the performance like everyone else. The reflection of his face and the old man behind him felt strangely
safe even though he imagined places like this were probably under surveillance. Maybe they were looking at him
through the strip of tin, adding to their registry of deviants.

He glanced at a shadow in the doorway and was met
by an exaggerated look. A man in his thirties with hazel
eyes, Latin-looking, he seemed to smile but his lips didn't
move, and then he was gone. Darcy buttoned himself and
left but the face stayed with him. Brows dark and full as

caterpillars, golden skin despite the winter, his hair chestnut-streaked and slightly tousled.

Darcy reached the top of the stairs and breathed himself back to the world above ground. To this new normality. The program-seller in her booth, almost asleep on her feet; smoke from a cigarette curling from her hand. It was as though he'd conjured the man with copper skin. Then Darcy noticed him walking across the tiles with easy strides in a herringbone coat and cream fur hat, a thick black scarf around his neck. As if in a trance, Darcy moved over the Persian carpets and through the vastness of the entrance hall, hoping the man was the sort who might look back.

Darcy, he heard from behind him.

Fin stood in her wrap, her coat over her arm in the shadows of the burgundy velvet curtains. She'd caught him in action. He took a last glance at his quarry despite her, the man gliding down the icy steps and into a fresh canopy of snow. He covered the ground so gracefully, Darcy wondered if he'd even leave prints.

You took my binoculars, said Fin. She lifted them carefully from around his neck. Were you gone on safari?

I just needed some air, he said.

She motioned with her program, down towards the dark stairwell with the Russian sign for toilets. People usually go outside for air, she said.

Darcy raised his eyebrows innocently. He barely understood it either, he just knew. He'd come here in part to avoid the old haunts and he was already finding new ones.

Fin rolled her program and pulled on her coat. I once had an orgasm on a horse, she said, but I don't hang out at the stables.

It stirred up an image in Darcy: the missionary climbing the slope away from him, being left naked in the grass.

You still go riding, said Darcy.

Fin clipped her binoculars back in her purse. Not here I don't, she said, as they walked out into the snow, Darcy remembered the nights he walked from school and visited the clearing, lay his shirt in the grass in a careful ritual, spread the arms out wide. Alone, he pushed against his arching back and recalled the salt smell of the missionary's sweat, the sensory memory rising inside him and a pre-pubescent jolting, a strange euphoric recall in the grass among the butterflies.

Mount Eliza, Summer 1969

Darcy rode beside his father in the kombi, taking the long way back from the Yamala shops, Darcy changing the gears with his right hand while his father did the clutch, but Darcy missed third when he saw the missionary walking along Humphries Road. The kombi in neutral, his father just let it roll, half on the bitumen, half in the dust. Is that him? he asked, but Darcy said nothing. Roll down the window, his father said.

The missionary stood with his white shirt sleeves turned up and a narrow black tie, loosened from his collar because of the heat. Darcy's father leaned across Darcy to the open window. I'll take you to the top of the hill, he shouted.

The missionary opened the door, stepped up into the rumbling van. Make room, said Darcy's father, and suddenly Darcy was sitting between them, putting the grocery bag down under his feet, and the missionary was saying a quiet American thank you.

I believe you two know each other, said Darcy's father, starting up the road, doing the gears on his own.

The missionary removed a black baseball cap with risen letters that said UTAH. He ran his hand through his shock of thick hair. We have met, he said, yes.

Darcy wanted to offer him grapes from the bag but he didn't. He glanced over, saw the awkwardness sewn in the corners of the missionary's eyes. Did you read the Book? the missionary asked him.

Darcy turned his gaze to the floor, the missionary's leather sandals, his dusty feet. I looked at the pictures, said Darcy.

So you're a Mormon, his father said, and for a moment Darcy thought he spoke to him, then he noticed the missionary nodding, fiddling with his baseball cap. Darcy stared at the tattoo of the thorns on the missionary's arm, he felt his knee against the missionary's pants and a ripply feeling spread over him. He thought of the Rose of Sharon that covered his mouth, the weight of the missionary rubbing against him.

Are you married then? asked Darcy's father.

The missionary's smile was slight. It's not compulsory, he said.

A truck ran past from the quarry and the kombi shuddered. We thought you'd have lots of wives, said Darcy's father, didn't we, son?

Darcy stared straight ahead, concentrating on the white line, the electric touch of the missionary's leg.

I met your wife, said the missionary. She didn't seem well.

That's none of your business, said Darcy's father, his change of tone sudden. Darcy eased his knee away.

The missionary turned the cap in his hands. I was on my way to see her now, he said.

Darcy's father stopped the van, leaned over past Darcy and opened the passenger door. I can take care of my family, he said.

The missionary seemed shocked, stepping down to the roadside, mumbling something about trying to help.

Then keep away from my boy, said Darcy's father. He jumped the kombi forward before the door was barely closed. Darcy didn't dare watch out the side mirror to see the missionary getting smaller in the dust. He probably just wanted dinner, said Darcy.

His father pulled into the driveway and parked. I think I know what he wanted, he said. He got out and slammed the door and Darcy sat there, still as the sun through the windscreen, to see if the missionary would still walk past the end of the drive. Instead, he saw his father with a stick. With it, he propped open the bonnet of the Austin and unhitched the battery, removed the stick and let the bonnet crash down. He threw the battery in the incinerator. He'd taken out the Austin's heart.

Fin had arrived and was already gone.

Darcy pedalled his bike along the dark gravel road-side, hiding in trees from the headlights. His breath loud in his head as he wended down the Humphries Road elbow. He knew where Toorak College was, closer to the beach on Old Mornington Road. The bike had been brought home by his father so Darcy wouldn't drive. His father who'd slipped away for cigarettes, which meant he was visiting one of his *girls*; his mother already too drunk to notice Darcy gone.

He planted his bike in the bushes and clambered through a gap in the woven-wire fence. Anyone could have climbed through. He had a photo of himself in a Fair Isle cardigan, his hair swooped low over his forehead. He wanted her to have it, for her to understand he hadn't wanted her to go.

The boarding house was just a long corrugated bun-galow painted green, down among the acacias. Fin, he whispered through the open window.

He heard the rustle of girls, a cough of disapproval and then giggling. Country girls from sheep and cattle properties, more titillated than afraid. As he crawled in, one shone a torch in his face. What have we here? she said.

All Darcy saw were green mosquito nets, girls pulling up their sheets. They sat up in their beds and whispered.

Where's Fin? he asked.

America. It's for you.

Inside, Darcy walked between the narrow cots to find her. The bed without the net. She stared up at him with her pale green eyes as he held the photo he wished he hadn't brought. He put it down beside her, along with a jar of barley sugar.

Fin sat up in her nightie, her thin arms still tanned from a faraway sun, her hair matted and long, the colour of white sand. She searched Darcy's face as he sat on the edge of her blanket. What are you doing? she asked. She looked at him like he was the one who needed care.

I came to see you, he said.

She sat up and kissed him on the forehead like a parent might. She smelled musty and sweet, just as he remembered. To him it was the scent of California. She told him she had been glad to get away. And somehow he knew she was the lucky one. Then she looked at the photo in the dark.

You look like a girl, she whispered.

Darcy nodded. He lay on the floor by her bed and slept there, dreamed he was kneeling among the Indians, beseeching at the missionary's feet, the missionary in a white robe standing up on the rock where Jesus stood, speaking his soft American, teaching of his return.

Darcy sat half-asleep at Fin's laminated counter. He ate a version of All-Bran bathed in milk that tasted vaguely of tin. He looked out the window, the morning cold but crystalline. Fin in her bedroom doorway slipping on sheepskin gloves, heading out already. I need to get to the embassy, he said.

I'll take care of your passport, she said. She grabbed a scarf from a coat hook without noticing the dog lead dangling down the wall. You stay home and paint.

Darcy drank down the remains from the bowl and stood. He didn't see how they'd issue new papers to her, or how she could charm his passport back from the railway station without him, but she was snatching her patchwork coat and fur hat. Remember to lock yourself in, she said.

I'm coming with you, said Darcy. He rugged himself up with his own scarf and gloves, reached for his fleece-lined oilskin coat, but by the time he had pulled the door closed behind him there was no sign of her. He ran down the stairs and out through the main glass entrance, caught sight of her in the ice-covered street getting into a small battered car. It was driven away by a man Darcy couldn't quite see, a man who must have been waiting.

Darcy forged through the whistling cold to the corner in hopes of a cab, fumbling for his foldout map in his ski gloves. He knew the embassy was across the river so he walked in that direction. At the lights he waited beside a man with a greatcoat draped over his shoulders, European-style, then he recognised the black roping eyebrows and golden skin, the man from the Bolshoi, his caramel hair now covered by a brown fur hat. He heard Fin's warning—*There's no such thing as coincidence here*—but he was already imagining the possibilities. A choreographer, perhaps, or a poet from the Caucasus, a diplomat from Portugal. Darcy put the map away, didn't want to appear like a tourist, and the man acknowledged him, as if he recognised Darcy too.

Darcy entered the park, the same one as yesterday, and when his friend followed without even hesitating Darcy felt a pang in his underarms. They threaded each side of a young woman who pushed a primitive baby carriage with a fogged-up plastic cover. His suitor stopped, kneeled to coo to the baby, but looked up at Darcy, the smile for the baby still on his face. Darcy divined being escorted to some embassy, drinks on a heated terrace overlooking the Arbat, introduced to local envoys. Perhaps he'd get his passport that way. He waited at a railing, trying to keep his senses, watched the cold light play where the pond was frozen. He knew this was a country where they tortured men for being with men, the warning in *Spartacus* was clear: *Severe penalties under Soviet laws.*

He focused on the end of the pond where it had thawed to a tinged green, a spurt bubbling up from a pipe, but in Darcy's side view the man stood a few feet away, watching him almost blatantly, fingers still clasping the edges of his coat.

Darcy looked away at a pair of ducks floating motionless in the reeds. At first Darcy thought they were decoys—

the ducks should have flown south by now—but then he realised they were real, hovering near a pipe that spurted steaming water. Darcy turned slowly; he couldn't help himself. And the man was smiling almost cheekily, his teeth too white to be from here, a small scar that broke the line of his right eyebrow saving his face from being too perfect. I saw you at the Bolshoi, ventured Darcy.

The man made a little gesture with his brown eyes as though such things were not unexpected. He seemed to understand. Faint smudges shadowed below his eyes as if he hadn't slept, a shadow of moustache above his untasted lips, his sideburns shaped and close-shaven. He didn't look Russian. Are you a dancer? asked Darcy.

I was once a dancer, the man said. A curiously accented English.

And now?

Now I look at you, he said. He allowed a disarming, pursed smile. Darcy thought of the uniformed boy in the railway station in Prague, the searching, desperate eyes, his cap on the cistern and how he made him feel; he thought of the man from yesterday, not far from this same place. But there was nothing afraid or desperate about the one who stood before him now. This was something different.

Is this part of Gorky Park? asked Darcy.

Mandelshtam, the man said, a word that sounded like a compound sentence.

Darcy moved along the railing and stopped nearer the winter ducks, and he was followed like a courted bird.

Mandarins, said the man, motioning with his chin at the pair of ducks, their bluish-green feathers and a crest of orange. One kept wetting its head and then shaking it. They are being a long way from China.

They are being that, thought Darcy. Many of us are
far from home, he said. The ducks manoeuvred among
the reeds where the ice had melted. Where are *you* from?
he asked the man.

Cuba.

Made sense, Cubans in Moscow, Vietnamese and
Libyans, Nicaraguans, Angolans, the patronage statues on
bridges. Darcy's feet were getting numb with cold but a
nervous pulsation ran through the depths of him, the
man's coat sleeve almost grazed his ski glove as they
walked. Darcy contained his desire to brush against him.
They looked at each other dead on. In Moscow, all is connected by politics, said the man.

Darcy had hoped for something more intimate. I'm
not here for the politics, he said.

The man raised his eyebrows with a false inquisitive-
ness. So why you are here?

I'm a painter, said Darcy, but he immediately thought
of the money belt, how he was afraid he'd been a smuggler
too.

Ah, said the man knowingly, like your friend. He
laughed.

Darcy's breath seemed to stop in the air, stunned in
front of his mouth. He gathered his thoughts as he picked
up a stone and skimmed it out across the glassy ice, but
the stone slid further than he'd planned, not far from the
ducks. They winged up into the white winter air. How do
you know about her?

I am to be keeping an eye on you, he said. So I know
a little.

Darcy's heart skidded like the stone. How much? he
wondered. Maybe he knows what I need to find out. He

tried to keep breathing normally, standing before a row of iron placards set up on frosted posts. He brushed the cold rusted letters with his glove. They appeared to be in braille; a nature walk for the blind.

For those who do not see, the man said philosophically, right beside him, but there were no blind children reaching to touch the leaves, even the ducks had flown, everything bare and frozen save for toxic water steaming from the pipe. Are you supposed to speak with me? asked Darcy, aware of his keeper's lips. Part of him wanted to kiss them and part of him wanted to run.

No, he said, nonchalantly, but I like the look of you.

Are you having somewhere you want me to go? asked Darcy.

I go to a wedding soon, said the man, his eyebrows raised again, full as cats' tails. It wasn't an answer Darcy had expected. My friend Sofia marries the general. I work for him. I introduce them.

They were walking now, chatting like friends in odd conversation. What kind of work is that? asked Darcy.

I am sometimes *druzhinnik*, he said, head of patrollers for hooligans and *blues*—then I wear an armband. He pointed to his empty sleeve, his coat still draped over his shoulders.

Darcy asked him what *blues* were.

Homosexes here are called *blues*, he said, but they have no official existence.

They passed a statue clad with what looked like medieval armour and Darcy realised it was a cosmonaut. And what are you called? Darcy asked.

His friend's ungloved hand appeared for the first time, his fingers dark and long, his nails polished-looking.

I am Aurelio, he said. Darcy took off his ski glove and his hand was shaken firmly, the warm fingers inviting him, a complicity in his touch. My house is near, he said. His eyes now seemed to have an almost olive quality, where Darcy would have sworn they were hazel before. Come with me, he said. Why not? You are in Moscow!

Together, they drifted back through the avenue of empty elms. An old woman raked the path. It was the same babushka from yesterday, even though he had entered the park from a new direction. The *baba* tucked her woollen scarves into her coat and leaned on her rake for a moment as if she was trained to look out for the likes of the two of them. The Cuban smiled at her, unconcerned, as if he knew her or wasn't fussed, but she didn't smile back.

She works for me, he said. Darcy thought about yesterday, the man in the trees and the tremulous whippet, the Polaroid.

On the street they wove elegantly among the bulky pedestrians who shuffled through the snow, leaden-faced, bodies bent forward with the weight of plastic bags. Darcy felt light by comparison, walking with Aurelio, excited about his prospects. Serve Fin right, he thought, off on her own frolic. He'd get to see a wedding on his second day in town. Darcy grew wary, though, as they turned down a narrow lane. He'd followed strangers into alleys before, but not in a country like this. Yet Aurelio seemed more preoccupied than dangerous, jingling his keys at a door under a tattered awning at the back of an old brick building. An adventure, he said, sensing Darcy's apprehension. No?

Inside was not what Darcy expected. The walls were

stacked high with rolls of cloth and cobwebs, a long sewing table, racks of garments and scarves on hangers, a troubadour's outfit. Costumes for the Bolshoi, Aurelio said. He grabbed a pinstriped jacket from a hanger, long and grey like a funeral coat. Try this.

Darcy removed his coat, pulled on the pinstripe and checked himself in an ornate full-length mirror. In a Goth sort of way it worked with his cords and combat boots, his black and white Collingwood beanie. Do not be worried, said Aurelio, it's a *come as you are when the ship went down*. Darcy assumed that was a Cuban expression.

As Aurelio brushed the dust from the back of the jacket, Darcy felt an energy against his shoulders, then Aurelio kissed his neck. Muted tobacco on his breath, tinged with something sweet, aniseed, fennel; perhaps he smoked cigars. His lips in the fine hair behind Darcy's ear, as if he knew his favourite places. Darcy arched his neck back. What time is the wedding? he asked.

It is now, said Aurelio, drawing away to reach for his scarf and some black leather gloves that lay on a stool like the wings of a blackbird. He took off his hat to replace it with another and his hair was luxuriant. He undraped his coat from his shoulders to reveal a double-breasted navy suit. Over it, he pulled on a tailored Kensington floor-length overcoat.

Darcy said he felt underdressed in his oilskin so Aurelio tossed him the greatcoat he'd just been wearing. A leather-scented cologne imbued the lining as Darcy slid it on.

Aurelio escorted him past an old treadle machine to a front entrance, out into the frigid street where a rusty Lada waited with a corpulent driver sandwiched behind the wheel, waking from sleep as Aurelio knocked on the window. Darcy and Aurelio both got in the back, Aurelio speaking in a language that sounded neither Russian nor Spanish. Darcy asked him what it was. You have no languages? Aurelio asked him, surprised. You English, having it easy.

But Aurelio was the one with the car and a driver.

Is this yours? asked Darcy, looking about as they rattled along.

Aurelio shrugged as if he couldn't help good fortune.

How did you end up in Moscow? Darcy asked.

Aurelio looked out the window and Darcy was afraid the question had been gauche. My mother is a friend of Castro, he said. He put his hand on Darcy's leg reassuringly and Darcy felt the hairs rise on his neck.

They both looked out at the river, at big discoloured wedges of ice too deep to be sliced by any sharp-hulled barge. Darcy imagined the climates they'd both come from, worlds with heat and beaches. I'd love to go to Havana, he said.

It is so far away, said Aurelio wistfully.

The traffic was light and it was now raining, groups of cream taxis flying past like large wet birds. A building draped in scaffolding and workers perched up high in the cold. Aurelio leaned close to Darcy, the sweet faint tobacco on his breath. Darcy found himself leaning too, as if they were on their own. Aurelio pointed. St Anne's in the ominous shadow of the Rossiya Hotel. The car slowed and Darcy looked up. A pale stone church, onion domes and limestone walls the colour of dirty washing, dwarfed by the towering building. He could paint the juxtaposition, baneful and clichéd.

As he opened the car door he heard the organ moan from inside the church as if it hadn't been played since the revolution. Aurelio offered him a square of fruity fennel gum. We go for the party, he said. A gust of cold air and the chill returned to Darcy's feet—he wasn't sure if Aurelio meant the Communist Party or the wedding reception.

They walked briskly across the rain-slicked cement and up some steps into a stone-cold church lit only by lanterns and candles. Darcy smiled at the unlikeliness, attending a place of worship in a communist country when he never set foot inside one at home. The crowd was sparse, the men in the usual drab suits and the women in dark shapeless coats, and Darcy thought of Aurelio's expression about when the ship went down.

The ceremony was already underway. Darcy pulled off his beanie and slipped into a pew beside Aurelio. Above them, the central cupola was boarded over; if there'd once been frescoes they'd been painted over too. Aurelio made a slight sign of the cross as he sat—a gay Catholic communist, maybe even Castro's misbegotten son. A secret of his own.

As the organ played Darcy removed his gloves and rubbed his aching fingers. The pew was cold. Aurelio pressed his knee against Darcy's and tipped his head to the bride near the pulpit; she wore white but no veil, a trail of silk and tulle floating down the steps behind her. My friend, said Aurelio. No bridesmaids or maids of honour. The groom stood a good head taller, slab-sided, square-shoul-dered, imperious in his military cap and uniform, a sword sheathed at his hip, curved like a narrow dragon's tail.

The general. His boss. But Darcy saw little evidence of high-ranking people, considering his stature, no minister either or priest, just an official celebrant, short and stout in a green uniform, speaking in muffled, dissonant Russian with the mike fading in and out. Candelabras framed a vase of red carnations on a table behind him. He lit the candles as the couple turned to face the guests; Sofia was beautiful, big-mouthed and Roman-nosed, her broad teeth showing, her smile full-lipped. She nonchalantly spat on her fingers and flattened her hair.

Is she Cuban too? asked Darcy.

Aurelio nodded, quietly chewing. Of course, he said, a smile like that.

Darcy felt the general's eyes rest on him with a kind of disdain—or was it Aurelio he was staring at? Darcy figured him in his sixties, Mussolini-faced and handsome in his military cap, snatching another glance at Darcy then glowering out beyond, as if on parade. Then the bride caught Aurelio's eye and made a subtle face, both mocking and desperate. She says he's like an animal, Aurelio whispered, making a claw with his fingers. He showed his unstained teeth. Darcy squinted to see the general's well-set features, the gold stars on the pocket of his jacket.

They took my passport, he whispered.

I know, said Aurelio.

What do you mean?

He shrugged. I know many things, he said. It is my job.

A man crouched in the aisle taking photos and Darcy craned his neck in case it was his Pentax but it wasn't. Aurelio began to translate the proceedings with the pressure of his knee, his breath near Darcy's face. Are you taking me to be your legal wedded husband? he said as the bride took the general's hand.

I hardly know you, said Darcy.

Aurelio turned to face him. You don't know anything, he said.

Mount Eliza, Late 1973

Darcy and Fin double-dinked, wobbled along the edge of Old Mornington Road, giggling, her young breasts against his back. She was ditching hockey practice, Darcy wagging his woodworking class. As they freewheeled down the hill, Darcy felt young in his school shorts and socks. She was already thirteen, her hair cut shorter, her hockey skirt way above her knees, wearing eyeliner to school, studs in her ears despite the regulations. Darcy'd sneak into her dorm even at lunchtimes now, calling *elly elly etdoo* from out in the trees as a warning. Her posh country roommates loved the conspiracy. If the matron or monitor came down the path, Darcy'd be out the cantilevered window before a knock on the door—or the flick of the switch if it were already dark; he'd be weaving through the trees to his bike hidden among the blackberries. But he had her with *him* now, taking her down to his secret clearing.

What are we doing? she asked.

I just want to show you, he said. He buried the bike in a thicket of gorse and they made their way down the wallaby trail.

Uh-oh, she said, but she wasn't afraid of scratching her legs. Show me what?

I dunno, he said. He wasn't sure why he'd brought her; it was as if he wanted to share it with her somehow, but the clearing was enshrouded by sword grass, it didn't look as pretty; the sun beat down on the grass and the wattle trees had withered back into themselves. A culvert had been dug and there was a pile of dirt. Others had been here, road-works people. Darcy turned and caught Fin as she ran down the gully slope to him. She buried her face in his neck and they held each other, innocent as lovers. Is that all? she asked. He felt her nipples firming like pebbles against his own.

Darcy broke free and took off his school shirt, spread it on what was left of the soft paspalum. Fin lay down on it without being asked and she looked up at Darcy smiling, almost daring him. Darcy kneeled. He realised that wasn't why he was here; he just wanted the missionary.

Fin took his hand and rubbed a finger in his palm. You don't like girls that much, do you?

At first Darcy didn't answer—it felt different being there with Fin. Darcy lay beside her. You're my sister, he said.

She raised her head up on her elbow and looked at him. Her fair hair with its tinge of red, her eyes their pale moss green. I'm still a girl, she said.

Darcy closed his eyes and remembered the bittersweet need in the missionary's eyes, how he whimpered and slumped and Darcy breathed into sweat that tasted salty like tears. The missionary wiping his butter from Darcy's belly with a pale green hanky, then he didn't look back as he climbed the slope through the trees towards the road. No Latter-day church was built on Two Bays Road.

Darcy stared up at the blinding white sun.

Mount Eliza, Summer 1974

Darcy noticed a burgundy Monaro parked near the gate on Baden Powell Drive. He went down to investigate. It was Fin, in a bikini, her bare feet up on the seat, next to a guy in Wayfarer sunglasses and greasy hair, a six-pack of Victoria Bitter between them. He slouched against the ribbed bucket seat with a smoke in his hand, legs splayed, worn holes in the knees of his jeans. Darcy saw the body-boards in the back seat. Fin hugged her legs. Wanna come down to Flinders? she asked.

I don't have my bathers, said Darcy.

Don't worry, she said, Jostler knows a secret beach.

A hand reached through the open window, past Fin, and shook Darcy's firmly. Darcy looked in and met the sunglasses, saw an ear pierced with a glinting silver star. This is Darcy, said Fin, but the boy just nodded.

Darcy got in and the car smelled of cigarettes and marijuana even with the windows open. As they drove, Darcy felt like a dog, the hot air on his face, happy, as they wound down Two Bays Road where the church never was. The view of the Mornington Peninsula sat low and hazy in the sun. Darcy imagined what it would be like just to get away forever. Fin, lying with the back of her head in this older boy's lap as he drove. He must have been at least eighteen, smoking a joint, one hand on the wheel. He passed it back for Darcy and Darcy took a drag and was spluttering, the smoke unpleasant in his throat. He waited for something to change, but all he felt was dizzy.

He watched out the window, smiling, as they passed Foxes Hangout, the dead foxes on the tree, then on through the orchards up the back of Red Hill and onto the dirt roads. A track through a farm over a cattle grid had Fin sitting up as the ocean unfolded before them, out beyond tussocks that poked grey through a luminous green that ran to the cliffs. Down to the right, a deserted beach that barely looked real.

Bushrangers Bay, said Fin. When they pulled up she and Jostler grabbed the boards as if they did this often and Darcy followed them over a grassy dune and down onto the stark white sand. A couple with a bucket down the far end looked for shells but otherwise no one. Fin, pale as the sand, lay down in the shade of a cave along the cliff and told Darcy to go out with a board. Jostler will teach you, she said. Darcy was nervous of water but he pulled off his cords and followed Jostler's tanned body, ran out in his shorts with the board and into the icy turquoise sea.

They paddled straight out even though it was rough and swimming out so far made Darcy more nervous, the swell higher than it had seemed from the beach. He tried to keep up, pushed out for what seemed like a long time, and then Jostler turned on the crest of a wave and boarded back out of sight, shouting things Darcy couldn't hear in the wind. Darcy turned too and crouched with his belly to the board to be swept in on a wave but it dumped him right there and the board flipped up and away as he struggled to swim over to it, a sense of the undertow strong. Jostler already back on the beach, motioning and pointing, but Darcy was breathless, out in the rip, drifting to the headland. The fibreglass smacked the waves, water freezing his legs and belly, spitting salt in his eyes like pieces of gravel. The strength drained from his arms and a sudden sense of being too tired to paddle, then Jostler returning and Darcy felt himself relax. All he could do was hold onto the board as a wave washed him into the rocks near the point.

Cold and aching Darcy scrabbled against the weathered edges, tossed by the waves, a cut on his leg. He saw Fin along the beach, running through the crab pools towards him, her face flushed with excitement. Jesus, she said when she got to him. I didn't know you couldn't swim.

Darcy sat gasping, in shock, as she kneeled down and hugged him, examined his cut. She dabbed it with a small, porous shell until the blood had stained it. Keep this to remember, she said.

Remember what?

How it felt like drowning.

Fuck you, said Darcy. He skimmed the shell out over the water and chased her, throwing shells, and they were laughing even though Darcy wasn't sure why. She went back to lie with Jostler in the shelter of her little cave and Darcy went and got the scuffed-up board, made his way along the beach and lay down near them, exhausted. Almost asleep in the sun, he checked his scraped leg, a glimpse through the thin blades of grass at Jostler on top of her, doing her. Darcy stayed low and felt himself, and he could tell Fin really liked Jostler, the way she was with her legs, and then she glanced over. She knew he could see. It was as if she wanted him to, and Darcy wished he could have lain over there with them, Jostler coming down on top of him—Jostler, not the missionary.

Then Jostler ran down to the water naked, patches of sand against his strong dark legs, and Darcy watched entranced, Jostler's half-erection floating out in front of him, hanging effortlessly with the rise and fall of the waves.

Fin appeared from her room, sleepy, her hair flat on one side and her lipstick faded. Darcy hung Aurelio's black greatcoat on a hook behind the apartment door. The dog's lead wasn't there. How did it go at the embassy? he asked. She didn't seem to notice the coat wasn't his.

I didn't get there in the end, she said. She was wearing her overalls with nothing underneath them and Darcy glanced at the curve of a small breast at the side of the bib and felt a sense of the ease with which she used her allure.

I didn't get to paint either, said Darcy.

On the counter, a tomato soup can filled with flagging yellow flowers and a screw-top jar of water. Fin sat on the arm of the sofa, studying Darcy as he studied the jar. At first, there seemed to be small black fish sealed in it, but as he held it to the light he realised they were small floating microphones. We found them in the bowels of the couch, she said.

Darcy could see where the cushions had been pulled free. Who is *we*? he asked. She turned her eyes to the window, didn't say. Her friend with the car, perhaps he brought flowers, swept the apartment for listening devices.

It's normal, she said reassuringly, and Darcy remembered he too had a friend with a car, yet a bitter feeling ran through him, of being out of his depth, microphones nudging up from the cushion-cracks.

It's not normal for *me*, he said.

Don't worry, she said blithely, they're not hydrophones, they don't record underwater.

And the flowers? he asked.

They're called yellow dogs, she said.

Who gave them to you?

A friend, she said, reaching down. Who gave you this? She held the dog's lead coiled up into a roll.

I found it in a park, he said.

It's winter. She said it cautiously. Why were you in the park?

Exploring, he said. He picked up a copy of the *Guardian Weekly* from a counter stool. LOSS OF CRUCIFIXES STIRS POLISH YOUTH. He thought of the church he'd just come from, the grey-painted walls, no icons or carvings, the crucifixes long gone. This guy followed me, he said. The one from last night, at the Bolshoi. He's Cuban.

Fin let the dog leash unravel and looked up at him, ran her fingers through her short hair.

He took me to a wedding, said Darcy—some general he works for.

Fin scratched her neck the way she did when she was nervous.

When I told him I was a painter, he said *like your friend*, and then he laughed.

Fin blanched, her lips pressed tight.

He's invited me to the country, said Darcy with false merriment.

You can't just go to the country, she said, there are checkpoints, but Darcy knew it wasn't just that—she didn't want him finding friends of his own. Moscow was her city. You'll need your passport, she said.

He said he'd arrange it, said Darcy. He sat on the barstool and leafed through the paper as if there would be news from home but there was only a photo of Nancy Reagan. He hated Nancy Reagan. He followed Fin's gaze out through the smudged window into the misty afternoon. Svetlana in the stark box of light wore a scarf. From beneath it, bleached strands of a fringe sprinkled her face. The scene reminded Darcy of an Edward Hopper, the Soviet version. Then her light went off and Darcy envisaged her waiting until they were gone, creeping over to install replacement devices. He turned the jar upside down and the microphones floated upwards like a pair of Hercules beetles. Hi-tech and wireless, they bobbed inches from his eyes. He was about to quiz Fin about the money belt when her bedroom door scraped open. A man with a nest of thick dishevelled black hair. Darcy put down the jar. The guy was gypsy-looking, familiar, but with black-rimmed Elvis Costello glasses.

Hello, said Jostler darkly. He moved past Darcy and snatched the jar up from the bench. As he pulled on gloves he didn't say more, just glared at Fin, a warning or a reprimand, and headed to the door. He seemed less swaggering but even more brooding. Darcy had imagined him up at Byron Bay, or Cairns, dealing weed to tourists, working in surf shops, not appearing here like some gypsy-intellectual.

His name's Jobik, said Fin.

It wasn't when he fucked you on the beach at Flinders. Darcy walked over and picked up the dog leash from the rug, rolled the leather around his narrow wrist. He felt Fin observing him, almost pityingly.

Be careful here, Darcy, she said.

And Darcy wished he hadn't shared about the wedding. Was the money belt for him? he asked.

No, she said. It was for you. She picked up the newspaper and headed to her room.

Darcy snatched the yellow flowers from the soup can, to hurl them after her, but she turned. That's what your mother would do, she said.

She'd throw the can as well, said Darcy. And then the toaster. They sniffed a laugh almost simultaneously then stopped.

She had a stroke, said Darcy.

The flower stems dripped water onto the floor. Fin said nothing.

It was only minor, he said. She just lay on her chaise pretending she was okay, her cigarette shaking, then she had a day in hospital. He thought how he'd visited her just once after that—to return her car. He'd told her he was going to Sydney.

Mount Eliza, Spring 1975

Darcy was baking a cake in the kitchen, whipping cream by hand, while his father poured a bottle of Remy Martin down the sink. The school says she's disappeared, his father said. He never mentioned Fin by name when Darcy's mother was in earshot, but she was sitting at the dining-room table and Darcy could tell his father wanted her to hear.

With some New Australian boy. Older. Apparently he took her off to Queensland. Did you know about this?

Darcy stood at the fridge with a bowl of cream in his hands, sinking. She hadn't said goodbye; he'd barely seen her since the day at the beach. Darcy moved to lean against the bench, told his father he knew nothing. But he'd seen Jostler just a week ago, the Monaro stopping on the corner of Mountain Road, offering a ride down the hill. Jostler, who'd come from the Somerville pub.

Darcy began whipping cream furiously. Yes, he knew Jostler. Darcy still remembered the holes in the knees of his jeans. He'd fantasised about being alone with him and some tinnies up at the old quarry on Two Bays Road. And now Jostler had taken her away.

His mother stood silent in the doorway as his father drained sherry from the stem of a tulip-shaped bottle. Apparently his last name is Garabed or something, he said. The police are searching for them.

Darcy mouthed the name: *Garabed.* I wish they'd taken me, he mumbled, but his father pretended not to hear, his mother glaring at the loss of liquid. A mix of envy and rage unbuckled inside Darcy, images of the endless beach at Surfers Paradise swirling white before him, Fin's head on Jostler's thigh in white sand as the clouds ran silent above, shadows on that phosphorous ocean. Fin knew first-hand about being abandoned, had left Darcy knowing how he'd feel. Jostler made her promise, he thought.

Darcy's mother drew on her smoke. She came, she went, she said sarcastically, and look at us.

Darcy threw the bowl of cream across the room. Most of it landed on the stove, dolloping down into the electric elements, some like semen on the walls.

Tut, tut, said his mother. Now we'll have to clean that up.

His father had an emptied bottle of her Gilbey's in his hand. He didn't look at the mess. Maybe we should go on a trip, he said.

Not to Queensland, said his mother.

Darcy hated her dismissal of every idea with a word or a wave of a cigarette. He felt a sudden desire to run from them, catch the bus to Surfers Paradise, or just walk out into the darkness, search the roads for the missionaries. He'd been right—Fin was the lucky one.

Ulitsa Kazakov, Wednesday morning

Darcy waited on the street, standing alone in Aurelio's coat under a black elm whose roots had fissured the pavement. Fin appeared beside him in her fur hat and headscarf, her lips pursed anxiously. Darcy liked how she didn't want him to go. She knew whose coat he had on now.

Fitfully she pushed at the fingers of her gloves. You shouldn't have told him where you live, she said.

He already knew, said Darcy.

Icy air funnelled alongside the stucco apartment block, stung his face as he stared at a car navigating the corner, the same rusty Lada from yesterday. At least let me see what he looks like, said Fin, in case you disappear.

Darcy didn't mind her protective and jealous, but her paranoia unnerved him. I can take care of myself, he said.

This isn't Dandenong, she reminded him curtly, and it made him feel more wary, his trust in the hands of strangers. The Lada double-parked.

His mother knows Castro, said Darcy.

Fin cast Darcy a sidelong glance from behind her scarf. That's a comfort, she said.

Aurelio rolled down the fogged-up window and there he was in wrap-around reflective sunglasses. Is there a chance of sun? Fin said. But Aurelio seemed larger than the life that surrounded him, a turtleneck sweater and overnight stubble, he could have easily been in an Aston

Martin, departing for the Alps.

Uninvited, Fin approached him. *Dobry utra*, she said. Aurelio removed his glasses and Darcy watched her embark on her charming Australian-but-fluent-in-Russian thing. Darcy got in the passenger side, the heater belching stale air, but Aurelio didn't greet him. He would forgive him, but he wondered if he could trust him. Darcy looked at his profile, waiting, noticed the ends of his hair poking from below his hat, that the space between his eyebrows looked shaven. Darcy's father said never to trust a man whose eyebrows met—but who could trust Darcy's father?

Fin's gloved hands gesticulated through Aurelio's window, her smooth unintelligible smoker's voice. *Spasiba*, she said, thank you, and Aurelio wound up the window, sat his sunglasses up between the brim of his hat and his harvest eyes.

He turned to Darcy, at last. We ready?

Gently Darcy took the sunglasses from Aurelio's forehead, put them on himself. They made the snow turn green, that light moss green of Fin's pupils. Sure, he said. He resolved to stay optimistic. Fin's arms gripped her shoulders, hugging herself in the cold, and he waved as they drove. Glancing back in the side mirror, he made out her slightly raised arm. Standing in the cold of the newly green street she looked puzzled, but he wouldn't be sucked into her suspicions; he had nothing to hide. Everything was green, he'd pretend it was beautiful. Why was she thanking you? asked Darcy.

She is worrying, said Aurelio. You are not with your passport. Darcy turned to regard him, the smudges now olive under his big dark eyes. Try to keep light, like yesterday, he thought; don't get complicated. And yet there was nothing playful about Aurelio now, steering with a military confidence, his hands solid in his driving gloves, as they turned from the street into the sparse mid-morning traffic.

Her Russian is surprising, he said, your friend.

Darcy surmised that gleaning information was probably part of this deal, but he refused to let the quid pro quo disappoint him. Fin had already put her spanner in the works, and he was niggled again by the memory of the money belt against him like a strip of swollen skin.

She studied Russian at university, said Darcy. He stared out as they crossed the lime ice river and passed the back of the Kremlin, the stone gates to Alexandrovsky Gardens. Too cold out there for birds except the occasional all-weather pigeon. He could pretend they were parrots through these lenses.

Did you meet her there, at the university? asked Aurelio.

Darcy nodded. Partially true. This, he knew, was exactly what Fin had feared, this conversation. *Keep it light, Darcy Bright, keep it light.*

Were you lovers? Aurelio asked.

Would you care? Darcy made an effort to smile.

Maybe.

Darcy'd have to guard his heart as well as his mouth, he knew this. Aurelio was different today, inquisitive in a less intimate way, but Darcy tried to ignore it. He'd say nothing of the money belt and nothing of Jostler who was now Jobik. He glimpsed a corner of the monolithic Rossiya Hotel and thought of yesterday's wedding down in its shadow, Aurelio and his friend Sofia; their eye contact mixed a subtle duty and flirtation. Was Sofia *your* lover? asked Darcy.

Aurelio smiled to himself as if it was hardly Darcy's business. We are connected by history, he said. He raised his crescent-moon eyebrows. Flirting, finally.

Darcy nodded, he understood about that, and while it felt better to be asking the questions, he still felt out of his depth.

The street seemed as wide as a landing strip, a slushy roundabout with the blunted shape of a workers' memorial, a determined-faced woman carved in granite, a sickle thrust from one hand and a flag from the other. She looked ready for anything. Darcy pulled out his map to get his bearings. So where are we going? he asked.

To the general's country house, Aurelio said. He is gone to Odessa on his honeymoon. He arched his back to get comfortable and Darcy found himself doing the same.

What will we do at the dacha? asked Darcy, pleased to know the word. An aubergine crow stooped on top of a lamp, burying its head.

I will get to know you, said Aurelio.

Will I get to know you?

Why not?

Darcy watched the stark city trees whip by, patterning buildings with their webs of twigs and bare branches. I know it sounds naïve, said Darcy, but is it true they cut the corners of gay men's mouths here?

Aurelio tossed his head back, laughed, then coughed. Who is telling you this?

I read it.

A story, he said, from the West.

Darcy feigned relief. How long have you been here? he asked. He pretended it was like a date, finding out about each other.

First I had scholarship to the Bolshoi, said Aurelio, and I was very strong. I'm sure, thought Darcy. But they only like Russian boys, so I am recruited to a special job. And today is my big day off, so I am with you. He gripped Darcy's knee and Darcy imagined Aurelio's dancer's body, Aurelio undressed. He wanted to stare at him but looked instead at the Byelorussian Station outside the window, foreboding and classical, surrounding three sides of a square; it looked different in daylight. That's where they took my passport, said Darcy.

I will do what I can, Aurelio said earnestly, tomorrow. Then he pointed out the *Pravda* building, a constructivist block of reinforced concrete and glass. *Pravda* is meaning truth, he said, and Darcy was relieved at the irony in his tone, his irreverence felt safer than his questioning.

At an intersection where snow ploughs stood fallow they turned. We're going direction Zagorsk, said Aurelio. Darcy couldn't read the signs and he'd lost track on his map; they could have been going to hell. A boy ran alongside them with old-fashioned ice skates over his arm and Aurelio regarded the stark multi-sided structure behind the fading figure. Dynamo Sports Palace, Aurelio said. Then they headed what felt like east past a plantation of high-rise flats, their cement-grey made green through the glasses, matching the sky. A fat man walked a cold, reluctant dog.

I'm not sure I could live here forever, said Darcy.

Aurelio understood. Why is your Finola in Moscow? Really?

Darcy felt Aurelio's coat around him—hearing her real name from his lips seemed strange. She has a grant from the Ministry of Culture, said Darcy. I came to help with one of her projects. He looked out as if uninterested, unsure if he'd already divulged too much. Buildings lower now, a tract of old wooden houses, snow-flecked shingle roofs. He'd only told what he knew.

She looks like you, said Aurelio, your friend. Actually, you are both looking Slavic. Like cousins of Navratilova.

We're just Australian, said Darcy, though he was sure Aurelio already knew that. He just hoped he didn't know they had American mothers. Being Australian felt more benign in Reagan's *empire of evil.*

Unexpectedly, Aurelio turned up a narrow windswept road and Darcy grabbed the leather roof strap, felt suddenly less certain. A tractor came out of a driveway and Aurelio slowed to swerve around it. Siblings of destiny then, he said. If he'd caught Darcy in the lie, Aurelio didn't acknowledge it.

They stopped at a guardhouse; Aurelio produced a laminated pass from his breast pocket and they were ushered on, winding quietly through a scant birch forest where a woman wrapped in a shawl collected wood. She stopped to watch them go by. It is close now, Aurelio assured him, and it felt like they'd entered a rarified place. They motored by a log house set back in the trees. Nabokov once was writing here, said Aurelio.

Darcy said he thought Nabokov wrote in exile.

Aurelio shrugged. Pasternak, maybe. Darcy couldn't tell if Aurelio was unconcerned with the truth or just trying to keep the trip interesting. They turned up another fresh-swept asphalt path and parked among the trees. Did you read *Lolita*? asked Darcy.

Aurelio leaned over, his mouth barely open, his stubble near Darcy's cheek. No, he said, and Darcy thought they might kiss but Aurelio reached to open the passenger door. He pushed the sunglasses up high on Darcy's hat like ski goggles.

Lolita is amazing, Darcy said. It always reminded him of the missionary, stamping a child with that. He wondered how he'd have been without it, if he'd have been in and out of so many strange men's cars.

Outside, the cold was piercing but it was nice to be rid of the city; no smell of fumes or sweaty polyester, just Aurelio's leather scent in the lining of the coat as Darcy pulled the collar up. He looked over at Aurelio's velvet skin and wondered if he felt the chill as deeply, his Cuban blood so thin the wind might blow through him too.

Aurelio unhinged the windshield wipers, put them in the trunk. People are stealing all things here, he said. Bad as Havana. He wrapped his burgundy scarf around his throat and ushered Darcy forward down a track flanked with low vines and fallen branches. Darcy wanted to reach for Aurelio's hand, to feel romantic, a longing that felt unfamiliar, no clear procedure like with the soldier in Prague. Where's the dacha? asked Darcy.

Aurelio pointed ahead, along a path hemmed in by firs and pines, Fin far away on the green-tinged street, left behind for once. With the crackling twigs underfoot and each crunch of snow it felt like there were others with them, but when Darcy looked back there was nobody. Then Aurelio stopped and put one hand on Darcy's shoulder, gestured to an expanse of snow. In the spring there is a field of yellow dogs, he said, as if he wanted Darcy to know it was prettier then.

Darcy thought of the vase of flowers on Fin's counter, a common variety, how he'd wanted to hurl them at her.

He saw the field was white now; Jobik must have bought her flowers from a hothouse. No wonder they had wilted. Darcy wished it were spring as he followed Aurelio over planks set above a frozen seep. Do you know what a wild-goose chase is? he asked.

Aurelio looked up as if there might be geese but there were only two military planes flying low but surprisingly quiet overhead. The dacha came into view. No evidence of a garden, just the ashy trunks of birches and the pine logs of the cabin, a weathervane with a rooster and a red star above a door. Aurelio searched for keys in the pocket of his coat, halted at laughter and banging from inside the house. Darcy tugged at his sleeve. I thought we'd be alone, he said.

Never mind her, said Aurelio.

A television blared as they walked to a shuttered window. Aurelio waved at a drooling girl who ate an apple wildly. She sat in a wheelchair surrounded by toys, their limbs torn off and their fluffy innards on the floor. She threw the apple at the television, then picked up a wooden spoon and started slamming on her eating tray. Her short brown hair was dipped to one side in a manner that was almost seductive. It was as if she couldn't see them out there.

That's Kapka, Aurelio whispered, the general's daughter; she's like a little girl.

He pointed up to a second-floor room with a filmy curtain. That's the room where I stay, he said and ushered Darcy up wooden ice-capped steps. Through an upstairs door they entered a small bedroom, but proceeded on to a small, beamed bathroom. The water's very hot here, said Aurelio. He turned on the taps to cover the sound of the retarded girl slamming her wooden spoon and wailing, and eased unselfconsciously from his coat and jeans, his coppery dancer's legs, his chest. He got in the shower and held his head up for a long time, let the water run over him like he was drinking from the sky. His skin slightly matt until the water hit it, then it glistened darkly. His body so smooth Darcy wondered if it had been shaven. He felt awkward, not certain if he was supposed to join in, but he found himself undressing, gingerly stepping into the steam.

Darcy hugged himself shyly as Aurelio turned and held him close, the pebbles of water on Darcy's back as he buried his head in Aurelio's chest, sensed the beat of his own heart. Aurelio soaped him and their bodies lathered and softened into each other like animals nesting, not as libidinal and eager as Darcy'd imagined. He felt Aurelio's big hands about him, the contrast in their skins and the flow of the water, and everything silent now save for Aurelio's breath in his ear, the softness of his touch. Darcy felt a surrender, a closeness that wasn't familiar, in this privacy, and a peaceful shuddery feeling rippled through him as it dawned on him that this was what he'd always wanted. He kept his eyes closed, to sense if it could be real. He thought of his time in the school showers with Benton in fifth form, how they'd meet behind the handball courts and make out in the late afternoons, but then Benton got a girlfriend and Darcy went down behind the courts alone. He kissed Aurelio's neck, and as the water washed over his mouth and eyes, he knew how afraid he was of this feeling, how Aurelio didn't seem to want more.

☆

As they drove back into the city, Darcy clasped the roof strap tightly, feeling slightly dissatisfied, the water no longer pouring, the world no longer green through the sunglasses that lay on the dash like another set of eyes. Do you take men there often? he asked.

Not men like you, said Aurelio. Something unabashed about him that Darcy wasn't used to. He wanted to give him the benefit of his misgivings, but he realised they hadn't yet kissed, not really, just been intimate in a way that made Darcy now feel disquieted.

Aurelio pulled into the slush at the approach of a siren. A bulging limousine with tinted windows splashed by, a motorbike escort in front and behind. A ZIL, said Aurelio, for Politburo. Other cars moved further to the side.

A classless society, said Darcy, and he thought of Chernenko's daughter and mentioned how he'd seen her at the Bolshoi, the night he'd first seen Aurelio.

Her name is Anyetta. Aurelio smiled. She is beautiful, no? Her mother is coming from Balkans. He said it as if the Balkans meant pretty, and it was true, she'd not inherited her father's bready features. My mother is coming from Spain, said Aurelio.

It made sense—the light in Aurelio's hair. Were you up in the box with Anyetta Chernenko? asked Darcy but Aurelio just looked vague and smiled, didn't answer.

Were you?

Aurelio turned off the road where a track opened onto a snow-covered mound and there was a view of the Museum of Science and Achievement. She's a friend of the general's, he said. A tone in his voice that sounded sad made Darcy wish he hadn't asked. He looked out at the distant obelisk, the crescent shape from Fodor's.

The Monument to Space Flight, said Aurelio. It shone in the clouded distance and bent up like a moon to the sky, a rocket on top of it. Your friend Fin, she told me this is what you wanted to see. He searched Darcy for surprise.

Darcy thought of how little of this he understood, Fin's flurry of Russian in the street. He stared out at an artificial lake slick with ice that housed the gilded fountain. I'm supposed to paint this, he said. He tried to imagine it in summer, the central marquee with its star-topped spire, columns like the Bolshoi, structures set against lawns, but all he could think about was why they hadn't been more sexual.

Is best from this distance, said Aurelio. He opened the Lada's window. The spread of pavilions, more theme park than museum. Darcy tried to sketch them in his mind, their angle and shape combinations, imagined their colours on a bright day, but the sun felt like a distant memory.

I wish we'd met in Havana, said Darcy.

You would be trouble there. He pointed out across the frozen landscape to a colonnade. That is the Serf Museum, he said, his breath a white river in the air in front of him. The only real colour now in the red flags that dotted the landscape like berries spilled in the snow. Aurelio showed Darcy the distant Atomic Energy Pavilion, as if hoping the structures might meet Darcy's expectations. Has a model reactor inside, said Aurelio. The Soviets were the first to make harness for atomic energy in peaceful purposes.

I hope it works better than their toasters.

For a moment Aurelio was offended but then he laughed. He moved in closer, his shoulder almost touching

Darcy's. If it were summer we could lie in the grass, said Darcy, then jolted as a large squawking bird left a nearby tree. He watched ice shaking from the branches. Aurelio put a large comforting arm around him. Don't be afraid, he said. If your friend is only an artist, there is no worry for you here.

A sudden thread of fear coiled up in Darcy's throat like a tendril as Aurelio leaned across to kiss him, cold lips on his, soft but dry, barely open, and Darcy tried to meet them evenly, the cool stale taste of Aurelio's smoky breath and the insinuation, *no worry for you here*. Still, Darcy opened his mouth to share all he had, but Aurelio drew away slightly and Darcy sensed he'd been too keen, too ready. Aurelio nuzzled him gently about his cheek, then held Darcy's head against him, a cold bronze button of his coat against Darcy's eye. I have not often kissed with men before, Aurelio whispered.

New Guinea, Summer 1975

Darcy's mother on the deck in her folding chair. Darcy crouched in the shade behind the engine room, too pale for this part of the world. He read *Lolita*, tried not to be seasick. The trip his father promised for a year wasn't what Darcy had expected—this rickety boat out from Rabaul, the motor smoking like a bush fire, out on the rough island waters, a native captain drunk and swearing in pidgin English. His mother silent since the plane left Brisbane—Qantas to Port Moresby, Air Nuigini to Rabaul—when all Darcy could think of was Fin and Jostler up in Surfers or Maroochydore, how his father wasn't taking them up there like normal people.

The sway of the boat and a sweet sickening smell like compost made Darcy nauseous. It was the scent of the tropics. His shirt sticking to his back and the salt spray from the water, his arms already burning even in the shade. The biting lips of the sun. Darcy's father in a safari jacket surveying the sea, as if he knew how to swim or might decide to buy an island. Darcy buried himself back in *Lolita,* let the pages get smattered by droplets, the faraway world of Humbert Humbert.

He tried not to stare at Orpheus, the young local guide, who now leaned against the cabled boat railing, the blue wrap around his waist against his mahogany calves. Darcy took out his Staedtler pencil and began to sketch him, a blank page at the end of the book. The shape of the boy, blue and black against the high infernal sky, the white glare of the pitiless sun. Darcy wanted to remember this for a canvas when he got home. He pencilled the dark Melanesian face, the smooth jaw and watery eyes, unruly twists of frizz. Orpheus noticed and smiled but Darcy just shaded his eyes, drew the dry lips and tawny teeth. He wondered how old Orpheus was; fourteen maybe, fifteen, about his age. He'd noticed earlier how the skin connected between Orpheus' toes in a pinkish membrane that almost looked webbed. Darcy's father had said it was because he came from a tribe of watermen, spending their lives fishing.

Our guide's a mermaid, said Darcy's mother, the first thing out of her mouth all day. Now she watched Darcy, winked at him, a nudge of her cigarette in the air. Darcy stopped his sketching, returned himself to Nabokov and tried to ignore the captain's cursing and the rutting of the engine. In his own head, he thought how Fin had left without even calling, Benton at the prize-giving night, acting like Darcy no longer existed.

He put down the book as they anchored in a cove off an island, climbing down into a dinghy. His mother with her sun umbrella, whingeing about her lumbago and how the doctor had told her to stay on her back, Orpheus helping her, confused, and Darcy felt embarrassed at being here. He'd always felt himself different but never privileged.

They splashed through warm shallows and traipsed across a deserted driftwood beach, dugout canoes as if planted for effect, the late afternoon, a trail through the rows of coffee plantations and coconut palms, heading to a *sing sing*, a clearing with huts and a small crowd of native

women in dry grass skirts, breasts drooping to their waists.
Isn't it marvellous? said Darcy's father.

His mother rolled her eyes and Darcy looked at
Orpheus, aware of their imperialism. A man up a tree with
a mask like a toucan, native men appearing from the
forest. At first, Darcy thought they had bloodshot teeth
because they had bloodshot eyes, or because they'd just
eaten raw meat, then he realised it was something they
were chewing. *Betel nut*, his father called it. Orpheus tied
his cloth differently now so it sagged like a loose-pinned
nappy, open as his smile.

Darcy's mother threw a stick at Darcy, told him to
watch the limbo competition.

His father held the broom. One woman got so low her
back touched the ground; one of her breasts got caught
on the broomstick. Darcy's father's face gleamed peculiarly
as he flipped the stick so the bosom fell down beside her,
almost to the dirt. The native men laughed, the betel nut
red on their teeth. Darcy's mother shook her head and sat
bored in her folding chair, lit a cigarette. Darcy went for a
stroll. Orpheus followed as though it was his job to ensure
no one strayed and then they stood together nervously
behind a hut.

Orpheus put two fingers to his lips and touched
Darcy's nose with them, returned to the festivities as if
nothing had happened. Darcy's mother stood up carefully, folding her beach chair. She put her hand in the
small of her back for support. *Chronic* she called her lumbago, but Darcy's father had insisted, as if this weird trip
would make her forget about Fin. She carried her gin and
tonic in a thermos and took Halcion. She told Darcy *hal-
cyon* was really a bird that floats in its nest on the sea. She

sometimes pretended her bed was a nest and after she swallowed a tablet she went on voyages. She said it felt better then.

As they walked four abreast back through the plantations, small plots of taro and sweet potato, Darcy wanted to reach over and hold Orpheus's hand, stay here on the island, away from these stupid white parents. But Orpheus walked with his broad feet bare in the leaves, his twisted hair and red stained teeth, walking as though they'd not had their moment.

The natives must think your father's an idiot, said Darcy's mother as if his father wasn't with them. Dressed up like Albert Schweitzer, gawking at their women. An angular dog with a gash on its flank, sniffed along behind them. Darcy's mother shooed it away with her folding chair.

I think it went well, his father said, in his *rah-rah* voice. Everyone seemed to like us. He didn't notice the betel nut spat all over his safari shirt. Orpheus said nothing. Darcy wanted to give him the sketch inside *Lolita*.

You didn't include Darcy, his mother said.

Darcy's father looked at him, almost surprised. You had fun, didn't you, son?

Darcy nodded but not at him, held the book to his chest. I was doing my own thing, he said.

You certainly were, said his mother.

When they got to the beach and Orpheus said goodbye, Darcy wanted to tear out the sketch but he didn't. His father was plying the boy with Australian notes, explaining the coat of arms, the emu and kangaroo.

Off Leningradsky Prospekt, Wednesday night

It was almost ten in the evening when Fin took Darcy out to see jazz. A concert held in secret, she said, because jazz wasn't sanctioned in Moscow. They glided up endless escalators, through marbled caverns of an opulent underground, tentacles probing the skin of the earth. Fin seemed edgy again. But what did you actually tell him? she asked.

Nothing he didn't already know, Darcy said. Even though it was probably true, an itchy disloyalty slipped over him.

Did he want to have sex in the end? she asked.

Darcy wasn't sure if it this was a joke, *sex in the end*, but she didn't look like she was joking. She wore black and her make-up was subtle, no flashes of colour tonight. He was too busy showing me the museum, he said, and the half-lie buzzed about his mouth like a wasp. I'll still need to get some pictures of the buildings. The shapes were interesting, that rocket spire, and the pavilions.

A cluster of workers trundled down the other side of the escalators. Their jutted brows and wide-set eyes came and went between the bronze-encased lanterns that hung from canopies like fruit bats, a muted waterfall of cast-down faces. At first Darcy wished he had his camera, then he just wanted to be where there was light. He thought how it would be stinking hot in Melbourne.

Out in the night he extended an umbrella for Fin. The

Sports Palace loomed, a dark iceberg lit blue in the distance, but they headed around the back of the station, past drunks who leaned on each other for balance. Fin covered ground without appearing rushed, cut abruptly between prefab concrete high-rises, structures bathed in snow, poorly lit, windowless, unearthly. They wove through patchy darkness, down a concrete stairwell to a bolted red iron door. Fin knocked in a rhythm.

People like us can ruin things like this, she whispered. The lock was wrenched and they slid inside, the mouldering smell of an underground place. Fin shoved roubles into a palm that extended from the shadows and they stepped down into a spare, smoke-ridden basement where a small crowd sat on rugs and cushions spread along cement ledges that rose up like opium beds in front of a makeshift stage. An upright piano stood as something holy. The mood, so suppressed and intense, surprised Darcy, giddied him. Guys with button-fly Levis and long hair smoked *papiroses*; one wore a baseball cap, another wore a bandana and tongued his woolly-sweatered girlfriend. Darcy was suddenly keen to be here, behind the veil of the culture, the curtain behind the curtain, but where was Aurelio now?

Look comfortable, said Fin. She removed her hat and mussed up her spiked hair; she didn't mind being noticed now she was inside. Darcy took off Aurelio's coat and looked about at the people in every available space, arranging pillows and sheepskins to protect themselves from the concrete. A couple nearby on a raggedy couch drank vodka, and a tape of Thelonius Monk played 'Straight, No Chaser' from a yellow boom box that sat like an animal on the piano.

Darcy squatted beside Fin on some kind of skin with faded chartreuse cushions, her fur hat now beside her like a sleeping black cat. Darcy reached for one of her Gauloises and lit it. She'd said you can tell foreigners by their imported cigarettes.

A man with a ponytail took the boom box away and as the lights dimmed Darcy caught Fin watching the door. A latecomer in thick corduroys and a long leather jacket edged his way along their makeshift row, ran fingers through a shock of jet-black hair. Jobik. What kind of name was that anyway? Fin quietly picked up her hat and Jobik crouched beside her, then sat. He put on his glasses and gave Darcy a wink that prickled Darcy's skin.

The pianist appeared and perched at the piano in meditation, his arms still in his lap, then flung his hands abruptly at the keys. In the surging discordant rhythm Jobik edged closer to Fin, sharing her pillow. As he pulled his scarf free she slipped an envelope into it. Jobik caught Darcy noticing and reached past her to shake his hand, but there was even more meanness in the curve of his smile and a challenge in his sinewy grip. His hairline seemed lower, his widow's peak, black eyes even in daylight. Darcy still remembered how it felt being left out in the waves to drown. He'd always assumed Jostler was Greek but maybe he was really some Tajik or a Kazak, a separatist. He didn't seem moved by the music. Darcy struggled to remember his last name, could almost see it on his father's lips.

The pianist stabbed at keys and hammers, and the open-fronted upright jumped. The audience feasted on what must have been rare, worth risking freedom. A people who'd learned to measure consequence. Darcy knew he hadn't mastered that. And if he'd risked his freedom bringing in the money belt, it was a risk he was now certain he'd taken for Jobik—Jobik who looked over and gave Darcy a narrow-eyed smile—and Darcy wished he didn't understand why Fin ran away with him. Darcy would have done the same; they shared a lust for dangerous people.

The jazz player flung a sweater in the hull of the piano and it dulled the shrillness, but when he used his wrists and elbows on the keys the off-putting chords and Jobik there with Fin became too jarring. Darcy grabbed the umbrella and whispered something akin to *izvinitye* before Fin could stop him, and made his way through the smoke. He closed the heavy red door behind him and stood on the steps. In the shock of cold air he waited, leaned against heat from a grate behind the concrete railing. The smoky discharge mixed with the frigid air. As Darcy lit a cigarette, he thought of Aurelio and how being with him had both buoyed and unnerved him. The jolting cadence of muted piano thumped dully behind him, a ghostliness about the looming buildings, a landscape worthy of paint. Perhaps he was here for moments like this, for inspiration.

Don't stand up there, Fin whispered from the bottom of the steps. She motioned him deeper into the stairwell and took a cigarette from her pocket, ignited it from his the way she always did. She hunkered with him as if they were outside a gig at Monash, taking a breather away from the others. But Darcy felt like he was the *other* here.

Where's your mystery guest? he asked.

Her lips pressed around her cigarette as a slow-moving figure pedalled through the dark on an old-fashioned bike, rising from the seat to push through the slush and snow.

A leather bag was suspended from the handlebars so that it looked like a scene from after the war. That's him, she said.

At first Darcy didn't believe her, he'd assumed it was someone old, but she told him there was a separate exit, that Jobik could never stay long. She held onto her wrist as she smoked and watched the deliberate, languorous progress of the bicycle out to the ill-lit boulevard. It merged with the colour of the night. Fin watched with the stifled anguish of a woman in a situation. Darcy could see the precariousness in the redness of her eyelids. Jobik had somehow dulled the green of her eyes, dug into her deeply and latched her darkness onto his. Darcy imagined the pungent pleasure of their sex, a cause she'd hitched her wagon to because of it.

I thought he was Greek, Darcy said casually, back home. An old man stooped through the snow with a wheelbarrow of boxes. Where's he from really?

Fin raised her eyebrows with her own false nonchalance. It's all the Soviet Union now, she said. She reached for a stray bottle top from the stairs, her cigarette balanced between her lips.

I saw the envelope, said Darcy.

The slightest tightening in her jaw. I wrote him a letter, she said, and it seemed plausible, yet Darcy put his money on a lie.

Is that what I smuggled in? he asked. Love letters? He flicked his cigarette.

Fin was silent. She pressed the bottle top into the leather of her glove, examined the corrugated imprint. Applause rippled dully from inside as the piano banging ended, clapping dampened by the closed iron door. Will he leave you out in the cold? asked Darcy.

Fin half-smiled at his attempt at spy talk. She spun the top in the air like a coin and it planted itself in the snow. Will *you*? she asked.

Darcy stood in his sheepskin vest, staring at the notice-board. Flyers for the Young Communists and the Bisexual Alliance stapled side by side. Each had the caption *We know you're out there*. That's how he felt: just out there, floating. A year and a half and he hadn't made a friend he could be bothered with, save for a few minutes at a time among the stalls and glory holes in the basement of this Ming Wing, or huddled with some footballer in a shower stall at the uni gym, cowering unnoticed against the tiles as the bursar appeared with prospective students, showing off the new facilities. Darcy turned, drawn back down the basement stairs to check for that Sephardic boy from law, giving head with his yarmulke still pinned on. But Darcy felt a presence close behind him. A soft patchouli smell.

Deciding between politics and love? A voice that chilled him, filling him with a wave of astonishment. He looked at her speechless, confused. Fin smiled, her lipstick brown, the same white skin but short, spiked hair, a stud in one ear only and a fine silver nose ring. Seven years since. She lifted her John Lennon sunglasses up into her hair, and the same green eyes gazed down at Darcy's snug tartan trousers, the flare and lavish cuff. Nice pants, she said.

Darcy wasn't sure if she was being sarcastic but he didn't care.

Where did you run off to? he asked, as if it had been a week, not years.

Queensland for a bit, she said, then California. I finished high school in Berkeley and did a year of college there. Her accent seemed more American. She wore a shining leather mini-skirt and hugged a satchel fronted with a square of butcher's grass. Darcy felt uncool, like he was still from Mount Eliza. Why didn't you write and tell me?

I had to get away, she said. I was dying here.

You were only fifteen, he said.

I knew you would have freaked, she said. And Jostler was afraid you'd come and find us.

Darcy stared back at the noticeboard to keep himself under control. Yes, he'd freaked, in a silence of his own that had lasted for years.

So what about you? she asked.

Not too much, he said. He'd painted and studied, read, won prizes at school, but mostly he'd been lonely; scrappy and dissatisfied. He rubbed his neck, aware of Fin watching, but he couldn't pretend to feel breezy. So why did you come back? he asked.

To find you, she said, among other things.

Darcy felt like his clothes were too tight for how he was feeling. You could have sent a postcard. He could hear the hurt in his voice.

She swivelled her nose ring. I'm sorry, she said. I couldn't risk it.

Risk what?

Family, she said, and they looked at themselves in each other's eyes, but the time and distance had made Darcy feel more different, more left behind. His mother drinking herself into a deadening stupor, endless encounters at beats and then the parks along the Yarra, now here. How did you know I was here?

I phoned our father.

Our father who art in purgatory, said Darcy; he'd gone to live with Ranita, a woman he'd met on his egg run. How did you find him?

Through the egg farm. He told me you were majoring in art. Darcy was nodding at the faint freckles under her eyes, her bohemian perfume. His father whom he never visited.

Was Jostler with you in California?

She nodded. I studied Russian and psych at Berkeley, she said. Now I've transferred to this place. She looked about as if it were daunting but she didn't look like she'd be daunted by much. And he'd imagined her up in Queensland all this time, never dreamed of her at Berkeley. He'd only been as far as New Guinea.

I've changed my last name to Dobrolyubova, she said. Finola Dobrolyubova. She seemed pleased with how it sounded. Dobrolyubov was a famous Russian social critic, she said.

Darcy watched the brightness of her new hair, the way she stood so easily in her tight black mini while the other Monash girls moved past in their three-quarter lengths, observing her.

I'm still Darcy Bright, he said.

Fin searched the noticeboard and smiled. Young? Communist? Or bisexual?

Darcy's throat as dry as a branch. Mostly he felt unsure. Gay, he said. I'm gay.

Ulitsa Kazakov, Late Wednesday

Quietly Fin rested a large primed canvas on the easel, placed a concertina of faded tourist photos on the ledge. Without a word of goodnight she slipped off to bed, left him to it. On the duvet-covered couch, Darcy was smoking, staring out at the grey rectangle of well-stretched linen. The artist left to paint. He conjured the museum he'd viewed from Aurelio's car—the snowbound spread of buildings and oversized fountains, Gothic and constructivist, the Monument to Space Flight sluicing the sky, and the way Aurelio's arms had held him, the warm but slightly stale taste of him. Closing his eyes Darcy summoned bare-chested revolutionaries on dark Orlov horses galloping down through snow-covered trees and setting the museum on fire. An image seen clearly, but he knew he'd have to be more subtle.

He stood and brushed the canvas with his palms. Taut but soft, unspoiled, nice for drawing. He placed Fin's gift of foldout photos of the museum on the end table. A sheet secured to the window now, tied to the hinges with shoelaces. He was alone. *When the soul wants to manifest something, she throws an image out in front of herself and moves to catch it.* He repeated it, tried to believe, imagined as he always did the rhythm of the arms of a juggler, the whoosh of the pins and the effortless reaching, the musicality of limbs. He imagined Aurelio dancing. Darcy rested his cigarette in Fin's kabuki ashtray, lit one of her red candles.

He pulled her paintbox from behind the couch. Oils and acrylics mixed, a compartment of half-washed brushes, flat ferrule and oval shaped, the familiar smell of linseed. He sharpened a woodless carbon pencil. He figured if he drew in the candlelight, amid the smoke that wove from the ashtray, he might capture the movement of buildings, fake himself into feeling intuitive. Without a drink.

He pinned the concertina of images above the canvas, along the beam of the easel, eleven pictures, folding out one at a time. He recalled the sea of pavilions, acres of them jutting from the snow like mausoleums, the sharp silhouette of the obelisk. Aurelio and his private view as they sat in the Lada on the risen clearing, the reticent kiss, everyone's signals confusing.

The carbon pencil ran well, gliding over the soft material. He swooped the lines of the shiny platinum form to the point where the gunmetal rocket would sit, a fin-shaped tower, bent and tapered. He drew with a juggler's cadence, the meditative speed of the pins, his concentrated eyes. It summoned the memory of Laika, a televised image from childhood—the expression of the dog in the Soviet rocket, launched into a Soviet sky.

He took the Polaroid of the whippet and copied the lines of its face, its narrow back and nervous haunches, forelegs perched on a nose cone and an expression of forlorn hope. He added the bulbous tourist bus from the fold-out card at the base of the monument, realistic enough but also oddly proportioned. Postbox red. A touch of Basquiat. He tried to keep the rhythm before it got discordant, the softness of the pencil in his fingers, but he thought about Fin and felt the river of movement fading; this painting her ruse.

Still he was in it, drawing pavilions small and fountains and obelisk big, both realist and abstract, less concerned with perspectives and angles, knowing if he stopped he might never finish and that if he drew all night he could have something by morning. The Stone Flower Fountain with huge ornate petals sprouting from a mattress of rocks and high cascading flutes of coloured water: garnet, turquoise, lapis, emerald, amber. He turned to the foldout photo of the wedding-cake building, Doric columns and the star at the top of the gold-painted spire, red flags from the portico, an Aeroflot jumbo with its loading ramps down like a pair of splayed legs.

Darcy stood back. It was a long way from McCubbin and not quite de Kooning, and it wouldn't exactly be Soviet Realism, the curious outlines and empty sky, too many shapes and juxtapositions; more like Soviet Surrealism. The candle on the end table collapsed down one side. He pushed his fingertip into the melted wax, felt the slight stab of heat as he stamped some red in the whippet's eye. It dried like a seal on an envelope, the intricate web from his fingerprint. It gave the dog more life.

Darcy's eyes were sore, his wrist and movement fading. This was all he could do now. He left the painting there, thought he should shower, but he wiped his hands on a rag and lay behind Fin in bed with his dark smudged fingers. He kissed her goodnight above the line of her T-shirt where the tattoo was, and then she was turning and he could sense that she'd been crying, her tears on his skin and her saying sorry as she kissed him softly, tears on his cheeks. I'm sorry, she said and he felt himself against her and thought of them as children, on the driveway at Mount Eliza, on the beach with Jobik with her legs up. She kissed him again and he thought of Aurelio and knew this wasn't what he wanted, his sister like this, but her sorries and tears had aroused him, his face in her hair and the scent of her shampoo, a coursing of grief deep within him. On the verge of inside her, he suddenly wanted to get back at her, at Jobik or whatever his name was, at Aurelio who didn't even want to kiss, but a sound came from Fin, far away as an island. No, she said. She was staring back at him through the dark, her lips parted, afraid. Not that.

Monash University, Winter 1982

Fin appeared in the smoke-filled dinge of the Small Caf, late as usual, wearing her calf-high boots with a short pleated tartan skirt despite the cold. They always met on Wednesday evenings, after his Portrait, Figures and Anatomy class and her Russian history. Afterwards she'd go to her psychology tute. Darcy watched her slide through the milling students, past the dopers at the big round table where they sometimes sat, everyone saying hi. Her hair plastered up on one side, flat against her scalp on the other. She fascinated Darcy, her punk-chic style, not unlike he imagined himself in drag. She flung her faux cowhide satchel over the chair, sat as if exhausted.

I need to do a psych test on you, she said.

Darcy sipped his coffee, pushed the second cup towards her. Must you?

She dropped her small oval sunglasses on the table. It'll only take a minute, she said. She extracted a set of ink-blotted cards from her satchel. All you do is tell me what you see, she said. She placed a card on the tabletop. The first thing that comes to mind.

Darcy was used to her talk of Chomsky and Jung, he usually just smoked and listened to her random diatribes, thought about where he'd go later for sex. Now he strained to examine the patterns inked on a card.

Monkeys playing drums, he said. He looked up at her,

wondering what he was supposed to see.

Look at the cards, not me, she said. She flipped over a new one.

A wildebeest with wings, he said, trying to impress her. He drank more coffee. The face of a startled cat, he said next. Aren't you supposed to take notes?

Fin stared at him through the smoke, kept turning cards.

Blood in the rain, he said, when he saw obvious lips. Two mirrored butterflies. She turned them faster. Purple lingerie on the torso of a man. Iguanas fucking. Twin vaginas, he said when they could have been more butterflies. She splayed the last card on the table. An orchid. It wasn't his first response; he'd seen another vagina.

Fin shook her head as if disappointed, gathered up the cards and shoved them back into her satchel. She flattened her skirt and lit a Camel with her neon lighter.

What does it mean? asked Darcy.

She turned and dangled one leg over the other, a boot extended, as though feigning her version of a therapist. I'd say you live in your shadow, she said. She licked her top teeth as if they might be stained with lipstick, conjuring something more. You contain an inherent duality.

Darcy wondered if she'd been stalking him. Tell me something I don't know, he said.

Okay, she said. I think I want to make art.

Darcy felt glad for the change of subject. He'd never heard the expression *make art*; it sounded American.

I want to do installations. Like Judy Chicago. You know, like 'The Dinner Party.'

Darcy had seen a photo of the triangular place settings meant for the women omitted from history. Sappho to Georgia O'Keeffe, he said.

But I'm going to do my own thing, she said.

Darcy thought how little she asked or knew about his art. The series he was painting from photos he'd taken, the rain-slick streets around the back of Ascot Vale where the abattoir smell lay in the air like a transparent fog. That's cool, he said. He had listened to her lectures about movements and struggles in places he'd barely heard of, Eritrea and Azerbaijan, the second wave of feminism, deforestation in Brazil, but she hadn't yet told him where she lived. She refused to discuss their family. And now she wanted to muscle in on his territory. *Make art.* He watched her blow cigarette smoke into the hazy cafe air, off in her own thoughts. She reminded Darcy of his mother, the way she let her head fall back.

There's something I think about, he said.

She looked at him, gauging him, the fuming green of her pupils.

Why did you really leave Mount Eliza?

She touched the corner of her mouth with the little finger of her cigarette hand as if there was something to flick from there. Then she cast her eyes over at the stoners with their bags and surreptitious bowls. Because I was pregnant, she said. If you must know.

Darcy felt the weight of their underlives, how they spilled over into each other, the memory of her through the sand grass, taking it deep on the beach at Flinders, the way one of her legs went up at an angle. Jostler? he asked.

A flush of pink under her eyes. Well, it wasn't you. She laughed in a husky way that didn't sound normal and then looked back to the veil of weed smoke that puffed above the next table.

Darcy was thinking about how she'd only been fifteen. Did you have the baby? he asked.

Yeah, right, she said. She pulled on her cigarette.

Where's Jostler now? asked Darcy.

Here and gone, she said, but her expression altered at the mention of him, clouded. He's become very political, she said. Don't ask me where he is now.

I don't even know where you live, said Darcy.

She pulled out a postcard and looped a telephone number on it. Darcy watched the grace of her white fingers as she handed it to him. I got this for you, she said. Large square letters adorned by a drawing of a penis with an arrow to a big, red heart. CONNECT YOUR GENITALS TO YOUR HEART.

Darcy stared at the card in his hand. Why? he asked.

Because you ask questions like you don't have secrets of your own, she said.

Ulitsa Kazakov, Thursday morning

Darcy woke up alone, feeling strangely hung-over. He got up and stood in the bedroom doorway. Fin was watching the Winter Olympics, adjusting the wire coathanger she'd rigged as an antenna. His sketch sat on the easel but Fin didn't mention it—she didn't mention anything. On the television, a Soviet cross-country skier with toes secured and ankles free, scooting through powder and into the trees. Sarajevo, said Darcy. He couldn't tell if it was snowing there or if the reception was poor. Then a woman was poised on the ledge for the slalom. Dark pencilled eyebrows and wisps of dyed blonde hair sticking out from under her ski cap. Fin translated the commentary, stony-faced. Ida Bogdanova, nineteen, from Moscow, three months pregnant.

The skier covered her face with Carrera goggles and a foghorn sounded. She plunged amid whistles and ringing and Fin leaned forward on the couch. The figure hurtled, bouncing between the pegs and leaning, scouring snow, then hit a mogul sideways and flipped end over end, skidded into orange netting. Onlookers scattered and the coverage switched to curling. Fin sat back deep in the sofa. What would that do to a baby? she said.

A Soviet curler rippled his stone smoothly across the ice. It floated off-course then drifted back, stopped close to the tee.

Abortion is the most common contraception here, said Fin. They call it *Three Nights in Sochi*.

Darcy felt a sadness creeping about him. That he'd wanted to slip inside her as a twisted revenge. He thought of Sochi, a town on the map, on the Black Sea. A resort town. Darcy sat down beside her on the couch. Have you ever been to Sochi? he asked.

They both stared at the screen. No, she said, I had my afternoon in Brunswick.

He thought of her at fifteen on the Smith Street tram with Jostler, the set of her teenage face as they dug up inside her. Remnants of that face now watching the snow-blown trees in the televised forest. Another Russian langlaufer swished grimly by and then swung from sight, absorbed into the pine trunks.

Why didn't you tell me, asked Darcy, back then?

Tell you what?

That you were pregnant.

I promised him I wouldn't tell anyone. I keep my promises. She looked at Darcy as if for the first time. Let's never mention last night.

Darcy felt an undertow of secrets held for those they were fucking or almost had. He found himself nodding. If you tell me what you're really doing here, he said.

Fin stood as if drawn to the window. She pulled at the sheet that half covered it. Come look, she said. Your Cuban's in the courtyard. And there he was, the telltale drape of his coat about his shoulders, his prints fresh in the snow behind him. He was headed to the building opposite but he turned, as if sensing them. Maybe he's come for his coat, said Fin sarcastically.

Aurelio was motioning Darcy down to join him and

Darcy grabbed his greatcoat and beanie, happy to end their conversation, but Fin did the same, pulling on her sheepskin coat and fur hat. I don't trust him, she said.

Darcy knew the truth—they no longer trusted themselves. They hurried downstairs, relieved by the distraction.

Aurelio leaned against the double-parked Lada, the collar of his Kensington framing his chin like the petals of a big, dark tulip, the shadow of his sideburns slightly thicker down his jaw than yesterday, smudges etched more deeply below his eyes. You were headed to the wrong building, said Darcy.

Aurelio regarded Fin cautiously. I was not sure, he said. He took his keys from his coat. You have been to the Pushkin? he asked. The Tretyakov Gallery? He'd turned from watcher to seducer to Intourist guide.

Fin said she'd love to go and broke into Russian. She got in the front seat and Darcy found himself getting in the back like an afterthought, deciphering only occasional names and movements: Kandinsky, Chagall, Isaak Brodsky, realists, avant garde. Aurelio didn't meet his eyes in the rear-view mirror; he slid his gloves from his long fingers and fiddled with the radio dial.

Darcy felt disoriented. He'd wanted to talk with him about last night's jazz but his mind was swamped with what almost happened with Fin. In the mirror he caught a glimpse of his own face; his hair stuck out like a shelf from being slept on, his Australian tan already gone. Aurelio kept his colour despite the winter and Fin kept hers too, porcelain white, pristine against her fresh morning lipstick, but even paler this morning, drawn, as she chatted away as if all was on the level.

They wended the wet streets to the river, a dirge

crackling through a speaker attached below the glove box, vibrating near Fin's knees—the place where Darcy's legs should have been. In the front they continued their exchange with such passion their Russian sounded like the quarrelling of lovers. Darcy listened to the music. I'm not crazy about Shostakovich, he said, to get them back to English.

It is Prokofiev, Aurelio said matter-of-factly, turning the volume down. Fin glanced back at Darcy but he chose not to receive her look, focused instead on the furry place at the nape of Aurelio's neck where he'd buried his face only yesterday. Then he watched out into the leafless streets—the whine of the wipers with the lament of the requiem was hypnotic and it was beginning to snow. They stopped at a light near the frozen drainage canal where men perched on buckets on the embankment, bundled up like bears. They contemplated dark holes they'd made in the ice, their fishing poles draped into them. Wherever there's water men are fishing, said Darcy, mostly to remind himself of his own voice.

Aurelio turned back to Darcy, a desire for forgiveness in his eyes, but the music stopped abruptly and there came an announcement. Fin reached for the volume. Andropov's dead, she said, wide-eyed. They all listened.

How? asked Darcy, afraid it had been the Americans, but Aurelio smiled; he seemed pleased.

He is been sick for months, he said. He wiped the fog from the window in front of him and put down his foot at the change of the light. The engine gushed as if it might flood. He drove faster now as if in his own world, making calculations.

I just saw him on the TV, said Darcy.

He's probably been dead for weeks, said Fin. They play old footage.

And they play dirge on radio to prepare the people, said Aurelio. Is hard to know what is real.

Together Aurelio and Fin seemed to know everything, except perhaps about each other.

Didn't Andropov write to the American schoolgirl? asked Darcy. It was the only thing he could remember.

He wrote romantic poetry, said Fin, and arranged the invasion of Hungary.

He was two people, Aurelio said, turning to her. Like you.

She's more than that, thought Darcy.

I'm an artist, said Fin. I'm allowed. A new torrent of their fluid-sounding Russian.

No, thought Darcy. I'm the artist.

The Monastery of St Peter rose up behind a high stone fence, a stepped belltower with a tapered green dome, a conglomerate of churches. Will it be Gorbachev's time now? asked Darcy to break them up.

Things get worse before they get better, said Aurelio, and Darcy heard them mention Chernenko's name. He thought of the daughter, how she might become more influential now.

News of Andropov's death had pedestrians hurrying to the metro entrance at Prospekt Marksa as if there were things to prepare. Their movement was infectious. Aurelio said he'd have to drop the two of them off at the Pushkin because he needed to return to his office now. Darcy felt both relief and disappointment. He hadn't imagined Aurelio having an office, just the dress shop.

Can you drop us instead at the Beriozka on Petrovka?

asked Fin as if a car was a bonus she couldn't let slide. She pulled her netted *perchance* bag from the pocket of her coat.

Aurelio watched Darcy in the mirror as if intuiting he'd still want to see the museum. I have some thing for you, said Aurelio with a certain sad amusement, dividing *something* into two separate words. He produced a small package from the sleeve in the door and handed it back to Darcy over the seat. More dull colour postcards. The Museum of Science and Achievement, the same shot of the arcing obelisk dwarfing the bright red bus. Captions in both Russian and English, the Atomic Energy Pavilion, colours unknown to nature added to the images like artificial sweetener. Pictures taken in summer. Aurelio looked in the rear-view mirror again, waiting for Darcy's gratitude. To help for your painting, he said.

Another shot of the People's Friendship Fountain, the gold-leafed women holding bouquets, the water festooning, not frozen or smudged with snow. The grass a torpid green. Thank you, Aurelio, said Darcy. The sound of the name felt round on Darcy's tongue.

Fin asked if she could look but Darcy continued flipping. The Stone Flower Fountain, he said. The huge ornate petals that sprouted from rocks with high cascading flutes of water. He envisioned his canvas with the rocket-shaped monument bent and shining into the ether, mounted with the Polaroid of the prick-eared dog. Multimedia might be interesting here, he thought; both real and surreal, an ode to achievement and Laika heading into space on her own, the pavilions below. He could imagine it.

Then he came upon a black and white picture, loose. Two men in a lavatory stall, shot from above. Had Aurelio left it accidentally? And then it dawned, a shadowed version of himself, his pained expression, eyes twisted closed, searching upwards. The one standing was Darcy. Shame and panic rose in a wave to his throat and came to his eyes.

Aurelio had seen what Darcy uncovered. He pulled over outside the nondescript self-service market as Fin had requested. That is why there is a problem with your passport, said Aurelio.

Darcy got out onto the pavement, stunned by the cold and the photo. He always knew there'd be a day of consequences. Fin stood behind him, watched the Lada motor away. I'm not convinced he's on your team, she said. Darcy didn't ask which team she meant. Let me see them, she said.

Reluctantly, Darcy let her flip through the photos, waiting until she came to the black and white. A photo, not a Polaroid. The railway station in Prague, he said. Together they stared—the guy in his uniform, down on his knees, his army cap on the cistern. One of Darcy's hands in the young man's wavy hair, the other gripping his own abdomen as if clutching a pain.

Fin gazed in disbelief. She'd warned him to be careful and yet there he was, captured from a hole in the ceiling. Darcy could feel her seething, an anger no doubt magnified by what she'd almost let happen the night before. They stared at the strange grey shapes. Darcy could hardly believe it himself; the shame of it made him feel woozy.

Where was the money belt? she asked.

Darcy pointed to his mid-section, just above the soldier's head. That's what Darcy was holding onto, the leather belt pulled up high, his arm hugged around it, holding himself, his face twisted up and his hair falling back from his forehead. He was too handsome to refuse, said Darcy. It was a thudding consolation.

He was in uniform, she said. Are you crazy?

Darcy didn't answer at first. It could have been that he was.

One minute you're acting normal and the next you're in a foul-smelling place with a stranger, risking everyone's lives.

At least I look happy, said Darcy, but he could feel his insides convulsing.

No you don't, she said. You look possessed, like you just injected heroin into a vein. He'd never seen her so incredulous. I hardly recognise you, she said. Look at your expression.

It was true. He looked more desperate than he imagined, as though he'd forgotten to breathe. He wondered how his face would have looked last night if he'd been caught on film with Fin. Fin turned the photo over like it was some unwanted symptom. Lines of Cyrillic letters on the back. Her mouth set hard inside her balaclava. Your name, she said. My address.

For a moment Darcy stood speechless; there was nothing to say in defence. It's too cold to have this conversation in the street, he said, but he knew they couldn't have it inside Beriozka and Fin wasn't moving.

Aurelio's part of a network, she said.

No kidding, said Darcy, then wished he hadn't been glib. Aurelio so cruisy and European, his coat draped over his Cuban shoulders. He didn't seem like he played by the rules, said Darcy.

You didn't think that odd? asked Fin.

He said he was Cuban. Darcy knew it should have seemed odd; Aurelio had even shared that he was involved with the *druzhinniki*, the rounding up of hoodlums, yet everything had felt so foreign it was hard to register what would have been normal. What would be normal now?

Fin slipped the photo into her pocket. I suppose you wanted something to happen, she said—well it has. She hugged herself against this new reality. The Soviets think homosexuals should be liquidated, she continued. They call it a psychic disorder. They treat it with electric shock. They've researched the transplant of straight men's balls. It's not like I didn't warn you.

You knew who I was when you invited me, he said.

I did, she said, but you promised. She was on the verge of tears, overwhelmed by what all this meant. Darcy held her to him in the wind. Last night she had been apologising to him. For what? For leaving him, bringing him here? Using him? Kissing him? Now, she pulled herself free.

I should have known you'd be trouble, she said.

Then why did you bring me here?

Because you were the only one I could trust.

They looked at each other and Darcy knew it had been the truth. He also knew they'd severed that now. They were both in trouble, with each other and the world. What about last night? he asked.

I don't know about last night, she said, shaking her head in a sort of amazement. Her face frowned up in a manner that made her seem older. But this photo is bad for all of us.

How many of us are there? asked Darcy.

Fin didn't say, she left him there outside the shop and walked off as if to tell him he was on his own. He felt as if he might stand there and wait for the night to come down over him. He was freezing, imbued with a deep sense of reckoning, a panic that stunned him quite still. If she'd trusted only him, she didn't trust Jobik, but what kind of solace was that now? He looked at a bug-eyed plastic flamingo in the shop window. *What now, Darcy Bright?* A stab of anxiety spread through him. Aurelio had declared Moscow to be a place where nothing was legal yet everything possible, but little felt possible now, just a sense of this, his watershed day. The day when Andropov died. He pulled out his plastic map, an instinct to be pragmatic. He could analyse all of it later—his frailties would still be his frailties, but the disapproval on Fin's face would haunt him, from when he'd kissed her through her tears last night, to the way she'd glared at him just now.

The street before him appeared quiet as a frozen planet. Andropov's death had everyone indoors now, burrowed in the buildings he passed. He imagined them around transistor radios, wary of a clampdown. There were no celebrations.

He had marked the Australian Embassy on the map with a pen; he knew it wasn't far. He could seek refuge there, request a replacement passport. He imagined climbing the fence and plopping like a fig into the cover of a garden. So he walked. The mind-numbing cold whipped off the river. A wintry expanse already lit from the rim of the parapet, a vessel marooned, resting against the cutwater, dark as a whale. And as he walked the experiences lined up before him with an unexpected clarity. The scene with the soldier was as it had been: gratuitous and easy, an adrenaline rush, it *had* been like a line of heroin. The poster in the Ming Wing when Fin did that test on him: CONNECT YOUR GENITALS TO YOUR HEART. In Prague it was more familiar, mouth to genitals, genitals to a vein in his arm. With Fin it had been different—tears on her cheeks and his anger, a wound somehow being mirrored. What he'd shared with Aurelio felt ridiculous now. How many red flags could one country fly?

He walked on the sidewalks cleared of snow but still crunching underfoot, the image in the photo reverberating in the headwind. Maybe he'd betrayed Aurelio also, but he knew, most of all, he'd betrayed himself.

When he looked up from the pavement and into the sulfurous cold, he wondered how many copies of the photo were out there, how one got into Aurelio's hands. Not far from Kropotkinskaya Prospekt 13, he stopped. A tepid green Art Nouveau mansion behind a high-spiked iron fence. The gate was electronic and the cars inside were buried in snow. From beneath a bare elm, Darcy noticed what looked like a Soviet guard shut in a windowed sentry box. All Darcy had on him as picture ID was his International Driver's Licence so he waited in case there were comings and goings, for a ruddy-faced attaché with a familiar accent, what a relief that would be. But the place might as well have been abandoned.

The guard observed Darcy loitering and Darcy observed him, imagined being sentenced to stay upright all day in a kiosk the size of a phone box. He wished the gate was manned by some boy from the barracks in Sydney, standing alert in the wind, but Australia, he knew, was no Soviet ally. So he produced his cardboard driver's licence and approached. What was left to lose?

The guard slid the door of the sentry box open and regarded the document blankly. Darcy pointed to where it said *Issued in Melbourne, Australia* so the guard would know he was in the right place, but it clearly wasn't his alphabet.

Po-angliyski? asked Darcy.

The guard shook his head so Darcy pointed at the photo, but in it his hair was longer and still streaked dark. The guard observed him with an indifferent suspicion. *Pazpot?* he asked.

I-do-not-have-my-*pazpot*.

The pistol nested in the guard's holster caused a clamminess at the base of Darcy's spine. There was no apparent phone or intercom, just a small oil heater to be leaned against, the smell of singed clothes. Not even a mail drop. Darcy thought maybe he had the wrong building. A flagpole on the roof but no suggestion of a flag, no familiar points of the Southern Cross or the Federation Star. He couldn't throw a stone and see if he might hit a window; it wasn't that kind of country and the ground was covered in ice. If he scaled the fence the bars would rattle and he'd be shot in the back. He motioned at the great stone house. *Australianski?* he asked.

The guard glowered, not understanding, so Darcy shouted *Hello* in the hope that someone inside would hear his accent but the sound was lost in the wind. None of the curtains opened. The guard touched his pistol as a warning. *Pazpot*, he repeated.

Darcy felt suddenly weary as he headed back towards Komsomolskiy Bulvar. For all he knew the Australian delegation had left—with Andropov dead, there could have been some coup or crackdown, or maybe the embassy was open by appointment only. If he could get into the Intourist Hotel he could ask at the desk for the telephone number but he wasn't registered there, he had no Intourist guide, only Aurelio. But Aurelio was nowhere now.

He passed the doors of St Nicholas the Weaver, its tent-roofed belltower and golden cupolas shining against the lacklustre sky. A city where churches were being converted to museums of atheism. A cardboard box flew up and scraped along the wall, tore off around the corner. Those still in the street had their hands in their pockets as they leaned into the squall. A siren interrupted, sharp as the wail of a wounded dog, then it was as quiet as a curfew except for the slush of the cars.

In the alley at the back of Aurelio's dress shop a sapling bent as though trying to hold onto its long lost leaves and a brindle cat leapt between square metal rubbish bins, its fur blown flat. Darcy couldn't see much through the half-painted window, just the mirror where he'd examined himself as he first pulled on Aurelio's coat. Scraps of material and a bodice on the work table, but no sign of life. Darcy banged loudly and shouted *zdrastvuytye,* the syllables butchered, all of them engulfed. He stood back in case someone appeared in the window above, Aurelio's mother perhaps, the friend of Castro, but there was just a filmy curtain bunched at one side. He shouted *Aurelio* and suddenly wondered if that was really his name.

A stocky man appeared in the mouth of the alley and, without being sure who it was or if he'd even been noticed, Darcy found himself running. He hurtled down a barely lit side street, narrow compared with the broad boulevards, past two stone lions atop a gatehouse, buildings with low gargoyles, an old part of the city. When he stopped for breath he kept walking on an empty lane with shopfronts. A washing machine in the window of one and a stack of folded blankets topped with a bouquet of plastic sunflowers. It wasn't as cold away from the river.

He sheltered in the doorway of a store with stuffed birds in its window, dead hawks and falcons, a display so dusty it could have been there since the time of the tsars. A horse's neck and head was mounted beside them. It was carved from a tree trunk, cut straight across its shoulders, part of it covered in bark. Then Darcy realised it was real, not a carving, but so old the horse's hair had fallen out and the leather was peeling. Its ewe-neck bowed upwards as if it stared at the moon, reaching for something, its Roman nose high and a wildness in its marbled eyes. He saw himself in the photo, even though he'd strained up with clenched eyes; with Fin they'd been wide open, reaching for something else.

In a cul-de-sac behind him he heard a dull thumping, a boy juggling bowling pins in the dark, three at a time. Some trick of the faded light or a dream, the image he conjured to paint was appearing in real life. The young boy on his own, a bicycle leaned against a tree and a pat-terned handkerchief tied on his head. The boy's ragged canvas pants and his fervent concentration on the rhythm of the pins had Darcy entranced. A secret response to the General Secretary's passing. Everyone lying in wait. The boy tumbled the pins much higher, then dropped one and slapped himself on the thigh, more self-aware than if he were alone.

Darcy looked up into the blank apartments, imagined inhabitants standing in darkness behind the shutterless windows or kneeling on beds they used as divans in the day-time, pillows laid along the walls, watching. If it was a subtle celebration of Andropov dying, for Darcy it was something else. If he'd believed in a god he'd have thought it a sign. But of what? Hope or innocence, or both of them lost?

Darcy wanted to dig for his pad and sketch the lines of the juggler but he just watched, intoxicated by the boy's gypsy flair, his circus pants, the bandana. His evocation of purity. Then the boy began swinging pins from ropes wound on his wrists and curled through his hands, and he spun them in opposite circles, flipping them fast and then faster, surrounding his body as he swayed. Whizzing like propellers extended from his arms.

Darcy had thought that everyone here looked lonely, that he could almost smell their disappointment, but the boy seemed different, reaching and dipping, possessed by a passion. Darcy used to imagine teaching horses to dance on a rumbling wooden floor so their steel shoes made a tapping sound that blended with flamenco music. He'd wanted to paint the Lipizzaners doing airs above the ground. But he'd become lost along the way. He searched up into the new-fallen afternoon dark like the horse did beside him, as if there'd be a moon through the low-ceilinged clouds. He was close to the age the Mormon had been when he appeared at the door on Baden Powell Drive, and the thought made Darcy feel strange.

The boy seemed to sense Darcy staring and abruptly he caught all his pins and packed them into his drawstring bag. Darcy held up his gloved hand to say he was sorry, he meant no harm. As the boy got on his bike and scraped down the street, he glanced back at Darcy in the doorway then blended into the dark and cobblestones. The juggling pins in his bag bumping gently on his back.

Monash University, Late spring 1983

The quad lay in shadows, dew on the grass, they appeared with the Ming Wing behind them like a juggernaut. Darcy kicked the forty-four gallon barrel that rumbled with books, keeping it straight, a drum accompaniment as it rolled over cement behind Fin as she shouted her spiel about witch-hunts. *The Malleus Maleficarum,* she yelled to Asian kids who roamed the campus at night, haunting the libraries, gathering now, intrigued yet ill at ease with their own books under their arms, evening lecturers turning their heads, on their way home. Fin dressed up as a punk medieval witch, purple boots that came up over her knees, her leather mini-skirt and a cape with an embroidered Harley-Davidson. She looked more like Robin Hood's dominatrix.

The Hammer of Witches, she said, that's what it means.

Darcy held up her placard that read WE ARE NOT THE EVIL-DOERS. He felt like a magician's assistant, but he'd promised to support her. He dropped the sign on the ground because he couldn't do everything, poured the fake copies of the witch-hunt book from the barrel all over the moist evening grass. Copies of anything by William F. Buckley Jr stolen from the library, now pasted with *Malleus Maleficarum* covers.

Darcy glanced up at the random assemblage of student faces, some of them wincing, trying to understand.

Fin pointing at men accusingly: A hundred thousand women killed, she shouted, her numbers that always felt plucked from the air.

Accused of infanticide and cannibalism just for refusing to weep in the inquisitorial courts.

She doused the insides of the now upright barrel with kerosene and threw in a match, started burning the books. Her face painted black with white lips, her eyes now lit by the flames with a ghoulish effect. A female teacher in a plaid skirt shouted, Hey, offended by books on fire.

It's an instruction manual, Fin yelled back. For the killing of women. Like you. Idiot women like you.

The woman walked off towards the Student Union and Fin stared at Darcy accusingly. He faded behind her into the shadows but, undaunted, she continued with tirades about female circumcision, Islamic women, Nigeria, Egypt, Sudan, infibulation, subjugation.

Elly elly etdoo, Darcy warned her as a security guard emerged through the glass doors of the Union and Fin stopped mid-sentence, abandoned her props, and they ran through the dark between buildings to the car park on Wellington Road with their smiling getaway faces. This was the fun he'd been robbed of, he thought. Then he realised that Fin was in costume, quite unrecognisable, while he'd been there as himself.

That went well, she said, laughing, as they leapt into Darcy's mother's Corvair and sped out towards Dandenong Road. She reached for her stash in the glove box to roll them a joint.

You call that art!

It's more interesting than what you do, she said, taking a first toke and then coughing. At least it says something. She passed the joint to Darcy and he took a hit, his chest pumping in as he held it, sputtering.

They had no idea what you were talking about.

Then it must be art, she said.

Darcy puffed again, resenting how she made his work feel dated, *painted*. He closed his eyes at the Chadstone lights and waited for the first hint of a buzz. And then they were silent, Fin already in her Fin world.

At Caulfield, they turned underneath the railway bridge and all became more vivid, the glare of the headlights along Balaclava Road, cutting across to St Kilda. The distant beat in Caulfield Park where he'd have stopped if he were on his own, the observant Jews at Orrong Road, on foot because it was Friday night, men in black hats, the women frumpy. Dad doesn't live so far from here, said Darcy.

Fin took another pull on her blunt as they passed a tram that screeched on its cables. Do you ever see him? she asked.

Not lately, he said. His girlfriend's nice, though. She's Israeli. He wanted to tell her how his mother was what she called *circling the drain*, that he had her car because she barely left the house, the Austin getting her back and forth to the drive-thru bottle shop in Frankston. What happened to Aunt Merran? he asked.

Fin took another puff, swallowed then exhaled. I saw her once, she said. In California. She was still in the house outside Montecito. She had a blind ram in the garden. It walked in circles with its head up in the air, sniffing towards her when she called it. It had holes for eyes.

Does she drink too? he asked.

She did that day.

They arrived outside Darcy's flat on Robe Street and parked. He hadn't told her he paid the rent from his grandmother's money, the small inheritance Fin never saw. He showed her his studio in the closed-in end of the balcony. His own exaggerated realism: the four of them on easels, like he had a gallery at home. The curved brick walls and the signs of the buildings. WHEELAN THE WRECKER and BERRIGAN'S FOUNDRY, streetlights and old Holden cars, a Falcon ute parked in the shadow of a railway bridge, everything slightly larger than life.

They're really good, she said. She picked up an envelope of the photos he'd taken of them, sets of pictures ready in envelopes with his resume, some shots of his portraits and pastels.

I'm applying for graduate art programs, he said.

Can I take a copy of these? she asked.

Darcy nodded, flattered. Sure. She put the envelope in her satchel. Your thing was good too, he said. I didn't mean to make fun of it.

It was kind of stupid in the end, she said. She went to his bathroom and washed off her white and black make-up, put on her red lipstick, and together they walked up Acland Street, Fin still in her cape and boots. They headed to Pokey's up near the corner, caught the end of the show, a part-Aboriginal drag queen singing 'Nutbush City Limits'. Darcy was high from the dope and for once he felt happy. The music was loud and the dance floor opened, Fin in her own little groove with her cape and her satchel, her hands in the air to the Eurythmics' 'Sweet Dreams', doing her Annie Lennox thing.

Darcy ordered a Bundy and Coke from the shirtless tattooed boy at the bar, the older men cruising, the glare in their eyes and the tips left wet on the bar. Darcy leaned there and listened to the Human League, tasted the liquor and thought of his mother as the rum touched his tongue, and vowed, as usual, that this was his last for the night.

He drank and then danced with Fin to the Thompson Twins, in a rhythm like they belonged together. If he were alone he'd go down to the beat near the beach, lose himself there on the weed and the Bundy, where no one said anything, but now he had Fin and he held her narrow waist as they bumped on each other on the crowded dance floor like no one else existed. He felt sexy in his tight Fioruccis, his narrow black boots as they slithered on the slick parquet. He circled on his own and looked up at the lights as they dazzled, mused about art school in Sydney, the night-life up there, but when he came back to the present Fin had disappeared. He went to the ladies room and shouted, looked around the club but there was no one he'd take home. With a good buzz on, he took another drink to go, for out where he knew the night would take him, to the paths along the banks of the Yarra, waiting under the Anderson Street bridge or in the bushes, to find someone to remember and forget.

It was already 7 pm when Darcy stood slender and pale in his boxers, reflected in the shadow-stained bathroom mirror. He stared at the black and white remnants of the photo from Prague floating in the toilet bowl, torn up by Fin and left here for him to pee on. But Fin wasn't here now. Darcy flushed and some pieces were swallowed, but part of his face just swirled and remained: a tight-closed eye, and the top of the soldier's burnt-sugar hair. His army cap indelibly placed on the rusted cistern, out of the way, as he'd lowered himself on that piss-stained cement. A second swirl of water and all was gone. Darcy'd been set up; he knew that now. The soldier was one of those *agent provocateurs*. He'd been set up in Prague and now by Aurelio, everyone part of something, Fin as well, except Fin and he had ignited a new secret of their own. All he did was kiss her on the back; why did she turn around?

Behind the bathroom towels, Fin had stowed her potato vodka from Poland, a gift, he assumed, from Jobik. Darcy sensed she'd kept it hidden because he'd sworn off it before she'd left Melbourne in September. He'd barely painted since. She told him he didn't need to become any more like his mother, but now the voice in his head said: *too many feelings to cope with on your own, come with me, my sweet potato?*

The vodka seared a hollow in his delicate throat and

it made his breath feel loud inside him, flooding his veins, liquid distilled from lava, a tasteless taste that usually brought tears as he walked with the bottle into the hot other room where the canvas sat sketched without colour on the easel. In the dog's red wax eyes Darcy sought all kinds of forgiveness, for his mother and father, the Mormon, the soldier, and he searched in its eyes for himself, asked how he should paint this, the charcoal in his newly warmed fingers. He had the pavilions, the fountain, he had what they wanted, the obelisk mounted with the shape of the dog, the only colour so far in those red torch-lit eyes. He remembered Laika as famous, launched in that rocket, but did she ever come back?

Darcy picked up the waxen puddle of the cinnamon candle from last night. He'd paint it for penance, not just for himself, he'd paint it in wax with the stash of Fin's candles. He pulled her collection from the drawer of the end table, red and cream and yellow, a royal blue, the paraffin scaly and rough in his fingers as he laid them out like paints on the ironing board. He covered the ironing board roughly with pages of *Izvestia*, newspaper photos of Andropov living and dead, and laid Fin's cheap oils and Russian watercolours alongside the candles. Melted wax and paint, it would be naïve and primitive, all he needed was heat.

The travelling iron sat on the board like an invitation. Its plastic handle folded into its shell, and he lay it on its back like a silver beetle, a miniature hotplate. Another swig and a burn in his pharynx that rushed to his ears and it made him feel close to his mother, snapping candles, ripping at wicks and pushing their nubs into the iron's heat. He grabbed a teardrop knife from Fin's paintbox, Fin who he wished hadn't turned around. He kneaded the molten wax with the blade, conjured the boy in the square and his juggling, but the vodka had eclipsed that, so he turned to the dog on the canvas.

He drank again and then knife-painted the wavering flag on the wedding-cake building, layering the ruffled red in melted wax. Already he knew it felt good. Blending in yellow he wax-painted the tourist bus a more brilliant red. He imagined all breeds of wax—beeswax, carnauba for polishing cars, floor wax, ear wax, tallow, shellac. The aeroplane bright yellow, even though the Aeroflot at the museum was white with a flag on the fin; he would make it a thing of his own. He carved its windows with the pickpoint of the palette knife, wiped the knife clean across Andropov's newspaper face. With the knife in his hand he felt a feverish accuracy, reaching for the oils, tubing silver on the palette to knife-paint the obelisk platinum. His version of the Monument to Space Flight. He marked the stones shiny with the knife edge, detailed them fine to the top where Laika stared out, curious and waiting. He would paint her last.

Straight from the candle sizzling on the travelling hotplate he waxed the sky above her with off-white and powder blue. The candle he used like a lumbering pen, then he smudged on some more direct from the iron. Gold ochre for Laika, you innocent thing; he worked on her with a fine-tipped brush, sculpting her shape from the whippet's, mounting her hopeful on a rocket through space, reaching for something. In green, he painted a pair of butterflies there, wings in the light from Laika's chasing eyes. Green, he'd heard, was the colour of the heart.

To frame it, he shaped the curves of the lavatory cistern

ingrained in his mind from the photo from Prague, the rusty cast-iron shape. On top he outlined the soldier's cap, its peak faced forward, emblematic, with a CCCP insignia and star. They would have their nationalism. Darcy stood back to see what he had and it was quite something, the shapes in the wax. It wouldn't be what they expected, it might even be better than that. Along the cone of the obelisk he signed: *forgive me.*

Darcy turned at the door being opened, Fin standing in the entry hall. His drawing hand tightened, anticipating her thoughts: *good that he's painting; he's fucked up my travelling iron; why did I bring him here, why did I turn when he kissed me?* She silently removed her coat, and he felt her assessing the shining dry wax and the shapes of the buildings, the eyes of the dog and the half-empty bottle of vodka, the mess, but she was looking at Darcy in his boxers. He wanted to cover himself.

I painted the dog for you, he said, and the butterflies.

Fin leaned on the velvet arm of the couch where the buggers and de-buggers had delved among cushions. Self-consciously, Darcy dabbed red wax in the star on the military cap that sat on the cistern up among the clouds, he carved its details with the pick. The cap was a military grey with a stretch of canvas blank above it. The colour ended mid-stroke near the edge. He put the brush down. He waited.

It's wonderful, said Fin. What about the corner?

Darcy stood back again and saw the canvas whole; the strip left uncoloured made it seem more modern, less exact. I like it that way, he said. The mix of wax and paint seemed vaguely kitsch but at least it was unusual. Fin approached him, lifted her hand and peeled a scab of red wax from near his nipple. He wasn't sure what it meant. It's really good, she said, the painting. She blew the wax from her finger. It's not what they're expecting but the curator's cool, he'll like it. She picked up the vodka bottle. No glass? she asked.

No glass, he said, a smile of apology. He'd rarely painted sober, she knew that, but he felt suddenly sober now. Are you okay? he asked.

She reached for her Polaroid camera on the bench and took a random shot—Darcy with the canvas in the background, the ironing board alongside like a flat-backed horse. I wouldn't say that, she said.

She peeled the picture and gave it to Darcy to dry, and they both watched his shape materialising from the cloudy turquoise liquid. Her blouse brushed his bare elbow as the picture coalesced in the streaks like one of the Rorschach images. His features arranged themselves in the tinted emulsion and red flags brightened from the painting, the silver of the obelisk and the anxious face of the dog.

I'm sorry about last night, he said. That was all wrong.

I can't deal with that now, she said. We have to deal with the other business.

I know you warned me, said Darcy. He looked at himself in the image, formed now, his eyes and mouth seemed somehow less generous.

We need to get practical, she said.

They both watched the painting. It was drying also; the wax gave it a depth and dimension. I went to the embassy, he said, but I couldn't get in. Maybe we should go to the Americans?

Quietly Fin screwed the lid back onto her vodka bottle; they were sparing contact with each other's eyes.

No one will touch you, she said, especially the Americans. Not now—and, anyway, there's too much going on. Everyone's afraid Chernenko will be the new General Secretary and that'll be like going back to Brezhnev. There may be changes in Poland, she said, but it's too soon for here.

Darcy looked at the words he'd written on the obelisk. Perhaps she hadn't noticed them. What about us? he asked.

I think Aurelio will be your best bet, she said. I don't want to be around you when you're drinking. As she left the room she turned momentarily. The painting's really amazing, she said. Thank you.

Don't give up on me, said Darcy, but she was already closing her bedroom door.

Nepean Highway, Winter 1976

Darcy knew it was too far to take the Austin on a rainy day, all the way to Melbourne. They followed the kombi, two cars behind, Darcy's mother too crocked to be out on the road. She drove in her housecoat with gin in her veins. Rain seeped in above the visor and the Austin felt small on the highway, like a dodgem car implanted with a brand new battery. It was going to be his car one day. Shouldn't I drive? he said, but his mother was on a mission; she'd already coerced him from the house in his pyjamas as if the kitchen were on fire.

You're here as my witness, she said.

You people are crazy, he said. He started to doze but his mother struck him hard on the arm.

I need you to watch, she said, so we don't lose him. But the kombi travelled high enough so they could see it ahead in the traffic, his father driving through the same rain, oblivious.

Perhaps you should go to Alcoholics Anonymous, said Darcy.

And she should go to Don't Fuck My Husband.

What about me? asked Darcy.

You should have gone to Nude Driving School for Boys, she said, but it's too late now.

Darcy looked out the window.

They caught up with the kombi well before St Kilda,

saw him turn up Chapel Street where the houses began to get bigger, more trees that weren't eucalyptus. Toorak, Darcy's mother said, disdainfully. On Albany Road they saw him pull over, deliver some eggs in a hurry. Look at him run, said Darcy's mother.

But he was already back and driving. He stopped off Glenferrie Road at a house with a modern extension in the front. Darcy's mother parked the Austin behind a station wagon and they watched him carry four cartons up the drive. Then she picked her teeth nervously with paper she'd folded into an edge.

If he's leaving he'd take more than eggs, said Darcy.

I'm going in, his mother said.

She disappeared up the drive and Darcy decided he should follow in case she got into trouble. But in the street he felt embarrassed, fourteen in his flannel pyjamas, his bare feet in the rain, tender on the gravel. He spied his mother at a window, around the side past a garden of collapsing wet lilies, and he wondered if she'd been there before. She stood on a fruit box and motioned for Darcy as though she were watching a cat having kittens. But it was cold without his shoes on. She stepped down when Darcy got there, sat on a bench by a small pond and lit a cigarette.

Darcy stood on the box like she had, looked in between the orange pots and leafy hydrangeas. His father sitting at a table drinking tea with a woman, his legs crossed to the side. He looked handsomer than usual, the woman smiling, a clasp in her brown-grey hair, her eyes on Darcy's father. A ray of light appeared through a skylight above them, from a sky that seemed full of clouds. A house so clean it made Darcy's house seem dirty, the kitchen big as their living-room. The egg cartons there on the bench, the teapot had a green cover.

Darcy's mother threw a small rock and Darcy turned. She pulled her coat around her, motioned him away with a flick of her head. Enough, she whispered, the weight already in her face. She dropped all her cigarettes in the woman's fishpond and smiled sadly to herself.

Darcy's feet were freezing as they walked back down the drive to the street. His mother pulled out her lipstick and wrote on the window of the kombi: *Careful Daddy.* Letters that looked like a child's.

What do you reckon? she asked.

Darcy didn't tell her he thought his father had looked happy. He drove home in his bare feet and she smoked her Virginia Slims. You're old enough to smoke on weekends, she said. He could hear from her voice she was crying. He didn't mention he'd been smoking since he was twelve, she never noticed him gone, riding his bike down the street where Benton lived, just to be near him, or to Fin's dorm, returning to the gully. When the Austin overheated Darcy didn't stop; his mother put an apple core in front of the temperature gauge.

At home they left the Austin steaming. His mother closed the curtains and went to bed. Darcy sat in his damp pyjamas on the wattle branch that ran along the edge of the single garden bed. He reached down and pulled out a capeweed. The soil smelled stale and sweet from the compost and chicken manure his father brought home. He knew in spring the capeweed would have a bright yellow flower like a daisy. He wondered who decided which were the flowers and which were the weeds, who decided whether his father would come home.

Then he heard the burr of the kombi and wasn't sure he was pleased. His father pulled in and parked under the trees, a red smudge on the window where the lipstick had been smeared. He leaned on the steering wheel for a moment before he got out, looking more spent than usual, then walked over and sat on the branch with Darcy, the sleeve of his shirt stained from where he'd wiped the glass. His good blue Arrow shirt. What did you get up to today? he asked.

Driving, said Darcy. He leaned over and yanked out another weed, shook dirt from the roots. I followed you. He didn't look over at his father. I saw you with the lady in the kitchen off Glenferrie Road.

Where was your mother?

She never got out of bed, said Darcy, but it was harder to lie when his father didn't believe him. And now there weren't enough secrets to keep things together.

His father looked over towards the house, the drapes drawn shut, clasped his knotty fingers. You're as stubborn as her, he said. He brushed at the smudges on his sleeve, kept watching the house as if it held an answer. Everything looked smaller than it used to, the dark brown weather-board and green canvas awnings. The incinerator smouldering with the wet leaves from yesterday and the faint smell of smoke; the fresh innards of a cantaloupe and eggshells on the compost.

What's her name? asked Darcy.

Ranita, his father said.

Darcy leaned down and touched the grass, felt it damp against his fingers. Does she have a husband?

She used to, he said.

Darcy thought how easy it was for people to leave each

other. The way Fin had gone, Benton dumping him without saying anything. Darcy stood and brushed the seat of his pyjama pants, took the capeweed and replanted it, pushed at the soil with his fist. She looked like she was from somewhere else, he said.

She's Israeli, his father said. From Tel Aviv. Her name means joy.

Darcy somehow doubted that; he'd never met an Israeli. Will you become Jewish? he asked.

I don't expect so, his father said, but as Darcy looked over at the lines in his father's weathered cheeks, he sensed this answer as a confirmation. His father would be disappearing soon.

They turned as Darcy's mother opened the curtains, the wooden rings scraping along the rod. She looked out into the distance as if the two of them weren't there.

Don't leave me alone with her, said Darcy.

Boyarski Prospekt, Thursday night

The wind whipped off the snow and bit Darcy's face as he got out of the taxi. He covered his mouth with his cold gloved hand and looked about. The banya seemed innocuous enough, even though the windows were cemented up, but no one entered or left, just hurried by in the dark with their heads down. It was nine forty-five, he was early, alone in Aurelio's coat in the gaze of a thousand frosted windows over Lermontov Square, a towering ministry skyscraper lit with a galaxy of eyes. Lost in thought on the couch, he'd noticed an envelope under the door. It had his name, not Fin's, pencilled on it, a note that read *Meet me tonight at 10 pm. Banya opposing the metro at Lermontovskay. Look forward on Boyarski Prospekt. Your passport is with me. Your friend always, Aurelio.*

Darcy braced himself and slipped between parked cars towards the scraped iron door. He knew a banya was a bathhouse. A ticket out or a ticket in deeper, he wasn't yet sure, but Fin had left him little choice. He opened the door.

Inside, a taste of sulfur settled on his tongue as he gazed at an old Tartar woman in the vestibule, her hair pinned up like a second set of ears. There was no caviar or salmon, no crowd to surprise him in the blue mosaic entry hall, to tell him it was all an intricate joke, life hadn't turned on him really. There was just a bluestone floor and steam wafting through walls where algaed tiles had fallen.

No Aurelio.

The woman searched Darcy's face as if she'd seen pretty boys here before and knew they were trouble. As he gave her a handful of kopeks she gestured warily to a stack of grey towels in a basket, to a locker room where the bench was covered in Astroturf. A row of pigeonholes and an elderly comrade wrestling with the elastic in his underpants. He cast covert glances as Darcy pulled off his boots and socks. The floor scunge was familiar from afternoons spent in public showers. He should have been comfortable here, but naked in the towel he felt a sickening uncertainty. Gingerly, he pushed open the steamroom door.

A young boy threw a bucket of water on a barrel of piled rocks and a wave of steam billowed. A plump-bellied Russian appeared through the vapours, his backside on the concrete; he was scrubbing the back of someone in front of him, leaning as if sanding furniture. For a moment Darcy thought it was too hot to stay; he shielded his eyes, beads of hot sweat coursed down his brow, salty and burning, scalding water dripped from the ceiling. There was still no Aurelio, no men on all fours being lashed with bunches of wet juniper leaves. Instead, apparatchiks with paunches lay about on raised concrete benches like beached seals. They noticed him but barely.

Two younger men watched him from the entrance to the showers, their heads shaven and rib cages showing, towels slightly low, seductive. A test or a trap, or maybe Aurelio was waiting in there. Darcy walked towards them, to where the air was suddenly cooler. Showers ran even though no one was under them. He went to the furthest and folded his towel on a ledge, let the cool water wash through his hair. One of the shaved boys came over and showered in the other corner, a sore on his shoulder and a small tattoo on his arm. He furtively shielded his uncut erection but Darcy wasn't triggered now, just light-headed from heat and steam, faint. He stared at the wall so he wouldn't respond, ashamed he might find the hollow-eyed boy alluring, and aware that he was likely being filmed.

A harsh light filtered through a crack in the white-washed dome, spreading against Darcy's leg and onto the wood-slatted floor. He closed his eyes into the pressure, a momentary escape, as voices rose and feet appeared on the concrete. A militiaman stood under the arch in uniform and a gust of panic rose in Darcy as he realised he was being motioned for. If it was a trap he felt almost yielding. What grated inside him was the quality in Fin's voice as she'd suggested Aurelio was his best bet, how she'd closed her bedroom door.

He slipped his towel about his waist as the soldier escorted him past the grey shapes through the steam and a row of old naked men along a wall, corralled by a guard with pockmarked cheeks and fogged-up glasses. Everyone's hair looked greasy. They glanced at Darcy uneasily, unclear if he'd been singled out or privileged. The militiaman moved him on through to the changing room and pointed to Darcy's pigeonhole; even that was no secret. All Darcy heard was the ceiling drip and his heart, palpable as a clock.

Wet in his Henley singlet, his jeans and multiple pairs of socks, pulling on Aurelio's coat, Darcy stepped back out into the night, into a floodlit darkness that was blinding by comparison, his sight adjusting to a car parked opposite, the Lada. He saw Aurelio in it, lighting a small cigarillo. He beckoned Darcy over with a flick of his head.

Darcy pushed his wet hair from his face and breathed, tried to regain his composure, but he was nauseous from the sauna, thirsty and confused, asking himself if he should run this time. Aurelio leaned to open the passenger door and Darcy slid onto the vinyl seat, into the now familiar smell of spicy aftershave and Cuban cigarillos. He saw the pistol in Aurelio's holster as Aurelio reached over Darcy to close the door, brushed his hand past Darcy, the way he'd done at the dacha.

You are looking like the wreck of the *Hesperus*, he said, slightly mocking, but he glared at Darcy, his expression urgent, not matching the tone of his voice. He passed Darcy a note and he read it: *Careful what you say. Don't talk about where we are being yesterday.*

Are you well? asked Aurelio, then pressed a finger to his lips, pointed to a small furry button affixed to the side of the radio.

Darcy tried to understand; Aurelio being monitored now, a small transmitter like he'd seen in the jar in the apartment. Darcy stared at it, not knowing what to say. It's just I'm still wet, he said.

No need for you being scared, said Aurelio. Darcy looked over at him, his brown fur hat, a fawn polo neck that looked like cashmere and a black sheepskin jacket. Clothes that weren't from here. You'll be drying as we are talking, he said. He pursed his brow intently, pushed his tongue tight between his teeth.

I don't know what's real here, said Darcy.

Aurelio picked a piece of tobacco from his tongue then brushed his mouth with the palm of his hand. There was a pleading in the way he stared at Darcy. What is real is you are in some trouble. Before I can give you your passport, we have to discuss, he said, almost in a monotone. I like you, Darcy Bright, and I can be looking after you. But you must help us. Aurelio looked away, his eye on the door of the banya. The situation is one as follows, he said. In lieu of the persecution there is a project for you. He spoke clearly, as if rehearsed for the transmitter. Darcy was transfixed by the small oval device. He wanted to ask who was listening, the general or someone else, but Aurelio was shaking his head. There is an influence person who is driving past the *pleshka*, he said.

Darcy had no idea what that was or if he'd meant persecution or prosecution. He searched Aurelio's face and it still shook in a slight warning. I will be showing you the *pleshka*, he said, it is in a different quarter of Moscow. He cracked his window to allow the smoke to waft outside; it hung languid in the icy air then disappeared. If you can be having sex with this man, and it is recorded, Aurelio chose his words carefully, it will be very useful.

Darcy's gut was acid—he was being pimped, for politics. *An influence man.* I'm not a hustler, he said. I've done things but not this. He didn't care who was listening. The hollow sense that it had been part of the pretence all along—the shower at the dacha, the kiss on the risen clearing. Those cold soft lips, for this.

Aurelio met the disbelief in Darcy's eyes. It is the way I can get the return of your passport, he said. Your only way out. He smiled but the torment was in his eyes also. Think of it as an adventure, he said.

The ache moved up to the pit of Darcy's chest as Aurelio produced a narrow stack of dull black and white photos and showed them to Darcy. This is what we have, he said. A woman getting into a taxi, numbers in pen across the bottom. A fat man in a rumpled suit having abrupt-looking sex with a woman on a bare wooden floor. A tall transvestite at what might have been the *pleshka*, getting into the back of a burgundy Volga, the licence plate circled in red. Why are you showing me these? asked Darcy. Aurelio kept flipping—two older men in anoraks kissing among hydrangeas in a park. It must have been summer. This is what we do in *druzhinniki*, he said. We spy on the *blues*. Especially important ones.

Lastly, the shivering whippet tied to the bench in Mandelshtam Park, and, blurred among the snow-covered trees behind it, the slender man with the grey-flecked hair and specs. Darcy obscured by branches. The babushka worked for Aurelio, Darcy remembered, the one he'd taken a Polaroid of. She'd shot a picture of her own.

It's him we want, Aurelio said. His name is Nikolai Chuprakov. We never seen him do a thing before, he said. All he does usually is walking the dog, and every Tuesday drives by the *pleshka* just looking. Aurelio quietly took the picture back from Darcy. He liked you, no?

Darcy stared at the glove box.

He's Chernenko's son-in-law, said Aurelio. He's married to Chernenko's daughter.

The iron door of the banya opened and the two narrow Russian boys came out in loose pants and torn T-shirts, their thin feet flat and bare on the icy pavement. One of them caught sight of Darcy in the Lada and his gaze tracked Darcy reproachfully. Darcy felt weirdly disloyal.

We call them *opuscheny*, said Aurelio. They are the degraded ones, just out from the gulag. Homosex prisoners. They get many times raped.

Darcy now realised he'd been summoned here to see them, to watch as they were herded out quietly by the damp plainclothesmen to the back of the white police van. They will go back now, they must eat all scraps from the floor. Many die, he said. He looked at Darcy with moist eyes now, apologetic. But I can look after you, he said, so this will not happen to you.

Darcy wished he hadn't said it twice. He remembered his first morning here, the panic-struck man in the park, and then the fine-looking woman at the Bolshoi. He watched the *opuscheny* climb docilely into the back of the van, their shaved heads like owls in the window as they were driven away. What if I say no? asked Darcy.

I cannot help you then, he said. He reached from the wheel to the sleeve in the door and produced Darcy's passport, blue with the Australian crest, emu and kangaroo. He flipped open the cover and showed Darcy it was actually his. Darcy pressed his fingers into his thighs, restraining himself from grabbing it. You cannot be having it now, said Aurelio, but if you are helpful, you will get this back. He stowed the passport in the door and started the Lada, slapped it into gear. I will now show you the *pleshka*, he said.

Aurelio quietly reached for the note and Darcy saw the word *yesterday*. As Aurelio folded it away, Darcy felt crumpled; even his tailer was under surveillance. Aurelio who hadn't seemed worried at all now drove and smoked in what appeared like a terrified silence. Perhaps they'd been seen at the dacha. The retarded girl sending morse code, banging her wooden spoon on the eating tray, cameras in the bathroom walls.

They didn't follow the tracks the police van stamped

in the slush but drove off in another direction. Darcy wondered who would be listening, in a room in a faceless
building, a group of white-haired men. He looked at
Aurelio as the Lada rattled through the perpetual sulk of
the suburbs. You will help make change here, said Aurelio.

They proceeded in silence, overtook a heavy snow-
plough, and turned down a narrower road, further from
the river, in a part of the city Darcy had not seen. The
night sky lay low as a trough, wanting to snow. Mostly factories, an industrial area, abandoned buildings, some with
broken windows, but no people visible. He could hurl
himself from the car but he wouldn't get far in the dark.

Where are you taking me? he asked.

I want to familiar your eyes, he said. So you can prepare. Aurelio pulled over opposite a narrow, dimly lit park,
beside an unused railway line, reversed into a place where
they were hidden among conifers. He turned the ignition
off and pointed at three women waiting under a street-
light in the distance; they leaned on a low wooden fence
under the cover of a tin bus shelter.

Travesties, said Aurelio.

Transvestites, Darcy corrected him.

A car went by, driven by a man alone, slowing down.

The same men are passing, explained Aurelio, but
rarely do they make a stop.

The three figures smoked cigarettes in a snowy
drizzle, one drank from a hipflask; they didn't acknowledge the Lada, just moved about to stay warm, hugging
themselves in their coats. They work for us, said Aurelio.
He raised his eyebrows as if to say *that's how it is—the
government uses them as lures and you will now work for
the government too.*

A black Chaika with embassy plates but no flag on the hood pulled over. It had tinted windows. The three hookers came down and leaned against it, then the tallest one was getting in. Finnish, said Aurelio. He could tell by the licence plate. They have a diplomat immunity, he said.

As the Chaika drove off, the two remaining girls stood in what had now become a slushy rain. But they are not right for everyone, Aurelio said. He turned and blew a plume of smoke at Darcy. The woman you see in the kitchen opposing your apartment will meet you the day after Andropov's funeral, under the elm on your Fin's street. It will be this car.

We call her Svetlana, said Darcy.

Aurelio smiled at the nickname, started the car. She will look after you, he said. Don't be worry.

They drove down past the two remaining transvestites, who were stamping their feet in the cold, one in a grey coat and matching scarf that looked like chinchilla, the other in black leather and fur. Outside too long, their cheeks were grooved and they were too tired to look pretty. Aurelio didn't greet them. He pointed to the snowy verge, around a corner. Darcy made out the remains of an old apple orchard behind a high-tensile wire fence.

Svetlana, as you are calling her, will tell you to wait here, he said. We think he will stop for you.

Darcy wondered how they could be so confident, those who were listening. I need to think about this, he said.

Aurelio pointed at the transmitter, his dark eyes narrowed, warning. If you think about it, you will be coming the first Australian *opuscheny*. He pushed his cigarillo into the pile of butts in the ashtray. And you see what happens to them.

I trusted you, said Darcy.

Aurelio put his hand to Darcy's mouth. And you should trust me still, he said, but his fingertips felt sweaty and cold. Darcy didn't kiss them. He turned away to the night outside and imagined the icy lips of the transvestites.

Frankston Hospital, December 1983

Darcy watched his mother from the door of the emergency ward. She looked like a tall palsied bird, propped up on pillows, her left arm against the wall behind her. The neurologist said she was suffering from neglect and it struck Darcy as ironic. As her left arm started to move it did unexpected things; flung itself over her head or unwittingly followed the movement of her leg. The nervous parting of her lips, the fierce narrow expression. He watched as she put on her cardigan backwards. Don't ask me what day it is, she said. She knew he was there without seeing him. They've asked me fifteen times.

What day is it? he asked. There wasn't a chair and he was glad because he didn't want to sit.

December twenty-two, she said, Sunday, her speech slightly slurred. I only remember because the nurse just asked me. She said it with a hint of shrewdness in her smile.

I brought your things, he said. He took her nightie from the pale blue overnight bag and placed it on the bed. It looked like a child's summer dress. I'm only in overnight, she said. For observation.

Next he placed her leather-covered radio on the table, but she didn't look at it. So you can listen to the cricket, he said. She'd never been musical, except for 'Moon River'— she preferred sporting commentaries, racing at Moonee Valley, cricket at the MCG. She was sliding down from the pillows behind her, so slow it was hardly noticeable. It made the hospital gown droop low on one side, her breast pale beneath her tan line. Have you been mean to the nurses? he asked.

They've taken away my buzzer, she said. The skin on her neck sagged dark like a wattle. She clutched her Medibank Private card in her right hand as though it was her passport. I guess Christmas is up in the air, she said. She turned to look at Darcy now and all he heard was Fin's voice on the phone from Moscow, urgent, *Please come.* And tonight he was driving to Sydney, to the College of Fine Arts, tomorrow his last chance to defer. He'd stay up there for New Year's Eve. Now he thought of the things his mother would have planned for their Christmas, stealing the top of some small roadside pine and stuffing it through the sitting-room window, her getting sloshed on gin and Pimm's, pretending it was fun.

They won't let me walk even though I can, she said.

Where's the doctor? asked Darcy.

They only have nurses, she said, her small eyes on Darcy as if she knew something he didn't. He thought of how the tickets had arrived in the money belt, and how he would stop off in Prague on the way, Wenceslas Square and the river whose name he could never remember, just that it wasn't the Danube. He'd never seen cities in snow. Across the hall an Indian family clustered around a shape on a gurney behind a half-drawn curtain.

People die in here, his mother said. Can you get me some Molly Bushell barley sugar from the chemist?

Darcy took a last look at her, her hand freckled and dark around the blue insurance card. Sure, he said, I'll bring it in tomorrow.

Ulitsa Kazakov, Late Thursday

The apartment felt hostile. Fin on the couch in her sage green overalls, one side fastened over a T-shirt. Darcy wasn't sure if she wanted him here or not, uncertain of everything now. As he shut out icy air behind him, he noticed the sheet off the window hinges, heaped on the floor. The easel was bare, the Laika painting removed.

Fin watched for Darcy's response. The only good thing he'd accomplished since he'd arrived, gone. The curator was here, she said. She stood; her lipstick was smudged. He liked the painting a lot, she said. Thank God. She spoke as if their near lovemaking had happened in a parallel universe but Darcy knew it was right there between them, a branch that scratches at the window if the wind blows, or a wolf that might follow them more closely now, cunning and patient.

A rivulet of water crept around the sash of the window, steamed as it met the heating pipe, and Darcy noticed the walls were naked too, the canvas of the mastectomy scar he'd tried to convert, the Polaroid of the babushka in the park just a square where less dust had gathered.

They confiscated what wasn't authorised, said Fin, following his eyes almost maternally, as though she hadn't meant to send him away. They own the insides of the walls, she added, that's what it's like being an artist here.

Folding her arms about the bib of her overalls, she told Darcy they'd taken her peasant dresses too, the one she'd lettered with quotes from Tolstoy, the one with the dream about drowning inscribed on the front.

Outside, the snow had transformed into a pelting, perpendicular sleet, nails being hammered from the sky. At least your painting will be in the exhibition, she said. A tarnished silver lining. You can add it to your resume, she added, I won't mind.

He thought of the other things he could add—brother, lover, hustler, spy—but a world where people had resumes seemed distant. His father once said it wasn't what was served up but how you experienced it, but how was he supposed to experience this, this cold mean place, these circumstances? He'd arrived with desires but this wasn't how he'd dreamed of Fin in the snow. It's not what you want, it's how it comes at you, he thought, how you catch it and fold it into your arms, if you can catch it at all. He remembered the juggler, spinning his wooden pins with a sensory joy, but self-contained. Darcy knew that his own joy lay in art and not sex, but he felt as if art was escaping him now. And he knew the Laika painting would never stay with him, not physically, but it had become like a junction box.

It didn't have a name, he said.

I told him it's called *Dogs in Space*, said Fin.

But it had been more than just that—it had been a line back into himself.

Fin looked at him sympathetically from behind the safety of her folded arms. We're guests of the Soviet government, she said, that's the arrangement…it's just lucky he liked it.

Did you see the words along the rocket?

Yes, she said, but I'm never sure what *forgive me* is supposed to mean. Accept me? She observed him with a sorrow in her face that was becoming familiar. If you ask me, she said, people want forgiveness so they can forgive themselves. All I asked was that you contain yourself here. I told you it was too dangerous. She moved the easel off to the side as if that part of the discussion was over. Of course, now they want another piece, she said.

Not from me, said Darcy. He poured himself a mug of kvass from a jug on the counter. The steam and fear had made him thirsty. Shouldn't we talk about last night? he said.

No, she answered abruptly, a flare in her eyes. She shook her head, asked where he'd been all evening, and then she went silent as Jobik appeared like a spectre from her bedroom and Darcy understood. This was who she was hostage to, more than listening devices or any regime, and more than Darcy.

Jobik kept from view of the window, took off his black-rimmed glasses and wiped them, looked over at Darcy with his deep-set mahogany eyes.

Are you the curator too? asked Darcy.

I'm not an artist, he said in a strange part-American accent. I'm sorry for your troubles here. He pushed a hand through his unruly black hair and raised an eyebrow to Fin, and with a nod let her know it was time to go. All it had taken was a nod and she was leaving with him. Darcy watched them rug up for outside and had a flash of the hookers standing frozen in the snow.

Aurelio's enlisted me, he said.

They turned simultaneously. Jobik's pupils deadened

but a shock of moisture glistened in Fin's eyes.

He has my passport, said Darcy, I saw it—but to get it back I have to be with a man so they can take photos.

What man? asked Fin.

Darcy drank some more of the kvass. Chernenko's son-in-law, he said. If I don't he said they'll prosecute. He showed me the *opuscheny*.

What do you mean? asked Fin.

It is what happens to the gays in the gulag, said Jobik. They get treated like dogs.

Can you help me? Darcy asked. Jobik? I brought the money belt.

But Jobik was shaking his head; he was leaving. Not now, he said. I can't now.

Fin stayed for a moment and Darcy saw the distress in her eyes. Jobik has problems, she said, and as she closed the door Darcy knew they were her problems too.

For a moment Darcy was left in an aloneness he remembered from far off, a boy in a garden before Fin had even arrived, a feeling he'd since avoided, and then he remembered last night. The thought of a drink almost repulsed him but he still found himself scavenging in the fridge for vodka. All he found were soft-skinned apples and, in the freezer, a sketch. Hidden from the curator. A sketch of a peasant woman kneeling with a baby in her arms, the infant held forward, suckling on the teat of a donkey. It had nothing to do with the landscapes of Moscow. Darcy held the icy picture and examined it. The rounded shape of a baby swaddled in white, its face disappearing behind the donkey's narrow thigh. The lines thoughtful, softer and more representational than Fin's usually were. Perhaps she'd copied it, traced it from a print to prove herself. A faint second figure was drawn in the background, squatting on a milking stool with a second baby in her arms.

Darcy thawed it with Fin's hairdryer, enough so paint would take. He didn't know what else to do. With a palette of her watercolours and a fine brush, he coloured where the dress fell from the woman's seated knees and looped along the stable floor. A light powder blue. The surface still wet so the colours bled nicely, there was no need to mix with water. He painted the donkey, its face, accepting the baby so placidly, one ear forward and one back. The nativity gone awry. He painted it softly like Munnings or Stubbs, forgetting about everything. It felt comforting to work in watercolours, to paint sober. Hints of pink in each mother's face. It calmed his nerves.

He was still painting in details, cream touches of straw on the stable floor, when Fin finally returned. She entered quietly and stood, her face swallowed in the entry hall shadows. Darcy didn't look at her. It's based on a story, she said and came closer, not seeming angered by what he was doing. It's a woman with syphillis who had twins, she said, but Darcy knew it had to do with the two of them, something she'd wanted to say but couldn't. She pointed to the figure on a milking stool, her dress now hinted with colour. The sister was a healer, she said. Her manner was soft now Jobik wasn't here; maybe that alone was her forgiveness.

Darcy applied a touch of pink to the second baby's face while Fin stood at the uncovered window. In the story, she said, they used donkey's milk because the mother's was infected. Then she approached the painting conditionally, as if it wasn't quite hers. Donkey's milk is more like a mother's, she said, from the teat it's the purest. She touched the infant's face.

How do you know all this? asked Darcy.

It was in a village near Archangelsk, she said.

A myth or a story? he asked. He dabbed at the dress with the remnants on the paintbrush. Again he'd left part of the picture bare.

What does it matter? she said. It was just that I couldn't stop thinking about it, so I drew it.

What happened to the babies? asked Darcy.

One died, she said.

He kneeled back to get a sense of it, the ghostly shape of the sister healer, crouched on the stool, unfinished.

I think it's about our mothers, she said.

Darcy drew his head back. He doubted Aunt Merran had ever looked out for his mother. He smudged some colour onto the manger with a linseed cloth. Maybe it's about us, he said.

Fin walked back to the window and looked out into the night and its new depth of snow. You shouldn't have kissed me like that, she said as if it were his fault. She stared into the gloom. It doesn't mean I don't love Jobik.

Darcy remembered her and Jobik together, an image that was always slightly intoxicating.

He needs me in ways you wouldn't understand, she said, but she sounded to Darcy as if she was convincing herself. He's the one who believes in something.

Darcy could tell she talked less of a faith than a crusade and he heard the subtle comparison. Does he believe in something good? he asked.

Fin stared out as if that remained to be seen. An ashy pallor seemed to veil her face all the time now. The shine had been washed from her. I hope so, she said. Did you know he's an Orthodox Christian?

Darcy was wary of anything orthodox, especially in the name of Jesus. The missionary had taught him that. You need to get away from him, said Darcy. We need to go home.

Fin's eyes turned back and fixed on the curious painting, nodding as if she knew. There's something I still have to do, she said. The more vulnerable she seemed, the grimmer their chances appeared. She was scared to death. He reached to hold her, afraid of how fragile she'd feel in his arms, but she pulled away.

Ulitsa Kazakov, Friday morning

Darcy slept fitfully, aware of a vague fear of waking, visions of the petrified face of the man in the park, his yearning eyes carved out of wood, empty sockets, the stare of Aunt Merran's blind ram. He woke to murmurs of Russian in the hall, a vague ache edging around his head. He lay fully dressed under the duvet on the couch with a panic that had seeded in him overnight, sprouting like an infestation of jittering insects.

Fin stood behind the couch. Svetlana will be waiting, she said.

Darcy stood, looked out the window at the apartment opposite. A figure appeared in the kitchen, an elderly *baba* who opened the window and sprinkled seed on the sill.

Fin opened Aurelio's overcoat. He inserted an arm at a time, an ache in his underarms already, the place where confusion and anxiety seemed to dwell. Outside, sparrows swarmed to Svetlana's sill.

Keep your wits about you, said Fin.

What about you? he asked.

Jobik will look after me, she said.

Darcy turned and looked at her with a sudden sense he might not see her again. There are those in more imminent danger, she said. It looks like you're working for Gorbachev's people. Think of it as a cause. For something like freedom.

She let him hug her this time. She spoke like an American and sometimes he forgot that part of them was. In the name of freedom and hardly breathing he held her for an extra second, felt her body tight and narrow and volatile, and yet he had a sense her core was stronger than his. We are just butterflies, his mother had whispered long ago, slightly tipsy, as she'd played with Darcy's hair.

He stowed the stab-and-pick can-opener in his sock, wrapped in three hundred roubles. He didn't show Fin, she would laugh. She sent him out but wouldn't look at him.

Alone in the hall, he had a momentary thought of fleeing down the back stairwell and then taking his chance, the scaling of fences out into the winter. There may have been those in more imminent danger, planes going down in the Urals, sinking boats in the Bering Straits, abominations, but Darcy just stood there as if his life had flown away. The bull-headed neighbour at the end of the corridor, observing with a dampened expression, eyes dug deep beneath his brow. Just sex with a stranger for a passport, thought Darcy, and then let me go.

Outside, a white gloom draped the morning like a drop cloth. A low porcelain sky, not even the ghost of a sun. Darcy glanced back up at the apartment window. A shirt hung stiffly next door and then he noticed Fin's small open hand pressed to the glass. It seemed melodramatic from where he stood, unlike her, but it reminded him of the part of her he loved. He wanted to wave but feared if he lifted his hand he might not make it. He pulled his beanie down over his ears.

In the small car park there was no Lada, just a beige Zhiguli. Svetlana inside it, heavy mascara and smoking, her fringe in strands like frosted vines from under a thick polka-dot scarf. She pushed open the passenger door.

You ready? she asked impatiently, a clotted 'r' and an absence of humour.

As Darcy slid inside she didn't say anything, just started the car. There's an old woman in your apartment, he said. She was feeding the birds.

Svetlana expelled smoke into her corner of the windscreen then reversed. I am finished there, she said, and Darcy looked at her light pink lipstick, her lime dress with a vague pink pattern under a heavy coat, a pair of dark glasses pushed up high on her scarf as if it were a different season. Not in the mould of police or militia.

She considered Darcy almost sympathetically. Do not be so afraid, she said with a hint of apology, and Darcy wondered if it was her job to make him feel safe.

Surreptitiously, he glanced about under the console for a furry transmitter but saw none, just an apple core under his feet. He wondered if only Aurelio was under suspicion.

I don't know your real name, he said. I call you Svetlana.

Then call me Svet, she said, as in *no svet*. She smiled and it made her look younger, the hints of cheek rouge, her red and white dotted scarf. He wanted to beg her to help him but all he asked was why she had this job.

Better than work each day in a factory. She smiled with a certain camaraderie.

As they crossed the river, he cracked the window to allow icy air off the water. I'm a painter, he said.

Svetlana nodded. You will not be painting today.

As they turned west on Zubovsky Bulvar, nearby the Chayka swimming pool, he felt the can-opener and notes pushed against his ankle. If I paid enough roubles and American dollars could you get me to Finland?

Svetlana chortled softly. I cannot get me to Finland, not even myself. She pushed her scarf back higher up on her hair. And it would not please your friend Aurelio.

Darcy thought of Aurelio last night, his slightly hunted look. Is he okay? asked Darcy.

Svetlana looked over. You miss him? she asked.

Darcy massaged his elbows with his gloves as if it might keep him together. Is he not *your* friend too? he asked.

Svetlana took another pull from her cigarette and shrugged. Darcy imagined being more like that, free of people, desires, Aurelio, Fin. Was he really with the Bolshoi? he asked.

With Ballet Nacional de Cuba, Svetlana said. Her fingers enfolded the steering wheel but her knuckles weren't tight like Aurelio's last night. Then he was with the Bolshoi for a short piece, she said. She seemed neither impressed nor judgmental. She turned from the ring road down smaller streets until Darcy lost his feel for where the river was. He concentrated on the landmarks; a modern statue, Pushkin maybe, stood on the edge of a fenced wooded park.

Is he Castro's love child? he asked.

They stopped at a light and Svetlana looked at him, confused, perhaps unsure what a love child was. These are not questions for you, she said. She stubbed the remains of her cigarette on the dash and pushed the butt into the ashtray. Darcy imagined unleashing the opener from his sock and brandishing it, Svetlana just laughing. A bullet in his arm from a pistol produced from the folds of her coat.

She coughed a sort of knowing smoker's laugh. In a way you are brave, she said, and he wondered if fear and the cold had somehow numbed him. And in a way you are foolish.

What should I do? he asked.

The cigarette poised in her lips, Svetlana reached and pulled a piece of paper from the glove box. Memorise yourself this, she said. She'd taken his question more literally than he'd meant it. A licence plate number. If he were a local he'd have deduced specifics from it—the year of registration, the region the car had come from. He committed the first three digits to memory: *Xu3*. He didn't tell her he was a transposer of numbers, dysnumeric Fin called him.

His car is black, Svetlana said. A Borgward. It is Swedish.

She motioned for Darcy to take a cigarette, nodding at the pack on the dash. A gesture of familiarity, or perhaps granting a last wish. He took a first drag, the smoke warm and ghostly in his throat. What if he doesn't like me? he asked.

He like you before.

He ran away, said Darcy. He remembered the man's afflicted expression.

They crossed a canal where a rowing eight leaned forward and back, oaring a skiff that somehow plied over the top of the frozen water, on tracks. A radio tower loomed up above and then they turned and drove down the road to the *pleshka*. Everything similar to last night yet not quite mirrored in daylight, except for the *travesties* at the bus shelter, one outside, draped against the chain-link fence, a black trilby hat and baggy trousers despite the cold, the other two perched on the wooden railing, buried in coats.

Svetlana reversed the car into the lane where Aurelio had parked, where passers-by couldn't see. You be the hitchhiker on the corner. She pointed. He usually passes by soon.

Darcy felt again the insects inside him, buzzing up from their slumber. Does he speak English?

He is studied, she said, you will talk to him. She adjusted the sunglasses on top of her scarf. Time that you go now. She retrieved the piece of paper from Darcy's fingers in exchange for a small device. The face of a compass, no larger than his watch. You press this. She pointed her pink-coated fingernail to a tiny red button. They want all sound and talking.

Darcy carefully pressed the button.

Once to start it and once to stop, she said.

The recorder seemed stylish for such a primitive country. He put it in his pocket as if it might explode. Stay hopeful, he told himself, but he felt as if he was heading to war without a weapon.

They will be watching you, Svetlana said. She tightened her lips in sympathy or pity, or just as a warning. Aurelio says you must please be careful.

Darcy dipped his head to get out into the cold, unsure how much Aurelio cared. He turned. Are we doing this for Gorbachev?

Svetlana regarded him curiously. Gorbachev who? she asked, and smiled.

The transvestites stared, silent and knowing, as the cold wind welled in Darcy's eyes. He was here to ensnare who they couldn't. He thrust his hands in his pockets as he turned the bend and stood where he was supposed to, waiting; the ache in his glands, a chill already in his feet. He cursed himself, then Fin and Aurelio, all that had led him here. He checked about himself for reference points: a disused railway line, an old apple orchard, a high-tensile perimeter, a prison perhaps. He felt the small recorder in his pocket, breathed and felt the iced air fill him; he was the perpetrator this time, a feeling that lay heavily, like an anger turning sour. He wanted to vomit in the snow.

He let out his breath at the sound of a car. The same as Svetlana's but a middle-aged woman who passed, ignored him standing there. Another and then a black car approaching, sloped like an old Vanguard, a driver alone. The licence plate beginning *Xu3*. Darcy pushed his fringe up under his beanie thinking he should hold out his cold, gloved hand, extend a thumb for a ride, but his hand stayed somewhere over his mouth. He just stood there.

Through the curve of the driver's side window he could make out the narrow face and horn-rimmed specs. It was him, slowing, then rolling to a halt up ahead in the slush. Darcy turned but his feet seemed frozen; the back window of the car, oval and small, mirrored the dull white sky. There was a pulse in Darcy's neck as he tried again to imagine himself on a Lufthansa jet on a runway. Cautiously he found himself drawing alongside the vehicle, a panicked stare reflected in the side mirror. Darcy wondered if it was his own but then he stood at a crack in the window. The face almost ferocious, as if Darcy was an apparition.

What are you doing here? the man asked in a clipped British English. Gingerly reaching behind him, he unlatched the rear door. Get in and keep low.

Darcy's first instinct was to shake his head no, but there was something like hope in the son-in-law's watchful eyes, a glimmer of understanding. Darcy climbed inside, lying down on a cracked leather seat, the warm car about him, the smell of dog and pipe tobacco. The son-in-law drove off. The same slender whippet laid his chin on the console between the bucketed seats, a stark recognition in everyone's eyes.

The son-in-law drank from a silver hipflask. Are you American? he asked, a soft vibration in his voice.

Darcy coughed softly. Australian, he said, knowing it was little consolation. The son-in-law took another swig, looking at Darcy in the rear-view mirror as if the road ahead was incidental. Who sent you? he asked.

Darcy felt again for the tape recorder, pocketed against his chest. He'd planned on saying the *pleshka* was in the *Spartacus Guide* under *cruising in the outskirts*. Can I sit up? he asked instead.

Nyet, said the son-in-law, not yet.

Darcy raised himself on his elbow. The dog was monitoring him, the son-in-law gauged the risk in the mirror, his wavy salt-and-pepper hair above the seat back. The ride was heavy and smooth and the engine rumbled dimly. A bundle of maps in the seat pocket facing him, an empty ashtray.

Can I see your passport? the son-in-law asked.

I don't have it with me, said Darcy.

The son-in-law slowed suspiciously at a roundabout and Darcy quietly switched on the tape in his pocket. You have so many maps, he said, a bleak attempt at conversation. Are you travelling a lot?

The son-in-law turned and glanced down. What you are doing in Moscow? he asked.

I'm an artist, said Darcy, but Svetlana was right, he didn't feel like an artist today. There was also doubt in the son-in-law's greying eyebrows, the way they strained into an arch of fear.

A fellowship to paint industrial landscapes, Darcy added. He peeked above the level of the window. Low undulating country dotted with wooden houses, patches of skeletal deciduous trees; the industrial landscapes were fading away. What about you? he asked. His voice sounded choked with weeds.

I am teaching at the university, said the son-in-law, staring out, his pipe tight between his teeth. The clouds were so low you could stand on the car and touch them. Distant people in the wintry fields, a cart pulled by a pair of Clydesdales through the snow. Soviets are now the most literate people in history, the son-in-law added almost proudly. He sucked at the embers of his tobacco, still pensive and wary behind his glasses. They sent you, didn't they? he said.

Darcy smelled the worn leather seats, heard the drum of the tyres on the bitumen, the fields an eiderdown of snow pocked by trees, flat and unprotected. No evidence of a car behind them. No, he said, I found it in the *Spartacus Guide* under *cruising in the outskirts*.

The car suddenly turned down a narrow side road and rolled to a halt beside a low drainage channel. The son-in-law left the engine running for the heat, ordered the whippet to the floor so he could sit on the passenger side himself. Breathing uneasily, the son-in-law ordered Darcy to take off his coat, then gestured with the stem of his pipe for him to climb forward between the seats.

Darcy paused, felt the can-opener against his ankle as he began to struggle through, over the console. He slipped behind the steering wheel as the son-in-law, his free hand shaky, reached back for Darcy's overcoat. Russian chewing gum fell from the pocket, a few roubles in an elastic band in the son-in-law's fingers.

They pay you? he asked, searching Darcy's face.

Darcy surged with misgivings, the insects again and the pangs in his underarms. Against his every instinct he mustered a gentle look, not of pleading but understanding. No, he said.

The son-in-law kept watch in the rear-view mirror, placed a narrow hand on Darcy, nodding almost imperceptibly. Can you take your trousers down? he asked. Everything risked for this.

As Darcy slipped from his Levis, he felt a rent inside himself in a way he hadn't foreseen, his jeans and thermal long johns slid around his feet, the can-opener pressed against his ankle, uselessly concealed in his socks. He looked away. In the distance farmers were high up on round bales of hay that had been covered in canvas. He lifted the bottom of his thermal undershirt to reveal the contour in his underwear and the son-in-law ran his fingers over it. Why are you doing this? asked the son-in-law.

Darcy couldn't say anything real without tears. Why are you? he asked.

I look for love, he said, removing his horn-rimmed glasses, then as the son-in-law lowered his face and kissed Darcy there, Darcy wondered how it could have been different, the way he romanticised things, this accidental collision with history. He gazed out in disbelief as a lorry approached with a hayrick, silent in the wind. A truck from the Second World War, the faint whine of its engine and a farmer peering through the frosted window.

Not in front of the peasants, said Darcy, and the son-in-law rose abruptly and said something in Russian. He grabbed his pipe stem and held it to Darcy's ribs. Drive, he

said, please, motioning at the wheel. Darcy turned the
ignition but the engine was already on. He lurched the
Borgward into gear and forward against the handbrake,
down the gravel lane. The pipe stem relaxed against him
as the lorry diminished in the mirrors and they came to a
T, a wide paved road. Darcy slowed to a squeaking halt. I
haven't driven in my underpants since I was a child, he
said, but the son-in-law frowned, distracted by two
babushkas leaning on a gate, their heads side by side like
two woolly birds. He gestured to the left but before Darcy
could turn a semitrailer with a load of concrete pylons
passed close and the Borgward was sucked momentarily
into a gap in the wind and then cast back out. He could
have driven out in front of it, but he knew he wasn't brave
enough for that kind of annihilation. Instead, he drove on
in his Fruit of the Looms and the son-in-law stroked him
gently. The whippet, sylph-like, turned away as if embarrassed, but there was no sign of anyone following.

Can we drive to Finland? asked Darcy.

The son-in-law reached for his flask and then for the
radio knob, dialed through the crackling channels,
speeches and *oompah* marches. He quietly turned it off.
When you come to a red grain silo turn left, he said.

Are you going to kill me? asked Darcy. Another truck
passed and Darcy looked back in the rear-view mirror; still
nothing.

Is that what you want?

Darcy saw the red silo and made the turn without
indication, crept the Borgward through the icy puddles.
No, he said. I want to get home to Australia.

The driveway was framed by an avenue of poplars
bare as twig brooms in the snow, and beyond, a small ever-

green forest. Why are we here? asked Darcy. He didn't see the house at first, surrounded by conifers, a place you might drive by and wonder who lived among the palisade of trees. Two storeys of black-stained wood, light blue shutters, some of them hanging on by a hinge.

I grew up here, in this house, said the son-in-law.

It was old but more impressive than the general's dacha. Darcy rolled to a stop in front of a chained and padlocked gate. The garden was overgrown, long winter grasses with rounded bellies of snow. Cumquat trees in collapsing whisky barrels and dormer windows extending from upstairs like afterthoughts. There was no sign of recent life.

The farmers used the banisters for firewood, said the son-in-law. There was once a circular staircase. He carefully took a tartan biscuit tin from under the seat. A crest on the lid, *Product of Aberdeen, Scotland*. He selected a shortbread for himself, gave one to the dog, and then one to Darcy. Pushkin visited here, he said without pretence, unlike the way Aurelio had tried to impress by mentioning Nabokov. The son-in-law seemed more composed out here. The only noise was the hum of trucks from the highway and the sound of them eating. Mid-afternoon and already the daylight was fading.

We had horses, the son-in-law said.

Darcy's feet were cold from the steel pedals, despite the air belching from under the dash. He pulled his knees up and removed his boots and rubbed his toes. I will warm them, the son-in-law said kindly.

Darcy pulled his thick double-layered socks free, the can-opener wrapped in notes, still concealed in their folds, now under the seat. He rested his back against the wood-panelled door and placed his feet in the son-in-law's lap.

Sucking quietly on his pipe as the afternoon darkness descended, the son-in-law rubbed them. Darcy thought of what he'd been recording. A conversation of two men getting to know each other. It made him feel sick to his stomach.

The son-in-law put down his pipe and blew smoke over Darcy's pale toes as if lighting embers, then softly kissed them. The son-in-law nodded to himself, clasped Darcy's soles, massaging them. He looked up at Darcy with tears in his eyes.

Does your wife know? asked Darcy.

The son-in-law shook his head slightly and Darcy masturbated himself dutifully, sadly, as the dim light gloved the house. The son-in-law just watched, held Darcy's feet and followed the movement of Darcy's stroke with his watery eyes, then a sudden flash appeared from among the trees. A camera flash.

The son-in-law pushed Darcy's feet from his lap, the whippet barked against the passenger door. The window rolled down, the son-in-law squinting out into nothing but shadows in the undergrowth. They mock me in my misery, the son-in-law whispered as if he'd known the moment would come. He let the dog out to chase through the trees. You knew, he said to Darcy, but Darcy was shaking his head as they heard the dog yelp. The son-in-law called it by a name that sounded like *Boyar*, then he stared at Darcy. You must go now, he said emphatically. The dog re-emerged from the trees and jumped back in, whined unnaturally as the son-in-law bent down and touched its rib cage. Go, he said without looking at Darcy.

Darcy was wrestling back into his jeans and boots, finding his way into the arms of Aurelio's coat. The son-in-law glowered out into the trees as if Darcy was already gone. Darcy was drawn to apologise, explain, but instead he found himself fumbling away through the grey towards the highway, the wind's fierce chill seeping back through him. He'd left his socks, Fin's socks, all of his money, under the seat. Then he heard the muted sound of choral music and stopped. As he turned, the shape of the whippet appeared from the early darkness. Shoo, said Darcy, shoo, but it wouldn't go back, it jumped up on Darcy lightly, craned its neck like a gargoyle, whining, its fine coat moist in the glacial air. Reluctantly, Darcy picked it up and folded it in his arms and picked his way back, seeking the edge of the gravel track, so dark now it was hard to make out the hump of the Borgward. The music was loud and the car door was open, the son-in-law slouched in the passenger side, his head collapsed as if sleeping. Your dog, whispered Darcy. The dog jumped in and cringed in the corner, its ears pinned back. The son-in-law was motionless. Darcy turned on the interior light. The pipe on the biscuit tin, blood from the son-in-law's chest flooding the front of his sweater from under his jacket, pooling on the seat beside him. A gun with a silencer lay on the floor. Nikolai, said Darcy.

Then Darcy saw a shape coming towards them through the trees and he found himself running blindly to the road as if he knew it by feel, leaning into the blackness, the mud crisp beneath him. Breathless, his cheeks damp with sweat, he turned back just once to see a flash of light behind him, then another, someone taking different photos—the insides of the Borgward, the son-in-law's blood congealing on the seat. A straggled formation of fighter planes formed high shadows overhead.

On the main road, Darcy put his thumb out into the

beams of an approaching semitrailer but the driver didn't see him. Darcy watched the red tail-lights recede until there was nothing but silence and dark. *The corrupt individual travels alone*, the words recalled from somewhere, but the dog was back by his side. Darcy kneeled and held its face, the whippet shaking, the smell of the son-in-law's blood on its breath. The lights of another truck like distant pinpoints, dividing the night as they got closer, then flooding the frozen asphalt to reveal Aurelio's small grey Lada on the roadside not a hundred yards up. Darcy stayed crouched with the dog in the shadows to keep out of sight as the lorry passed with the lengths of the shadows and spaces, then there was only the sound of Darcy's breath, the noiseless road, the dog. For a moment Darcy imagined driving the son-in-law and the Borgward back to the city and smashing through the embassy gates. He picked up the dog and its body folded up as he buttoned it inside his coat and waded out through the soundless night, stumbling up the road to the Lada. The dog's heartbeat against him.

The car was unlocked but no sign of Aurelio, no keys in the ignition. The dog let out a whimpering bark and Darcy let it down and it slid inside the car. Darcy reached into the snow at the road's edge, rubbed his hands then pressed his icy fingers to his eyes. Stains on his cheeks from where the dog had been licking, the son-in-law's blood on his hands for a passport. Aurelio out there taking photos.

He got in and the whippet curled up at his feet. Darcy hugged himself, stunned in the thick-shadowed night. Fear like throbs of bile. Aurelio climbing through the roadside fence now, scraping his boots on the wire. Another semitrailer shunting past, bathing them in light. Aurelio seemed unlike himself, dishevelled, night-vision glasses around his neck, his hair all tangled when he took off his hat.

He is dead, he said.

Darcy nodded.

Aurelio nodded too, but for a long time, then turned the key in the ignition. Did you touch the gun? he asked.

Darcy shook his head and leaned forward awkwardly, the hem of his coat about the dog, turned on the heater. He was a nice man, he said. The way he spoke so matter-of-factly made him realise he was in shock. His hands against the vent in the hope of heat, staring.

Aurelio suddenly slammed the car into gear then reached down and ripped the oval transmitter from beneath the dash, tossed it out into the dark like a stone. I will say you did that, he said.

The dog shifted in the blackness at Darcy's feet, but Aurelio didn't notice. Darcy said nothing, his fingers thawing, Aurelio drove. They monitoring me, he said. They threaten me. Article 121. Criminal acts. They know about us. He steered out onto the bitumen and drove too fast for the ice on the road.

Who is *they*? asked Darcy.

My father, he said. *They* is my father. The general. He looked over at Darcy but Darcy had nothing to say, one hand on the dog's head, but he heard the words like a rock in his gut. The dacha, the room, the retarded girl was his sister. The wedding. It all made sense and yet it seemed so unlikely. Can we just go away somewhere? he asked. You must know a safe place.

We are not in Sweden, said Aurelio. We are not in that kind of country. He drove back towards the city. You do not know my father, he said. The last place we went we are followed.

They both watched the white lines disappearing beneath them, swallowed under the car like endless cigarettes. Where are your gloves? asked Aurelio.

Darcy was confused, he didn't know about the gloves, left with his socks and the can-opener, his money. I took them off to drive, he said, but it made no sense. He'd taken them off to masturbate.

You were driving?

He wanted me to, said Darcy. He took me to another place first, out among farms, but a lorry went by us. Aurelio passed a dilapidated bus that seemed lodged in the snow.

Where's the recorder? he asked.

Darcy fished out the tiny tape machine from his damp denim jacket, handed it over. As Aurelio steered he tried to turn it on. Darcy's muffled voice: *You have so many maps*, then something inaudible, then nothing. Aurelio regarded him, bewildered, thumped the steering wheel, then seemed to hold himself in, shaking his head at everything gone sideways.

He was a teacher, said Darcy, at the university.

Aurelio looked over as if knowing Darcy wasn't suited for this. Darcy felt the dog nuzzling his feet, the memory of the son-in-law blowing warmth on his toes. He was just lonely, said Darcy, that's all. He shouldn't have lived in this country.

Aurelio rubbed his eyes then looked at Darcy, his brown eyes despondent. Do you think he had a choice? asked Aurelio.

Darcy stared out into the Soviet night. Not now, he said.

None of us has choices now. Aurelio lit a *papirosa* and sucked on it tightly as they drove back towards the city in silence. The lit windows of villages then the relentless concrete apartment blocks, lapping the outskirts like towering tombstones, the dog a curled-up creature, still unannounced at Darcy's feet. Images of the slumped body, the pistol on the biscuit tin. Darcy felt bloodless himself, his breaths came to him irregular and shallow, the consequences passed like the car lights. What about my fingerprints in the car? he asked. He didn't admit to the socks, his money.

At first Aurelio didn't reply, walled in by the night and a canopy of sullenness. He lit a second cigarette. Suicide, he said, a scrape in his voice. They can process as suicide.

Who is *they* this time? asked Darcy. Aren't *you* the militia?

We are independent, said Aurelio.

Are *we*?

Aurelio pulled up outside Fin's apartment on Kazakov, his face half-lit from a nearby street lamp, his aspect so tired he'd barely be noticed in a room. I have to go, he said.

Darcy felt another movement at his feet and, as if by invitation, the dog's slender head appeared, timid and anxious, at the gearstick. Aurelio shouted a Spanish oath as the dog moved up onto Darcy's lap, Aurelio reeling with fright. What are you doing with this?

Darcy pulled his coat back around the whippet's tapered body, holding it like a captive bird against him. The dog that had chased Aurelio into the dark and torn back to the Borgward whimpering. He belongs to Chernenko's daughter, said Darcy, as if something had to be salvaged.

The dog eyed Aurelio carefully and Aurelio looked at it in disbelief. You must keep this hidden, he said. Stay in that apartment and wait.

What about my passport? asked Darcy.

I have only a photo of you in Chuprakov's car. And photo of him dead. Same car, but later. His English was deteriorating. You are my friend, but we have no choices. You must do what I say. Trust me, he said. Fin's words when she'd phoned St Kilda the first time, to make her invitation.

Aurelio held out a hand to touch Darcy's cheek but the dog emitted a long low growl. I did trust you. A pleading shrouded Darcy's voice. He held the whippet to him as if it were a weapon of his own.

It is my job, said Aurelio. They punish me too.

But Darcy had slid beyond any sense of jobs and consequences, he felt faint now, his mind askew as he closed the car door behind him, looked back through the misted window. Aurelio's big haunted eyes, searching to be understood, and tears came to Darcy's that turned to frost on his lashes. He let the whippet down in the snow and it stood there, silvery, like a stolen ornament, suddenly unafraid.

The donkey drawing looked out from the easel, called Darcy back. It was too late to say sorry or return to a car that was gone.

Fin yelled out from her bedroom. Darcy felt too cold and stupefied to answer but the timorous whippet pricked its ears. The usual cabbage steam in the corridor had been overtaken by something in her room, a smell of suet. The whippet was sniffing under the door.

Darcy pulled his freezing feet from sodden boots, shaky, his bridges ached, toes caressed by dead hands, Aurelio gone. Shutting the whippet out behind him, he guardedly opened Fin's bedroom door. She stood alone in her Joan Armatrading T-shirt, the portable hotplate on the ironing board, tins of lard. She was pouring from a pot into a mould but she stopped, rested her eyes on Darcy, shocked. What happened, little brother?

He glimpsed himself in her mirror, faint mud smeared around his eyes, cheeks daubed with the dog's saliva.

It didn't go well, he said, brushed past her into the bathroom and turned on the shower, hoping that water might scald him of feeling, rid him of the ache in his chest and the pain in his feet. As he stripped, Fin came in behind him and together they regarded the mud and slush on his jeans, the telltale absence of socks. Did you have sex with him under a bridge? she asked.

Not exactly. He stepped under the water, so hot it felt cold, pouring into his upturned mouth. Fin waited for details, a streak of lard in her umbered hair, and Darcy felt her watching him through the plastic curtain, then he noticed the shape of the dog behind her; baleful and silent, it stood on the threshold. It must have nudged the bedroom door and now its front legs lifted lightly onto the lavatory seat, it dipped into the bowl, long-necked as an ibis drinking. Fin shrieked and jumped aside. He's mine, said Darcy, stepping from the shower.

Fin turned on the taps in the sink to add to the noise so they could talk. She placed a towel around Darcy's shoulders.

Nikolai Chuprakov shot himself, he said. This is his dog.

Fin cocked her head. The pink rims of her eyes seemed to deepen to red as she opened them wide. Chuprakov is dead? she whispered.

In his car on the farm where he grew up, he said. Speaking the words and seeing Fin's shock seemed to tranquillise Darcy into a false, heightened calm as the shower cascaded behind him and the truth took hold in the green of Fin's eyes.

And you have his dog, she said.

I couldn't just leave it. Darcy didn't tell her he'd looked after it briefly once before. As he dried himself, Fin kneeled for the curious dog, stroked its spine. It belongs to the next General Secretary's daughter, she said.

Darcy thought of the woman in the indigo suit at the Bolshoi, up in the balcony. The Lady and the Dog, he said.

Jesus.

Darcy put on Fin's sheepskin slippers, tried to keep his thoughts from careening.

Fin pushed her sallow red-tipped fingers through her hair. How did you get back here? she asked.

Aurelio, he said. He took a photo of me in the car with Chuprakov, then photos of him dead. Darcy now felt a deliberate tone in his voice that was tinged with accusation, implicating Fin. He wanted to blame her.

What are you supposed to do now? she asked.

He told me to wait for him here, said Darcy, unless you have a better idea.

Fin's face seemed even paler against her hair and flat brown lipstick. Did you get your passport? she asked.

Darcy stared at his garments curled up on the floor; jeans and sweatshirt and woollen jumper. I just saw a man bleeding to death, he said. He picked up his clothes and stuffed them into the shower, let the water wash away evidence. The dog looked up at him, showing the self-conscious whites of its eyes.

Fin dipped a Q-tip in dark make-up. Aurelio's last name is Sarfin, she said. He's that general's son.

Darcy stood dumbstruck. Who told you that?

Jobik found a source, she said. She ran the Q-tip over her eyebrows. General Sarfin was stationed in Cuba during the Missile Crisis, she said, leaned and petted the anxious dog.

Darcy dried his hair, felt himself being drawn back into her world. He thought of Aurelio's face through the frost-rimed window of the Lada—right country, wrong general, driving his father's car, carte blanche at the dacha, the sister with the spoon.

His mother still lives in Havana, said Fin. Darcy looked over at his own sister crouched in the steaming bathroom, regarding him in bewilderment as he took his Longines watch from the basin and put it on.

Get dressed and come with me, she said. Maybe Jobik will help you this time.

Darcy turned off the taps. It's not safe for me to leave now, he said, unless you can get me into an embassy.

I can't go to the embassies, she said.

The ache twinged in Darcy's underarms. Why's that?

I just can't right now. She went back into the other room. I'll wait here with you, she said, and they worked in silence, carving dried casts with what looked like dental instruments, tiny picks and cutters. The room smelled like an abattoir. The ancillary piece Fin promised the curator, a sculpture of the same museum. Art from dried lard, the innards of a pig—Darcy had once told her it hardened like marble. She remembered everything; what he remembered was the son-in-law, his poet's eyes and owlish glasses, his old-fashioned English, his torturedness.

Fin turned on the radio, her hands caked, her neck streaked where she'd wiped it. Dirges for Andropov played still. She'd poured hot lard into Russian Tupperware the shapes of horses' hooves, hardening. He took the teardrop painting knife he'd used to shape wax and chose a dry hoof-shaped cast, began to carve small columns, indents for windows, the Atomic Energy Pavilion. All he could do was look at what was right before him, no sense of the future, he'd flapped his wings in Prague and led himself to this. His breath now warm inside him, butcher's grass resting on top of the trestle table, the lake in the middle cast with blue-painted lard, tacky as folk art. He watched her pin the foldout postcards on the wall for shapes and reference. She looked over. I've made mistakes too, she said.

He moulded a tray for the People's Friendship Fountain. Was wanting to sleep with me one of them?

At least I've always known how to say no, she said.

To Jobik? he asked, but didn't look up for an answer. Instead he glanced about anxiously—the ironing board in here now, the dog by the bed on the sheepskin rug. The son-in-law who wouldn't be teaching, not quoting from Turgenev and Dostoyevsky; he'd not told Darcy what he taught, but Darcy imagined it had been literature. He also imagined the scene of the suicide, if it was still unattended, what Aurelio would be telling his father now. The way the general had stared straight at him then right through him: the new recruit, the one in the photo, was now in the fold. Aurelio doing his job.

Dust rested in the air and on the blades of Fin's scissors. The faded places on the wall where her peasant dresses had hung. She cut squares from a roll of chalky plaster bandage and for a time all Darcy heard were the subtle sounds of their instruments.

We could never have been everything to each other, said Fin. She dunked plaster in a plastic bowl of water on the ironing table. But you being here, I feel kind of broken in two, she said.

That's how I've always felt, said Darcy. Since I was a kid. The parts in him that lived in their separate compartments: sex, love and affection, trust. In Aurelio he'd sensed them just barely coalescing. He reached for her fine-toothed pick and tucked foil into the crevices of his building, making the lard look gilded, his fingers tipped with bronze. He looked over at Fin with nothing to lose. When I was nine, there was a Mormon missionary, he said, down in the gully.

Fin didn't look up at him.

He laid me out in the grass on my shirt and rubbed himself off on me. I felt like it was my fault. I followed him down the drive in the car.

The gully where you took me? she asked. She cautiously layered plaster on two toilet rolls taped end to end, moulding the swoop of the obelisk. She focused thoughtfully on her work. Do you think that's why you're like you are?

Darcy uncupped a new mould. I recreate it, he said, the intensity, the adrenaline rush, public places. He knew it needn't define him. But it had.

She took her blade and cut the edge of a section of silver foil. Did anyone know?

My mother guessed, he said, but she was too drunk to know what to do except taunt me.

Fin turned on her hairdryer, melted the foil on the blood-veined lard, gilding it with heat. Then she stopped. You don't think that made you gay?

Darcy shook his head. I've never wanted to be with a woman, he said, other than you.

She turned the hairdryer back on. The way the heated foil hugged the lard had the dulled effect of pewter. He could read her mind: *what sort of family is this?* Again she flipped the dryer off. I'm sorry, she said.

For what? asked Darcy.

The other night, she said, and back then.

You couldn't help back then, he said. He thought of their American mothers, Fin on the drive in Mount Eliza, just left there, the same drive Darcy rolled down in the Austin and where that had taken him.

I'm sorry I disappeared, she said.

Darcy nodded to himself and looked at her make-up,

the colour in her transparent brows, the line carefully traced around her lips. The prospect of being alone here lay about him like a prison, the way she'd brought him here. He reached for some of her wet plaster bandage, aware of the subtle shake in his fingers, laid the plaster to soften the edge of her man-made lake, to firm up where her building met the butcher's grass. She placed her implements on the trestle and folded a sheet of bronze-leaf foil then went into the bathroom.

Darcy watched her cigarette burning low in a saucer. The dog walked over and licked from a bucket of lard, and Darcy closed his eyes to the sounds of her getting ready, the running of the tap, the click of her make-up case, her mirror check. He fashioned a small wax dog and perched it on the nose cone of the obelisk, and painting it red he found himself crying. The whippet watched him from the sheepskin. Fugitive and guardian.

Fin appeared in her skinny jeans and a snug-fitting cardigan, her hair a new brunette like a Russian Sloane Ranger; all she needed was a string of pearls. Are you sure you don't want to come with me? she asked. She pressed her lips and spread her gloss evenly.

Darcy knew she was going to Jobik. I'll wait here, he said, for Aurelio. He looked at the half-finished sculptures, some mottled cream, others bronzed or silver. I'll finish this. He spoke uncertainly, not quite avoiding the break in his voice.

If things go wrong, she told him quietly, there's a restaurant called the Jaguaroff. It's in a lane off Solyanka, behind the church; it's listed in Fodor's but please don't write it down. She blew him a kiss as if she'd be back in a minute, leaving in her plain leather coat without so much as a haversack or handbag. He didn't dare look at the door.

Darcy found himself left with wax and lard caked on his hands, strangely still, her paintbrush in his fingers. The dog regarded him carefully, trustful. Everything fell suddenly silent as if a temporary deafness had come over him. He listened through the walls for sounds in the snow, from the wallowing darkness. Instead of freedom, he felt a frantic dread of being alone.

Ulitsa Kazakov, Early Saturday morning

Darcy dreamed he was in California, driving too fast on a winding road, birds thumping on the windscreen, blue jays, blood and feathers, eucalyptus and orange groves, a cottage in the distance. A sea of round lilies that turned out to be melons. He dreamed Aunt Merran waved a long-leafed vegetable over a fence, calling out but not to Darcy, to a blind ram with its bedraggled head twisted up. Aunt Merran's hair a dirty grey, long and loose. Darcy sketched her with his left hand, shaky and childlike, as the ram ran around in suspicious circles, sniffing up at the air. Eyes sunken deep in a woollen face, eyes that came at Darcy. If I left he'd die, Aunt Merran shouted, her farmer's tan and weathered face; she walked away with undulating hips. A cumquat tree looked like a large umbrella floating above the fence. But Fin was your daughter, said Darcy. The veranda sofas sprung and uncomfortable and the drumming of rain on the corrugated tin. You'll look after her, Merran said and Darcy drove away fast on a road through a jungle lined with emaciated men in rags, shaved heads and bleeding tattoos. He jolted awake in a sweat, his heart in his teeth at the squawk of the keys in the shifting locks. He leapt up from the couch where he'd been lying, the whippet held close for protection, watched a gloved hand slip inside the front door, reaching for the light, a hand that remembered the switch by feel.

Aurelio? he whispered.

Svetlana, she said. She stood in the entry hall, buried in the collar of a coat dusted with snow, a pistol extending from her glove. She pointed it at him with a thin-lipped smile and Darcy's breath went loud and quick inside his head. Where's Aurelio? he asked. The words faint, struggling from him as he gripped the whippet's fine coat, its skin taut in his fingers. Its collar.

You must let this dog go, said Svetlana. Her fringe was plastered wet against her forehead, no colourful scarf or sunglasses now. She produced a bone-shaped biscuit from her pocket. *Boyar*, she said, then something in Russian, the treat in one hand, pistol in the other, the name Darcy'd last heard from the son-in-law's lips, had him holding tight to the quivering dog, its heartbeat pulsing fast in Darcy's palms, its white-rimmed eyes looking back for permission.

Svetlana jolted the pistol, impatient. I shoot you right here and not one will be come to see you, not one. And Darcy believed her but still he held the dog hostage. Is Aurelio in trouble? he asked.

Svetlana squinted. We are all in trouble, she said. All of us. You were the honeytrap, but you gave us no honey. She moved a step forward, brandishing the treat and weapon, trying not to scare off the now cowering dog. Don't be hero, she said.

I need my passport, said Darcy.

You need more than passport, she said. Give this dog.

Darcy released his grip on the whippet's rib cage and Svetlana eased the handgun onto the end table and whispered to the dog in Russian, coaxing it to her. Warily, the dog stepped over the frayed purple rug and delicately sniffed at the treat in her hand, then, without looking back at Darcy, took the treat and chewed. Svetlana shoved her pistol in her coat and pulled a choker leash from her pocket. She looked older, her mascara washed away. Where is your Finola now? she asked.

Gone, said Darcy. She's gone.

You didn't leave with her? She regarded Darcy with a kind of pity. Get yourself out of here, she said. I can maybe say I never saw you, but still they will be coming. She reached to place the choker chain about the whippet's slender neck but it reared quietly away from her on its spindly hocks and growled. She calmed it, tried again, extended her arm. It let out a yelp, darted at her leather-gloved hand and bit her. Darcy did nothing to stop it, just shrouded himself in the duvet. Svetlana cried out and the dog barked up at her, baring teeth and making a second quick lunge, the sound of another dog somewhere in the building, a big dog howling and then a third shrill yap started. Svetlana held her wounded hand to her chest and pulled out her pistol with the other, retreating out into the hall, her face twisted up with pain. She didn't shoot Cher-nenko's dog, just took her injury away in a cacophony of barking. The other dogs kept on but the whippet peered back at Darcy like a finely hewn bird, a heron or egret, concerned.

Darcy pushed his fingers deep into his temples as the dog approached him timidly, the memory of blood from Chuprakov's wound and now Svetlana bitten. Darcy moved past the dog and locked the door then rushed into the bedroom, knocking over a canister of lard. He pulled open Fin's wardrobe and searched the pockets of her quilted patchwork coat, where he'd seen her fish for cash, felt along the hem. The dog behind him playful now, its paws on Darcy, but Darcy said *no* and it sat like a sculpture as he fingered Fin's winter dresses, her short leather skirt, stopped when he heard someone pass in the hall. He waited, a glimpse of himself so gaunt in the mirror, and the dog sniffed back into the other room, but there was no one. The other dogs had gone quiet. Then Darcy saw Fin's fake fur stole, curled up on the floor in the corner like a black cat. He reached down and felt the touch of something solid and square inside the silk backing. He shook the solidness down through an opening. A burgundy passport, an emblem and Cyrillic letters, a bundle of cash clipped inside. Different currencies, roubles wadded with American dollars. Darcy didn't count but he knew it was a lot, imagined stashes everywhere, Jobik's people, Chechens, Estonians, rebels, whatever they were. The passport embossed with an indecipherable stamp and a photo of Fin with short peroxided hair, without makeup. It wasn't as if it couldn't be him. He drank what was left of the tin-tasting milk from the fridge and grabbed at the crackers, poured some on the floor for the dog, then pushed what he could into his daypack, Fin's suede mittens and extra socks, buttoned himself in Aurelio's coat. Beneath his scarf the leather leash was now back on the hook from the first day, hanging like a promise, and the dog looking up as if ready, a liability or saviour, a charm.

Darcy didn't lock the door. He headed down the back steps with the dog jumping up on him, out into the still-dark street where there was no white Zhiguli, no Svetlana, just a wind that cut into Darcy's face like a flurry of spinning razors, the dog looking up with its eyes closed against it. Darcy felt exposed and paranoid; checking behind, he leaned into the bite of the gale and tried to remember the name of the restaurant, a car's name. He'd looked it up in Fodor's but kept his promise, not written it down. But now his mind was all fuzzy. A lane off Polyanka or Solyanka? He'd forgotten the name of the church.

He scanned the parked cars for men in pairs or solo, cleanshaven and waiting; he couldn't risk going back to check. And the restaurant wouldn't be open now, anyway. He looked down at the dog beside him, almost airborne in the wind, the weather both for and against them, this visibility, the taste of ice that stung Darcy's lips. His hand in his pocket with the end of the leash, clasping the small roll of money, the sharp edges of the passport. No point in the dress shop, he'd already shouted Aurelio's name from that knife-cold alley. The money, the chance of a bribe, or flagging down a US consular official, explaining how his mother grew up near Montecito. But it wasn't yet seven, no embassies open, then he remembered it was Saturday, they wouldn't be open at all. Without written travelling permission he wouldn't get far on a train.

Out on Ulitsa Dimitrova he walked among the early pedestrians, trudging, their heads low and covered. Darcy and the quick-walking dog moved through them, turned and cut through towards Polyanka on a street that passed near the Church of St Gregory. Maybe this was where she'd meant. He dipped up a narrow cul-de-sac to see who had followed and in the shelter of an alcove he kneeled and held the dog close to his coat. He saw no restaurant there, just a man in a well-lit second floor window, sitting in his dressing-gown, sipping from a teacup at a simple breakfast table. His little finger extended as he lifted a tea kettle with what could have been a cosy. A reddish-haired woman appeared at his side and served him a plate from a pot on a stove. Darcy imagined it might have been porridge, that they were expats, English, maybe one of those Cambridge spies, the defector and his Russian wife, one was still alive. Darcy blew his breath into the scarf that covered his face, the only warmth whispering from inside him and he breathed it on the dog, trying to remember the defector's name. The woman eating her toast in the window, what if that was them?

Kim Philby, Darcy shouted, startling the dog, but his shout wasn't as loud as Darcy had hoped. The woman stared out and Darcy started to walk forward like a child returning home, but above him he saw the silhouette of a man on the steep-pitched roof, roped by his waist to a chimney. He swung something and there was a shot; the dog jumped, pigeons rose up in flight from the eaves.

Darcy cringed breathless behind a metal rubbish bin, but if he'd been hit he couldn't feel it, nothing but snow on his knees and the dog right there with him. Another shot reverberated and Darcy peeked up; it wasn't a rifle but the echo of a hammer strike, sledging out birds from the crowns of the chimneys. But now a guard stood attentive in the glass doorway to the building, and upstairs the woman was drawing her curtains closed.

Darcy broke for the main street. Back out among the sluggish cars, he jumped in a taxi at the lights and let the dog jump right in with him. Hotel Metropole, said Darcy, checking the back window, car lights in the dark, grim faces through the wiped arcs of the windscreens. Anyone could have been anyone.

Nyet, said the driver, *Nyet sobakoy*. He stared at the dog on the seat but Darcy held out the roll of notes in the

palm of his hand and was driven on through the muted
fuss of the first morning traffic, past the grey mass of the
Variety Theatre, the great stone bridge and the shadowy
river, and then the black embankment. Darcy sat, relieved
to be in the smoky heat of the cab. He asked the driver for
a *papirosa* but the driver just grunted, didn't turn around.

'otel Ukraine, he said in the rear-view mirror.

Nyet, said Darcy, anger flooding through him, the dog
standing up on the seat as if incensed. Metropole, said Darcy.
You heard me. He knew that's where the foreigners stayed.

Metropole, the driver nodded.

He looked out at the Kremlin towers lit with gold
through what was now a blizzarding snow. The rifle shot
that wasn't had torn his nerves. He watched a red star that
dangled from the rear-view mirror and thought of his
mother, drunk and unattended, recovering from *left-side
neglect*. He could feel his breath laboured. A boulevard
lined with snow-blotched flats and barely lit shops, the
blue street lamps flickered themselves off even though it
wasn't yet daylight. He could search the lobby for Western
businessmen, tourists, give his name and tell his story,
then he'd try the Americans. If that didn't work, the
railway station. He looked out but couldn't recognise a
landmark now through the wipers. No GUM or the
Square or the towers of the Kremlin. Hotel Metropole, he
shouted. They should have been close to the Bolshoi, near
the Place Sverdlova, the Moskva. Stop, said Darcy. *Stoitye.*

Taras Schevchenko, the driver was saying, Taras
Schevchenko, pointing towards a statue in the shadow as
a towering sixties eyesore rose up in the windscreen; no
grand arcades or ornate grills—it wasn't the Metropole.
All Darcy knew was that Taras Bulba was a famous race-

horse from home, and this driver had a deal with the Hotel Ukraine, dropping foreigners there. Darcy thrust out some roubles that fell from his hands into the front seat, got out while he could, in the hope of divine intervention.

He and the dog ran through the snowfall, handed some notes to a doorman in a sagging green jacket so he would let the dog in. The lobby unfolded, flocked with what looked like dressed-up farmers, queues of them checking in and congregating. A clamour of the guttural mother tongue and piped folk music. Darcy stood with the dog on the edge of an endless green carpet littered with cheap canvas luggage, wind-burned men with wrinkled bloodshot eyes, crow's-feet like claws of eagles, some shrouded in sheepskin, others in boxy suits. People who didn't seem to notice the dog but Darcy knew he couldn't blend in here. No other Westerners. The wrong hotel. A heat rose up his spine, against the back of his wet coat. A clock. It was still before eight. He found a deep corduroy lounge chair in a vestibule among a group of milling women in bright woollen headscarves. One sat nearby and smiled at the dog, wrestling to glove her large hands. Darcy had no smile left in him. He removed Aurelio's coat. It felt heavy, like a shawl of dread.

Then he noticed, beside him, a pair of glassed-in booths, old-fashioned black phones. He imagined the sound of his mother's cigarette voice, a chance to tell her he was here and he was sorry. A row of surly clerks behind counters, he noticed a prettyish one at a separate desk just feet from him, a benign pale face alone in a tight blue cardigan. He searched her grey Slavic eyes for signs of benevolence. Her blonde hair was tied back loosely and she passed her eyes over Darcy and smiled, lit up at the sight of the dog. On a whim, Darcy stood and approached her, an ache in his neck ran through his shoulders as he leaned on a chair back in front of her polished teak desk and she petted the whippet. I need to make an overseas call, he said. He knew he spoke each word too carefully.

Number of room? she asked, nuzzling the dog now.

Darcy leaned in, forced his fear back down so it lay lit like kindling on his voice box. I stay at Hotel Metropole. He sounded croaky, his English broken.

You have Intourist guide?

With my group, he said. I must call my mother. She has a sickness. She is Australianski.

The girl seemed wary, but Darcy reached forward nervously, touched her hand as he took a hotel envelope from her pile. A photo of an old man sitting, cradling a trumpet, lay beside them on the desk.

Your father? asked Darcy. She nodded as he slipped a sheaf of roubles from his pocket into the envelope, proffered it to her quietly. For your father, he said, smiled as best he could. He wished his forehead wasn't sweating, that the tingle didn't run along his lip like an alarm.

She nodded with an odd muffled smirk, whisked the envelope out of sight under her desk. Darcy followed it into her lap. To call my mother, he said. For calling international.

Why you have a dog? she asked. She touched a plastic flower pinned to her lapel.

My friend, he said. He was afraid she'd wanted sex, not money, but she pushed a small red pencil at him.

You give me number, she said.

Darcy took the pencil, concentrated, whispered to himself as he wrote. The numbers lay scratched on the paper like an inculcation. His mother, oblivious, eight hours behind. Almost midnight on Baden Powell Drive, another planet. He stared up into this girl's ashen eyes. *Spasiba*, he said, pleading.

In the telephone closet all he could do was stare at the phone, a dial without numbers and a frayed brown cord. It didn't seem like it had the capacity to reach far away. He glanced out only once, to the dog on its lead, anxiously watching with the girl at the desk. He pictured his mother, alone in her dark bedroom, a species apart in her light summer nightie, recovered from her stroke. A last drink in one hand and a lit cigarette, ready for bed, unsuspecting.

When the telephone beeped Darcy sucked in air as if the floor was a trapdoor to water. He lifted the worn receiver, listened. A clicking sound, an echo and then the familiar Australian ring that made him feel heavy, his breath loud now and uneven; the phone rang and rang. He imagined it there on her bedside table, her clock radio, the latest Dick Francis, but no answer, no message machine. Darcy's heart sinking. He tried to spot the dog and his grey-eyed confidante but the desk was now unattended. Then he heard a new click. Hairlo? His mother, her husky drinker's voice, confused by the beeps.

Mum, it's Darcy, he said and heard the echo, biting his lip at the sound of her, the remnants of her American vowels, the way mothers know sons. Overcome with a rush of blearing tears. I'm in Moscow, he said. I'm in trouble.

How did you get *there*? The sound of him staving off sobs seemed to strike her quite lucid.

Darcy looked down at the damp, muddy square of linoleum, his sodden boots, uncertain what to say.

Darcy Dancer?

He pressed his fist against his cheek, knowing this would be recorded, he took his chance. They took my passport, he said. I'm afraid I might disappear.

Disappear! He heard her confusion, her own swallowing. What are you into now?

Please help me, said Darcy. The tears coming back, afraid if he started he might not find the words. I need you to contact the embassy. Write down these names.

His mother wasn't fighting tears, she was stunned silent, then the sound of her scratching around her bedside table for a pen. What are you talking about?

Write these names. Nikolai Chuprakov. Tell them he's dead. That I didn't kill him. Tell them Fin's here. Remember Jostler. She's here with him. They're involved in something.

His mother coughed. In Moscow?

I'm sorry, Mum, he said. I should have told you. But now I need you. Tell them I'm in the hands of a General Sarfin. His son is my friend. They will say I killed Nikolai Chuprakov.

With that the line went dead.

Darcy knew he'd said too much as he wiped his eyes on the arm of Aurelio's coat, stepping quickly from the booth of this wrong hotel, ready to flee, but his cardiganed friend appeared through the crowd. He avoided her apologetic smile, sniffing as he nodded. Where's the dog? he asked but she shook her head as if in apology.

Darcy said nothing, just slipped through the peasants to the large double doors. He did a half-halt when he saw the exit framed by two men in black-lapelled coats like his own, one man bearded, the dog muzzled in a cage like a captive thing being loaded into a van outside.

Darcy briskly changed course to a revolving door, pursued by the beard who crammed into the compartment behind him, and the revolving stopped. Darcy made a rush against the faltering glass and it flung him outside to the cold, to a hand that enveloped his face in cloth, damp against his nostrils, stinging his eyes, the shriek was his own at the fact of his capture, his head in what felt like a sack, the septic taste of a toxin and a roaring that pounded inside his ears. Then, for a brief suspended instant, it all felt as fluid as a dream, he could no longer feel it as real or fight it, hoisted by his arms through the snow, his feet kicking faintly but only the air. He tried to shout his name but could feel he was only mouthing, coughing up a foul astringency, asphyxiating, a suffocating glove. As the cloth flapped from his face he searched the air for the dog, for witnesses, fighting his tongue for the shape of Aurelio's name, the side of his face wet against an ice-blown roof of the van that came right at him, the feel of iron wrist bands as they clamped his hands, forced him into the back seat at an unnatural angle with his knees up, the ribbed edge beneath his hip. The slamming of a car door, then another, and they were driving through furry falling snow that drifted up high through a smeared piece of window. Ravens on the passing branches, a hint of blue above a jaundiced building. Daylight.

Lubyanka, Saturday, 9 am

Darcy came to, his face in his arms on a rough wooden table. A poisonous gagging taste, a cut on his lip that stung, a pungent animal smell. A tap dripped somewhere close, an echo then a whining. Darcy turned. A *baba*, standing in a corner outside the spray of light with a bucket in the shadows, mopping about the animal cage where the dog turned about itself, a black leather muzzle. Dog pee ran onto the floor.

Darcy went to stand, to comfort it, but the *baba* raised her mop and said *nyet* so Darcy just dabbed his lips on his arm, on denim, his jacket, but not Aurelio's coat. His daypack gone; Fin's passport, the money, gone with it. He looked up at a single bulb above him, two chairs in front. There was no clock, no window. *Da*, said the *baba*, *Lubyanka*. She bent over her bucket and hoisted the handle, left with the mop in the air like a braided head on a stick.

The battered metal door opened from the outside, a clanging in the passage. Fluorescent lights switched on brilliantly and Darcy clenched his eyes as a wooziness swept over him. He squinted up at the sound of footsteps, the general looming there, wide epaulettes and medal ribbons, his jacket pulling at its buttons, and Darcy smelled a different smell and knew it was his own sweat.

Can I use the bathroom? he asked.

The general's eyes were caustic. It is not a hotel, he said. He lowered himself carefully onto a chair that was too small and placed a manila folder and a silver lunch box on the table. His dome head large without his hat, his hair a white shaved shadow, his eyes heavy-lidded; Darcy saw nothing of Aurelio in him but the fullness of his still-dark eyebrows.

The general allowed a damp, bloodless smile then pulled some black-rimmed glasses from his lunch box. You may be having questions, he said, but I will be asking them. His English clipped, his deep tone almost seductive, the moist-lipped mouth. He was different close-up.

Darcy felt an urge to retch but there was no liquid left in him, just a nasty toxic aftertaste. He carefully removed his beanie and endeavoured to sit up straight. He wanted to tell the general he had attended his wedding but realised that was all part of a recruitment that went wrong. Where is Aurelio? he asked.

The general didn't answer, just delved into the folder then, almost casually, he placed a photo on the table. The photo from Prague.

A wave of fear rose up and Darcy breathed into his beanie's damp stale wool. More photos placed across the pitted table like a flush of cards. A shot of him standing alone on the roadside at the *pleshka,* waiting, the perimeter fence behind him. No sign of the son-in-law. Darcy looked up helplessly.

We have in this country Article 206, the general said. Criminal hooliganism with exceptional cynicism. Prison for five years. Or Article 121 *muzhelostovo.* He pointed to the photo in Prague. Another five.

Darcy beheld his own black and white face turned to

the heavens, twisting up in its fleeting shudder. He pointed at it but didn't look up. That was another country, he whispered, but when he raised his eyes this time the general's expression was not just callous and weary, but also oddly amused, the arm of his glasses swung gently in his hand.

Darcy turned to look at the dog, which just watched him balefully, and he thought about the son-in-law. Has the Australian Ambassador been notified about me? asked Darcy.

The general placed the glasses carefully on the table. No questions, he said, and Darcy's right hand fell like a rag onto his lap as he searched the general's big flushed face for sympathy. I'm a friend of your son's, he said. I was at your wedding.

The general acknowledged this with a fist slammed down on the photos. Darcy reeled back but the general just smiled again, his bottom teeth crooked, the colour of butterscotch. He set a newspaper cutting on the table, a small photo at the bottom of the page—Chernenko's daughter on a lawn in front of a large stone house. You know this woman?

Darcy shook his head, his palm scruffing back and forth through his hair in frustration, a sudden welling of fear. I don't know her; I just know who she is. He looked up so the general would see his sincerity.

You know her dog, said the general, gesturing to the restless whippet. Again the cruel amusement flashed in his eyes.

The whippet stood with its head tucked low and its haunches curled under itself; it looked like a narrow wheel. I saved the dog, he said. Nikolai Chuprakov killed himself.

Did he? asked the general.

Darcy didn't let himself cry. You know I am innocent, he said. Don't make me a scapegoat.

You are *muzhelostovo*, the general said, the syllables spat with disgust.

Then so is Aurelio, said Darcy.

The force of the slap from a huge pink hand stung Darcy so hard his head swung sideways, almost dislodged him from his chair, but he withstood it in silence, without cradling his welted cheek, even as the tears brimmed in his eyes.

You think we are not listening in, said the general. The general smoothed his index finger over the newspaper photo of Anyetta Chernenko, examined the remnants of the print on his fingertips, then he placed a photo of Fin on the table, taken in the street outside the apartment. She leaned into the window of Jobik's car, sheltered by her black umbrella, and Darcy saw himself there, on the pavement behind them, his hands in his pockets.

Darcy cupped his burning cheek. That's my friend, he said softly.

We will see, said the general. Soon will be arriving the Consul-General from Turkey. He has questions for you about your *friends*. He pointed at Jobik's car. Fin in her sheepskin coat and fur hat, Jobik's face hidden.

I only met him once, said Darcy. It was his first lie; he hoped he hadn't wasted it.

Tell that to the Turkish, the general said, glaring as the peep-window whined open. A pale woman's face shadowed through the grate. Fin, thought Darcy at first, but then recognised the face from the cutting, Chernenko's daughter, the high Slavic strength in her cheekbones, her blue eye shadow, staring in. Darcy stood to approach the door, wanting to let her know the truth, that it wasn't his fault, but the general grabbed his silver lunch box and shoved his chair back. Please get her dog, he said, motioning at the whippet in the cage.

Warily Darcy walked over, unclipped the metal clasp and reached for the leash that lay wet among its tapered feet. The dog shook like a spinnaker, didn't want to come out of the cage. Darcy didn't pull, just waited until it stepped forward. He led it quietly to the door, then he found himself kneeling, his head against the burnished silver coat, saying goodbye.

Boyar, the woman said and Darcy looked up at her, tall above him in a full-length brown fur, her stunned blue eyes. *Spasiba*, she said.

Darcy stood and placed the leash in her slender gloved hand. I took care of him, he said and she nodded, her mouth set in a strange effort at a smile, her eyes moist and shiny.

She not speak English, the general said. He took her arm and guided her down the corridor, but as she turned the corner she glanced back at Darcy. I thank you, she said.

Lubyanka, Saturday, noon

A narrow bed, wooden slats and a worn grey blanket, an iron door. The greasy floor powdered with lime. At the oil drum in the corner Darcy held his breath against the smell of those who'd come before him, pushed the lid free and peed, then slid the iron cover tight. He clenched his elbows against his aching rib cage, pressed his hands into his eyes. He'd passed a boy in the hallway in filthy fatigues and with almond-shaped eyes, Cyrillic letters on his cheeks, branded. A haunted sawn-off face shown on purpose, so Darcy could see what he might become. Outcast and emaciated, a foreign *opuscheny* a thousand miles east of here, no *troika* through the snow with Aurelio to a secret dacha in the Urals. He was here on this uneven cot, shawled in a stagnant blanket, staring up at a dim bulb on a wire that dropped from the cement ceiling. They watch from somewhere, he thought, though the door slot was covered. On the opposite wall was a heating duct covered with chicken wire, but it blew an icy breeze. His feet were still freezing.

He walked. Five short steps, he turned, then four. He remembered the night he arrived in Moscow, how they had passed this place in the taxi, a huge mustard building with a thousand cells inside. He remembered feeling young then, light and expectant. Fin had told him it's good to seem naïve, *spike your hair and be yourself.* He lifted his numb feet and gleaned the difference—Fin only *appeared* naïve. A shriek from somewhere, a muffled sound like a belt buckle in a washing machine; Darcy conjured a con-sular official—a broad Australian face with a grim, hesitant smile—coming to collect him and feed him cheese and Vegemite sandwiches, a plane lifting off to that faraway, flyblown place where he'd never belonged but now yearned for. He felt a howling inside him. The raspy telephone voice of his mother: *What are you into now?*

He veiled his nose with the blanket to reduce the stench, kept walking in a kind of stupor. The welt of the general's hand buzzed on his face and rang hollow in his ear, electricity came in surges, the bulb bright then strug-gling, the peephole still a grey flap of iron. He imagined Fin in a plane on a runway, some passport in her lap. At Monash, she'd always pretended everything was wry and amusing, how they'd taken the piss out of anyone studious, *regu-lar*, as they called the diligent dags from the private schools, the Asians kids haunting the library, buried among the metal reference shelves. Children who'd been raised to heed warnings, who hadn't been quite so free-range, or adulterated.

Darcy slumped on the bed and closed his eyes tight to fake a prayer but he wasn't sure what to ask, or how, his arms just hung like fallen branches in his lap. At a shift of the locks, the door lurched open and Aurelio stood in a drab felt suit, grey and unfashionable, a ladder-backed chair in his hand. Unshaven, his caramel hair slicked back, greasy. Darcy just stared, a sense of himself peering out bruised from the blanket like a junkie or a mendicant, a pulse in his palms, as if his heart had moved there for shelter. Aurelio moved into the room, his hazel eyes blood-shot and his cheeks slightly sunken. What happened to you? asked Darcy.

Aurelio sat in the chair and glanced back at the door, then reached to touch the welt on Darcy's face. My father is cruel, he said, tears glittering in his eyes, but Darcy was dry-eyed, the sight of Aurelio like this, his brow damp with sweat and the yeasty smell of beer on his breath, clasping Darcy's hands with clammy palms, not smooth and dry like they had been. Aurelio touched the cut on Darcy's lip, almost childlike; he leaned forward wanting to kiss.

Not in here, said Darcy.

Aurelio sat back in the chair and clutched his elbows. Aurelio, who'd always seemed to make his own arrangements, the golden boy of Moscow, his eyebrows now made him look sad. He'd lost the look of privilege, swanning around the park, the costumes in the dress shop, his complexion sallow now.

Aurelio, said Darcy, I need you to get me out of here.

My father knows about us, Aurelio said. And now Chuprakov is dead.

I know, said Darcy, but I need your help.

Aurelio arched his brows and delivered a loose sympathetic smile. Darcy felt an old allergy to drunkenness, watching his mother on the couch, knowing there wouldn't be dinner. He pressed his hand to the welt on his cheek.

My mother met Castro, said Aurelio, but he is not my father. He reached into his jacket and produced a shiny black wallet, a photo. This is her, he said. A small colour shot of himself as a child, beside a woman. Darcy rested his eyes on it in the palm of Aurelio's broad hand, his mother young and dark, lean, in a tropical dress, a magenta ribbon in her hair. She stood on wooden stairs. Aurelio beside her, a boy in a khaki suit and sandals, the same large eyes and luxuriant brows. I want you to have it, said Aurelio.

Darcy had a flash of Fin in her African print dress, unwanted in the driveway, under the flowering gum. I need your help, not your photos, he said.

I want you to remember me, said Aurelio.

Darcy rubbed his hands through his own matted hair—this was all Aurelio had for him. He took the photo and held it in a hand so pale it looked dead. His feet so cold, his boots as if lined with shards of frozen glass. Thank you, Aurelio, he said, but I need to get home. He stood up and walked again as if warmth lay in movement, afraid if his toes went numb he might never feel them again.

I am wanting to help, said Aurelio, but you must understand me. He swigged from a miniature vodka bottle, swallowing all that was left. I am in *druzhinniki*, he said. I working for my father, proving him I am not a homosex.

I—am—in—prison, said Darcy.

I see this, said Aurelio. But the maid at the dacha, she is my friend but my father pays her for confirm. And now he knows what we do. And then Comrade Chuprakov. That was my project.

Darcy sagged back on the cot, covered his face with his hands. All he remembered was the wild gaga girl with the spoon, Aurelio's warm body in that upstairs shower; he'd seen no maid. He thought of the son-in-law splayed in the dark, his chest like a sump.

The general left Cuba when I was three, said Aurelio.

Darcy turned to him. Why are you telling me this?

Aurelio held the small bottle half under his coat as if it were a secret. So you will remember me, he said. I was young in the Ballet Nacional de Cuba. He announced it as fact, devoid of ego, extended a long left arm, allowed his fingers to hang in the air, the movement both weary and graceful. I was an artist too, he said, like you, but of dance.

Darcy felt as though bricks were being piled on his chest. He knew it was a special thing, for Aurelio to say it, but Darcy smelled the stench from the corner, felt the raw ache in his feet. He thought of the girl in the Hotel Ukraine and how he'd wanted to trust her, her disconsolate eyes when he asked for the dog. What this place did to people.

Aurelio gazed at the floor as if it held some marvellous pattern. I come into Moscow at fifteen, he said. To Bolshoi. We rehearse *Spartacus*. Composer was Khatachurian, and director Preben Montell.

Darcy shook his head, names he'd never heard of. He picked up the photo from the folds of the blanket, imagined Aurelio as a dark-haired boy at the ballet barre in Havana. Your father said the Turkish Consul-General wants to talk to me.

My father is saying what he wants.

But what do you know? asked Darcy. Tell me what you know.

Aurelio searched up at the ceiling now. They are wanting your sister, he said, and her friend Jobik. They allegate he is murderer of Turkish Consul-General in a city you coming from. Aurelio took out another tiny bottle and upended it, let drops fall onto his extended tongue. They say your Fin was the driver.

A new seam of fear travelled up Darcy's spine. He cast his eyes low, to his Blundstone prints in the urine-stained floor. He never saw Jobik in Melbourne during that time, but he could just imagine Fin on Queens Road in St Kilda, behind the wheel of the rusted Corvair, Darcy's car, his mother's. He clutched his hands as if to hold himself still. The hollow sound in his ear, like a train coming in to a station.

She's a dangerous girl, said Aurelio.

She's my sister, said Darcy. He shut his eyes, wishing he didn't believe what he'd heard but he could picture it too clearly. Fin waiting out by the tramline, the borrowed Corvair in the shade of the elms while Jobik slipped up some steps to one of those Georgian houses, the Consul-General bidding goodnight to his driver, or greeting his wife at the door. Darcy remembered the photos, slain Turks on the front page of the *Age*.

Aurelio shook the bottle as if to prove it was empty. Jobik, he is having a history of blowing things up, he said. Turkish things. He is working for organisations. He spoke vaguely, as if this was irrelevant now. Armenian organisations. He stood to leave but Darcy reached for his arm.

Listen to me, he said. I am a foreigner. I cannot be held here without my country knowing. You must tell the Australian Embassy.

Aurelio reached down tenderly, touched Darcy's swollen cheek. This isn't England, he said. One time there was Jamie Brodkin, coming to start a homosex movement. Posters in the streets. He wanted to make a parade. Aurelio turned to the slot in the door. They told his family, but when his family come to take him home, his body had disappeared.

Darcy shut his eyes and all he saw was his mother, her first morning drink in hand, staring at her bedside table, strange foreign names scratched on torn paper, wondering if she'd written them down in a dream.

Darcy curled up in the damp, fetid blanket, too tired to sleep, his mind spinning out like a wheel. The hanging bulb went out as a knocking began from beneath the bed, four beats then three, then a flurry. The grate in the door opening, the guard's eyes looking in. Darcy turned to the bricks, to the wet day at Monash when Fin stole his car keys and then disappeared, even though she hated to drive in the rain. Images of her and Jobik on a blustery Melbourne afternoon, the Corvair parked in a dark garage near Albert Park, the two of them breathless and silent, waiting for the sirens to pass, or fucking on the strength of it, the sound of the explosion still resounding in their ears. The kind of killings Darcy'd heard of on the news, as if they'd happened far away, like history from school, Johnny Turk mowing down ANZACs by the thousand on the cliffs of Gallipoli, everyone's great-uncles. Darcy had a vague memory of the Armenian massacres, same country, same year, 1915. But Fin had never mentioned them.

The bulb came back on. A creak at the door and the wrenching of locks. A *baba* shuffled into the angle of light. Darcy squinted at her; the same old woman from the interview room, in her pale blue coat with her bucket, her unfeeling eyes. She placed the bucket on the chair with a sliver of white soap and the ripped end of a towel.

The bucket like an altar and the cement like ice beneath his knees, Darcy dabbed his bruised cheek with tepid water, pushed his wet hair back over his scalp, his head still unshaven, no grey prison pyjamas. He thought again of his mother. Would it be Sunday there or still Saturday? Who would she tell?

The *baba* placed a beaker of watery porridge and a metal cup of tea on the floor then left. Darcy wolfed the porridge and tea without tasting, then promptly threw half of it up on the cement, a whirring in his head. There was a guard observing through the half-open door, a narrow gaze, a head too small for the brim of his cap, a sparrow's mouth. A handgun in its holster and a truncheon he knocked against the door. If it was morning already, Darcy knew he'd lost all track of time. He wiped his lips, unsure he'd be able to stand.

The guard viewed Darcy with a blankness he found unnerving as they waited behind tall iron gates. Under a yellow light a distant prisoner was pushed into an empty cell and as the light went off, Darcy realised it meant they could pass. No display of the cadaverous boy they'd shown him in the hall, no tattooed *opuscheny* this time. They entered an open elevator cage that ratcheted up. The muted stench of the drains. Darcy stared down at the guard's black boots and focused on breathing, keeping the vestiges of oatmeal down. He scuffed along a corridor, a guard now in front and one behind, and thought of Aurelio's last words. Your face it is sore but it is nothing. Maybe my father likes you.

In the interview room, the general was already seated, his silver lunch box beside him, an astrakhan coat draped over the back of his chair, a picture of Lenin now hung directly behind him. The general stared up at Darcy from the folder of photos, but didn't say anything, softly tapped his glasses on the table and nodded for Darcy to sit in the same wooden chair as before. Just a creepy, knowing smile. Darcy looked over to where the dog had been. The cage was gone.

The general rose slightly but didn't get up as a man in a pair of rimless specs appeared, a brown felt fez with a small tassel. He had a pursed mouth and crow-black eyes, and a cold sweat rose on Darcy's back as the man removed his fez and placed it fussily on the table, smoothed his neatly parted toupee. He acknowledged the general but didn't shake his hand as he sat beside him, assessed Darcy. I am with Turkish intelligence, he said.

Say *Dobry den* to Consul Tugrul, said the general.

Darcy felt like a sheep emerged from a river. He avoided the perfect hairline, the moustache trimmed close along the thin upper lip. He looked instead at Lenin.

This is for you, said the Turk. He placed a photo of his own on the table, and Darcy noticed the clear-polished nails. A colour shot of Jobik in a baseball cap, leaning on a chain-link fence, a bombed-out building behind him. Jobik was younger, posing cockily in a tight-fitting T-shirt as though the bomb might have been one of his own. The fluorescent light buzzed in a way that had Darcy struggling to concentrate.

You must know something of this man, said the Turk, inquisitive, patient, his English almost perfect. If you can help us, maybe General Sarfin can help you. We extend you a leaf.

Darcy looked up at the general, who seemed slightly bemused, as if aware Darcy had nothing to offer the Turk, but Darcy tried to put himself back in the kitchen on Baden Powell Drive, his father telling him that Fin had disappeared to Queensland, but he couldn't yet conjure the last name. He swallowed. When I was a boy in Australia, he said to the Turk, he went by the name of Jostler. I knew who he was but I didn't really know him. Darcy looked up again at Lenin and it appeared like a gift in three syllables. His surname was Garabed, he said, back then.

Yes, said the Turk, nodding. Arman Garabed. He's the leader of the military wing of the Dashnak party. He spoke slowly, as if trying to sense what else Darcy had for him. He reached across the table, curled a long narrow hand about Darcy's forearm, and squeezed the muscle tightly. What else? he asked. He let Darcy go.

The light from the bulb seemed to increase as though monitored from elsewhere. Darcy looked down at the whorls in the wooden tabletop. He remembered Jobik in jeans against his burgundy Monaro, on the beach at Flinders, how he almost drowned. He said nothing.

The Turk produced a sheet of paper and read from a list. Sarik Ariyak, he said, Turkish Consul-General, Melbourne. August 1983. Again he watched for Darcy's response.

Blinking, Darcy pretended not to understand; the sound of the sea returned in his ear, the light now brilliant as halogen. He shielded his eyes as the general pushed another photo across the table—Fin smoking a *papirosa* on the steps of a theatre that wasn't the Bolshoi. Wearing her red twenties dress, the print with black fireflies on it, under a green coat. The Turk ordered Darcy to stop his nervous humming, his tone increasingly hostile. He now stood over the table, over Darcy and this new photo. He lit a dark unfiltered cigarette. Then what do you know about her? he asked.

She brought me here to paint, he said.

The general grunted, examining a separate photo.

A picture for an exhibition, said Darcy. I painted it for her.

We know she is not much of an artist, said the Turk. He balanced his cigarette on his lower lip and turned the matches in his fingers. A turbaned horseman adorned the matchbox cover. How long do you know her?

Darcy looked at the general again, a curve at the corners of the general's mouth. She'd only changed her last name three years before, but maybe the Turk didn't know. I met her at university, said Darcy. He counted it as truth— they'd met up in the Ming Wing, Fin by his side like an apparition.

The Turk put his cigarette down on the edge of the table and reached into his leather folder for a piece of paper. Monash University, he said. Clayton, Victoria. A hotbed, no? He put the paper down. Before that she was at Berkeley, California. He paused. Were you religious? he asked.

He saw Darcy's puzzlement.

The Dashnaks are Orthodox Christians, he said.

Darcy shook his head cautiously. I was a Marxist, he said. But I'm not sure now.

The Turk fished for another document, showed Darcy a sheet of red paper. Sixty-one killed since 1973. He pointed at the page. Attachés, consuls, ambassadors, wives. Vienna, Vatican City, Ottawa, Paris, Los Angeles. He reattached his cigarette to his lips, took another pull. Funded by Armenians from west of the Bosporus. From United

States, Australia, you can name it.

Darcy couldn't remember if the Bosporus was a river or a mountain range but the Turk was treating him like he knew these things. How many did Jobik kill? asked Darcy.

The Turk looked slightly deflated. That's what we want to know, he said. He flicked ash on the floor. In 1979 the Archbishop of the Armenian Church in New York was shot dead. He searched Darcy for a hint of recognition.

I thought you said the Dashnaks were Christians, said Darcy.

The skin around the Turk's wrinkled mouth tightened, the smell of his cigarette was strong. The Archbishop supported Soviet Armenia, he said. He reached for the general's silver lunch box, turned it to face Darcy.

Darcy sat perfectly still. You can't suspect me of being with a party I've never heard of, he said softly.

The general smiled lazily, folded his arms, as the Turk removed a zippered plastic evidence bag from the lunch box. What about this? he asked.

A panic ran up inside Darcy like he'd never felt, his throat closing. The money belt held up like a ragged leather pendant, the back of it hacked open. A sleeve in it after all. The Turk's weathered finger like a small gnarled branch, poked at it through the plastic. What was inside dis? he asked, his accent suddenly thick.

Darcy struggled for air. Airline tickets, he murmured. Some money. My passport. The leaf they'd extended sailing down into a well. It was a present, said Darcy. Delivered to my flat in a padded yellow envelope.

Do not pretend you know nothing, said the Turk. You are not so stupid. He dropped the evidence bag back in the tin and his chair scraped on the floor. As he walked around the table and stood close, Darcy felt himself cringe. I was stupid, he said, but the Turk leaned down and twisted his ear, the foul cigarette right next to Darcy's hair.

There is no immunity in ignorance, the Turk whispered. Your friends are killing my people.

Darcy let out a stifled cry as the Turk reefed his ear and looked in his eyes, his pupils narrow and black. Sarik Aryak was *my* friend, he said.

Darcy looked up at him beseechingly—No, I don't know—but the Turk jabbed his neck with the lit cigarette and sizzled it deep and Darcy remembered the name of the restaurant as his mouth yawed open with an otherly howl and he flung himself down to the cement, writhing in agony. The Jaguaroff, he tried to say but the word was sewn into his screaming.

Darcy lay restless, his eyes clenched, his breathing erratic, the cigarette burn throbbing. He'd slept for a spell and dreamed of his mother in the dark, her scrabbling around for a pen and then scrawling names in red all over her bedroom walls—Russian names like *Davydov*, *Katkov*, *Kosygin*, *Bogdanova*, *Chekhov*, all of them wrong. At a creaking he woke in fright, disoriented. Through the thin weave of blanket, a broad shape at the end of the flimsy prison bed, seated quietly with his black-framed glasses on, the general looming silently, as a parent might watch a child.

Darcy lowered the blanket, edged up, a tremor that began in his chest, juddered out into his arms. The general in a black dinner suit, his bow tie hanging loose down his shirtfront. He raised an imaginary glass in a cupped hand, as if toasting. Anyetta Chernenko says many thank-yous for being shepherd of her dog, he said.

Darcy smelled anise liqueur on the general's breath as the general pulled up his dinner jacket sleeve, smiled ruefully at Darcy's Longines watch, its silver band stretched about his massive wrist. Visiting hours, he said, showing his yellowed teeth.

Darcy half sat up on the slatted wooden bed, his aching back against the cold brick wall. He clasped his knees up under the raggedy end of the blanket, then noticed Aurelio's coat draped on the chair back, the roll of currency on the seat. How do you say in English? said the general. Your *things*.

Darcy found himself rocking slightly, suspiciously, the chance of being released, the general placing a thick pale hand on Darcy's covered foot as if to still him. First we have some business, he said.

A siren wailed somewhere and Darcy hugged the blanket tight, up over the sore on his neck, in a kind of hopeless defence, but the general reached forward, carefully pulled it down to inspect the wound. Ah, yes, he said. Consul Tugrul is quite cruel.

Darcy nodded in nervous agreement but recoiled even further; he'd known the feel of the general's great open palm in the same interview room, slapping him almost through the air, but it was coupled now with a memory, the missionary looming over a small boy's body. He clutched the stringy blanket like a rope out at sea as the general reached to touch his cold unsteady fingers, as though fascinated by fear, his hand almost twice the size of Darcy's.

You are shaking, said the general.

Darcy looked up at the general's moist, late-night smile, tried to slide his fingers from the touch, but then he felt the blanket tethered tight over his knees, stretched like a threadbare tent. Death felt like a not-so-timid visitor, waiting outside in the snow. He felt the quiver deep within him, to be left bloody on this greasy floor, ruptured.

I did not come to hurt you, said the general. I need you. His great square knees shifted over, corralling Darcy's huddled feet.

My mother is contacting the Australian Embassy, said Darcy, his voice just a shadow.

I thought you were Polish, said the general with a lascivious smile. He extracted the burgundy passport from his jacket pocket, and shoved the photo of a black and white Fin up against Darcy's blistered lips. Kiss her, he said. Kiss your naughty sister.

Darcy drew back from the tasteless laminated page against his mouth, blood from the cut on his lip as it smeared Fin's small, determined face. *Fin, what have you done to us?*

You agree she is with Armenian Dashnaks, the general said. He removed his glasses thoughtfully, put one arm of the frames in his mouth. I am supposing she gave a place to find her? He seemed to choose his English words carefully, as if he had only a few, his tongue remaining on his lower lip. His hand gripped Darcy's ankles like they were sparrows in a vice.

Darcy's own lip throbbed; he squirmed to free his ankles, the whirr in his ears began like the dull sound of propellers approaching. He knew this was his window, the restaurant—*if things go bad*, the Jaguaroff sat like a jewel in his sore dry mouth. Maybe I can find her, he said.

Where? Where are they? The general's whisper so vehement, the blood vessels pushed at his skin, his scalp darkened red. Garabed's men. Tell me where or I will fuck it out from you. Is that what you want? Darcy's ankles felt close to snapping as he fought the general flipping him over, writhed against the weight and screaming, the blanket deftly stuffed in his mouth like a choking sock and held there, the general's fingers cupping Darcy's chin from behind like a claw, the breadth of his wrist across Darcy's eye, the sharp metal catch of the watchband. Darcy contorting, trying to breathe as his belted pants were forced to his thighs and the sound of the general unharnessing, climbing up over him, on top of him, the weight of a piano as Darcy now shoved against the putrid blanket, heaving for air, shunted over the cot on an angle and pinned there, the general whispering like a madman in Darcy's ear. Do you scream when you are doing fuck with my son? In my dacha. The general the size of a fist shunting near the base of Darcy's spine, forced lower as Darcy's eyes crunched deep in their sockets, the suffocating bulk on top of him, his bloodied lips contorting against the fleshy hand, the general prying apart Darcy's narrowed buttocks. Darcy's chin twisted against the bricks, the wrong red names that ran the length of his mother's bedroom wall, and the fervent spittled anise whispers in his upturned ear. You like fuck with men. You think you like that? I show you fuck with men. Thrusting but not finding, like a blunt axe determined to split a narrow log. Then Darcy heard urgent whispers through the slot in the door, footsteps and clanking in the corridor. The general withdrew from him, the weight of a hand in the small of Darcy's back, and Darcy pulled the blanket over himself, heaving for air, and lay like a rag, his face against the wall.

The general, panicking, tucked in his studded shirt-front and fumbled for his glasses, his fallen bow tie. He towered over Darcy like a fuming building, wrenched Darcy around so he could see. Next time I clean you up pretty and rip you out a new hole like a real Polish boy. Sweat fogged up the general's glasses, the savage way he turned his mouth. Where is she?

Darcy lay very still, the tremor rippling all through his body, but all sound suddenly gone from his head. He knew he had been lucky this time, the unexpected voices in the hall.

She told me she'd meet me at Andropov's funeral, he said, in the square, and if not near the Ploshchad Revolyutsii for the opening of the exhibition. It sounded like the truth.

The general's face untwisted slightly but a squinting doubt lingered. There will be many at the funeral, he said.

Darcy braced himself against the cot. She said she would find me.

The general leaned down and pulled at Darcy's greasy hair and Darcy closed his eyes again, flinching. We will be watching you like a glove. Set foot near any embassy, talk with any person and I finish you next time, I split you in pieces. The general took a long last look into Darcy's eyes and then prepared to leave. Rearranging himself, he lumbered towards the voices outside the door. Fin's suede mittens, small as a pair of bats, floated from the pocket of his trousers to the floor.

Lubyanka Square, Sunday, 10.30 am

Darcy stood under a high white sky in a wind that chased snow across the square and stung the wound on his neck through his scarf and coat collar. He felt like a hunted species, let go briefly for his tormentors to observe him, in case his kin might emerge from the tundra and lick at his wounds. He never imagined he'd be homesick. His breath and the sky and buildings—everything smoky and white as frozen milk. His sight blurred, searching for the oxidised Lada, but what could he say to Aurelio now? The rabid anise-breathed whispers of the general still fresh, the cavernous sound that now lodged there, a violence behind him like a twisted slingshot, shoving him out into this gelid square as if Fin might dart out from among these sallow figures in black fur hats and usher him off to her coven.

The aches in him deep, his bones as if splintery, he ventured towards the metro entrance, to a single snow-swept food stand, the frosted street lamps like arrows planted in ice. A woman with plastic shopping bags, her face enveloped in a woollen balaclava, the two brown-hatted men in an angle-parked Volga, a sense they all watched. No choice other than to proceed as he'd said he would to the multitude amassing in Red Square. He bought three steaming *piroshki* from the street vendor who winced at the sight of his cheekbone, bruised black and red as a tsarist flag, but she said nothing, just handed him the first one, steaming lamb and onion buried in pastry. *Gde Jaguaroff?* he wanted to ask, but didn't speak either, didn't chance it, the mustard-coloured building still glowering behind him like a monstrous warning. He stuffed another in his mouth, let the mealy cheese and cabbage heat burn deep inside him, then he kneeled and dipped the napkin to moisten it in the snow. He wiped his face as best he could, dabbed at his cheek and pressed the dampened paper against his neck. He knew he had to keep moving, on among the Muscovites, the other *piroshkis* pushed deep in his pockets for warmth, his scarf up over his mouth to keep his lips from the fresh pellets of snow. He knew if he didn't lead them to Fin there'd be no limping out here into this winter a second time; he'd be splayed in his own pooling blood or shipped east over the Urals on a train, the prettiest face in some gulag.

Aurelio, he whispered, glad his lips could still shape the word, but the name was drowned by a crackle from tinny loudspeakers hooked on trees, dirge music piping out into the morning as if it were Darcy's own death being mourned a day prematurely. The venom from the general's lips, the repulsive jolting, had Darcy starey-eyed out here in the wind, far from weeping, the fact of it grasping hold.

He merged with a huddle fanning from the window of a Beriozka, where the proceedings in the square were being televised. On the screen, a tribune beneath the clock on Spasskaya Tower with a rose-wreathed casket, then a podium with dignitaries dribbling into their seats, waiting. Armoured vehicles motored past, columns marching with guns in the air past the striped onion domes of St Basil's. Raincoats and umbrellas covered the square like a field of wet flowers. Alas, poor Yuri, thought Darcy. Vodka so cheap they cleaned their windows with it, called it Andropodka. Alas, poor everyone, he thought.

If he steered them to Fin, he knew he'd not garnered himself any guarantees, just two venues and a couple of hours, a chance in hell. The KGB like a giant bear, pawing at him, no doubt suspecting he'd strung them along. His breath felt shallow, barely reaching his chest in the gathering crowd drawn down the avenue to assure themselves Andropov was gone. Craggy plaster faces strung on a line between the spindly birches and, beneath them, a mask seller who wore a plaster Brezhnev, secured by elastic. He wagged his finger at Darcy, making a speech, and a few people laughed brittle laughs.

Darcy saw a young girl who cradled a big cream handbag leaning against her mother for warmth, and he yearned for her innocence. This quaint-faced girl examining those wooden dolls within dolls, Lenin inside Stalin, Khrushchev inside Brezhnev, men inside men, but there wasn't an Andropov yet. She stared over at Darcy then moved in closer to her mother, spooked. He ate his second *piroshki* too fast, felt like he was gagging, the timid retreat of the child had him off-kilter, as if seeing himself from the outside. With a false possibility but not a real plan, just the sense enough would never be sufficient—it wasn't just Fin they wanted, it was Jobik and his associates, and the general's own desire to slam Darcy's face into a smeared concrete corner. The same general at St Anne's that first day, the Cuban bride whose smile lit up the sanctuary. *She says he's like an animal*, Aurelio whispered, as if it were a good thing, but where was the new bride last night, her general on the end of Darcy's prison bed? An animal, yes, but what sort exactly? How much did Aurelio know?

Darcy tried to stop his mind, thoughts like the sails of spinning windmills. He looked up from the footprints before him to the distant Tomb of the Unknown Soldier, plastic roses in the snow beneath the eternal flame and a boy on the kerb in uniform chatting up a girl in a leather coat that had *I Shot JR* painted on the back. A Fin kind of girl, a photo if Darcy had still had his Pentax, but it was too late to capture the ironies now. He'd missed the Moscow he could have visited, the one he'd hoped for, the majesty of her winter, but the sight of the couple reminded Darcy it had existed all along, the distant swirl of confetti eddying about newlyweds in fur capes near the tomb, celebrating on a Soviet day of mourning. The sights invoked in him a strange invigoration as he rounded the corner into the square, to the pageant of Andropov's funeral unfurling in real life, a quilt of wet umbrellas extending towards the domes of St Basil's. The din of the dirge now eclipsed by a battalion of soldiers doing that straight-leg step across the frosted cobblestones; it gave Darcy that shivery feeling like Germany, the trammelling force of them, a thousand uniforms, generals. He waded into the depths of the crowd, weaving sideways but quietly forward, as if searching for Fin. The idea of disappearing seemed rash but suddenly possible—return to the apartment, the list of restaurants in Fodor's. Find the Jaguaroff, get there alone. He knitted himself among dripping umbrellas, furs and stolid faces, his heart thumping up into his clamouring head. He hunkered, stock-still amid the rugged-up multitude, breathless, his eyes anchored on the distant platform, the casket wrapped in a rose-covered Soviet flag and, behind it, the rows of dignitaries.

Darcy pretended he was Russian, one of the pairs of myriad eyes that preyed on a distant Gorbachev, a tailored jacket in the front row, the purple stain on the brow just visible. He didn't chance to check if someone pushed through behind him into the now-restless concourse. The speech at the funeral would be delivered by the new General-Secretary, the replacement, that's what Aurelio had said. Gorbachev was the only man in the front row who looked under seventy-five, the Soviet saviour, but Darcy feared the general worked for him. He closed his eyes in a spell of giddiness, a sense of desolation, as if he could already feel a hand on his shoulder, a gun to his ribs. He focused on Gorbachev, Raisa beside him—he'd seen their photo in *Pravda*—then he made out Margaret Thatcher, her rooster's face and hair in some elaborate rain scarf. He found himself yearning for the sight of his own hawk-faced prime minister, a rugged Australian frown, but Darcy's doubting mind was riling up: *why would they have let me plunge so deep into this crowd?* Imagining the toxic feel of cloth over his nostrils, being hauled away from that wrong hotel, he gazed at a new row of artillery rattling over the cobbles, the chance of dissolving into this maze as the columns of soldiers turned like clockwork to salute the canopy of roses. A collective murmur as an old man struggled to the podium.

Merde alors! said someone nearby.

Darcy turned, the chance of a French reporter or exile, but a well-groomed woman met his glance. Svetlana, without make-up, in a fur scarf and cape, only three umbrellas away, her bitten hand cradled up into her coat and a glare that was chilling, the faintest shake of her head, a warning. Darcy's own gaze dragged down to the icy cobblestones, slick underfoot, glinting as if they were precious. They were all over him. A piercing ache struck up in his glands, the giddiness again, but he focused on the pretence of Fin's arrangement—he'd proceed to the exhibition, his painting up on a Soviet wall. He thought of Laika's cocked head, a dog in a rocket hurtled through space, how they probably knew her capsule would explode, they knew before they sent her.

Darcy looked over again but Svetlana was gone, just a voice that wheezed and echoed through loudspeakers, a face projected now on a huge gritty screen on the Kremlin wall, eyebrows combed up like seagulls' wings, like Brezhnev's. It was Chernenko, a glazed look in his eyes, puffy cheeks and rounded chin, white hair pasted back from his forehead. Medals and stars pinned on his jacket and a sudden grim silence crept through the mourners, their chance of change like grit in frozen teeth.

Darcy stared paralysed, imagined the son-in-law sitting up for Sunday dinner in the company of this old asthmatic, pretending. The son-in-law who'd whispered smoke on Darcy's toes, tried to warm them. As if some ill-omened blackmail could undermine this, accelerate history. The general, even if he worked for Gorbachev, seemed far more odious than the poor old salt from this man's lips. The dull acceptance of the great harvest of people had Darcy wishing for this as their moment of revolt, a rush for the barricades, comrades mown down by the thousands. But no shout came from Darcy's mouth, nor anyone else's—they all knew it would be answered by the *thuck* of a silenced bullet. Margaret Thatcher wouldn't even know their name. Darcy knew he'd be forced to pray for his own moment at the exhibition, in a crowd where he might be heard. There would be foreigners, artists, sympathisers.

A half-hearted clap rumbled through the gloom like the muffled sound of a thousand books being shut, applause at a funeral. Chernenko's speech finished as abruptly as it had started, the last gasps of the union petering to a halt, he'd run out of gas. Euphonious music now blared from the speakers, as if a new era had just been ushered in. Darcy hunted among the iced-over faces for the man who'd cursed in French, the vague hope of Aurelio, or even Fin and Jobik in some disguise, but those about him were dispersing already. Darcy just stood, his feet painful again, gazed up at the misted screen. Gorbachev reaching quietly for Raisa's hand, leaning forward to congratulate the frail Chernenko. Darcy wondered which of them really knew the general. Then he noticed Chernenko's daughter behind her father, not hugging him or shaking his hand, just there. Tall, in the same full-length fur, her face strained as if in a trance. The only one really mourning. Darcy felt a kinship with her, the way he did with the sadness of women, as if she were Garbo in *Camille*.

The sound of snow-sweepers returning to work, like gigantic beetles belching fumes, the bearded city kneeling by the solid river, the burnished cupolas of the beautiful church muted in the failing light. Darcy felt his pyrrhic promise of Fin unravelling quietly ahead of him, like the early aubergine darkness climbing down over the square, a sense that all had been building up around what wasn't here, gravity pulling things inward. Darcy hugged himself, nowhere to go but on to the Ploshchad Revolyutsii. He almost understood these people as they headed home to demonstrate behind closed doors. A snow shovel leaned against a barricade and he wanted to wield it like some crazy Bedlamite, slam it down against the stones and let it clang, let them come for me, let them come. But he knew instead he should be listening to his instincts, in case he was given his moment, or it was given to Fin or Aurelio to magically steal him away.

Still, he moved across the well-worn stones amongst these dry-eyed people as if being herded towards a corner. The distant funeral platform was emptying, none of the brass had been targeted by Jobik, in the name of Jesus or genocide, the Turkish Consul-General no doubt skulking in the back, preening.

Andropov's coffin remained like an afterthought, upstaged, the military battalions marching away like mechanical ants towards the river. A snaking line to Lenin's Tomb was already re-forming, comrades returning to their roots for solace. The ornate facade of GUM like a stage-curtain backdrop facing off against the Kremlin walls. The distant clock said twelve. It seemed to have stopped. Darcy surged with a last-ditch desire to run, get inside the infinite department store and get lost amongst a new crowd. The best place to lose a tail is GUM, Fin had told him. She said the KGB will run over you in cars if they have to, but they can't do that in a department store; you go up and down the stairs between floors. Darcy understood now why she'd known such things. She'd pointed out wreaths around the busts of heroes in the shadows of the Kremlin battlements and quoted Trotsky and Lenin. *They labour in vain in the vineyards of equality.* But Fin was too cunning to run; she just disappeared.

Darcy felt himself shivering harder now, walking on to a place where Fin wouldn't be. Death might come as some kind of release, he thought, the silenced shot. The last thing he'd see would be pigeons roosting in a bare tree like dull grey ornaments beneath the Hotel Moskva. He stared up at the featureless building, everything at right angles, not quaint or leaning like he'd imagined Europe, but windows from where his bullet might come, singing through the air. The burn on his neck throbbed, the memory of the cigarette shoving him forward, Fin's carrier pigeon, the sight of the ripped-open money belt in that Turk's brown hands, the hundreds of rooms now glaring down; a city surveyed from the safety of windows, naked eyes squinting into their binoculars. His only hope would be darkness.

Darcy ate his third *piroshki*, full now but thirsty. And then a Cyrillic banner came into view, hanging above the portico of the Exhibition Hall. The opening of *We are Building Communism*. The entrance loomed, well-guarded but not crowded, and Darcy wished he were arriving under other circumstances—his first piece in an international exhibition, albeit under Fin's name—but as he walked up the stone stairs, ashamed of the general's welt on his cheek, it felt as if he were being shunted by transparent bayonets.

A grey-uniformed woman with a clipboard and a wrinkled bark face talked at him in cacophonous Russian. Darcy Bright, he said huskily. He had no identity card like the locals, no idea what would happen if he didn't get in, but a snub-faced man in a full-length leather coat, holding a walkie-talkie, rested his pale rapier eyes on Darcy, nudged the woman as if it was okay. The woman smacked a silver star onto the lapel of Darcy's coat and the man stamped him with a withering stare. With it came a wave of nausea, as Darcy moved self-consciously into the monstrous anteroom, furnished with a bust of Lenin that rose twelve feet high. A red flag billowed behind him, rippled by a fan. A group of poorly dressed, low-level officials, warmth, but not the artists and diplomats Darcy'd imagined. Still, he found himself quietly whispering the word *help* with each exhaled breath, a prayer or a mantra, in case a sympathetic ear might guess he was Western, in trouble.

He passed Michelangelo's David, a fake that towered in an alcove, and Darcy whispered upwards at the curves of the great white thighs and the small marbled phallus, the white ruff of pubic curls. Nearby a zaftig woman in a large tan smock with black braided hair turned at Darcy's mumble, averted her face and moved on despite the plea in his eyes as they met hers. A man in a loose-fitting pinstriped suit and ponytail swanned between pillars, glanced oddly at Darcy then slipped beneath a rope to join the dignitaries grouped about a rough marble bust of Chernenko. Darcy went over to the rope and saw the prosperous few without the restless many, cordoned off, hobnobbing Soviet-style, right on the heels of the funeral. Waiters in evening attire with silver trays circled the anaemic statue of Chernenko made younger, his cheeks chiselled. Darcy held a sleeve up near his face and loitered near the archway, scanning for his painting, or the unlikely advent of Fin. He had a sense he was just being played with, tested. Darcy both hoped Fin would emerge somehow and prayed she'd know it was too dangerous.

She might once have burned manifestos in an incinerator here, in this place where Khrushchev or Brezhnev made a famous attack on abstracts, but where was she now?

In the middle of the other room amidst the privileged,

a monstrous depiction of Brezhnev hung, buffalo eyebrows and bulbous cheeks, in the fashion of a bad Soutine. Then Darcy saw through to a far wall, The Museum of Science and Achievement, small by comparison, the oil and wax shiny under the lights. Laika, half wax, part photo, part gold, perched on the nib of the obelisk rocket. The pin-stripe man was pointing to it, explaining to a group. Perhaps he was the curator, Fin's friend.

Darcy stepped to the entrance of the cordoned-off section as if he too might be ushered through, drink champagne, but the stone-faced guard ignored him. Darcy wanted to tell the curator the wax had been applied with a small travelling iron; a new medium, a new technique. Then he realised Chernenko's daughter stood among the little set of those listening, her hair now uncovered, swooped up in a barrette, not thirty feet away. Had she worn this pale blue evening gown under her coat to Lubyanka, then to the funeral? She didn't seem in mourning now. She turned to reach for a passing flute of champagne and for a second they locked eyes and Darcy thought she might come over, but the general appeared beside her, in the same black suit, and Darcy's hope turned to stone, a rush of sweat forming like a liquid skin.

Darcy sidled away, pretended to look at a plain canvas of a rocket launch, an oil pipeline threading across the Siberian snow. He hated Soviet Realism, its lack of heart or dimension, the sense of his own talent commandeered by Fin. He turned to check who tailed him, noticed Fin's *Achievement in Bronze* on a low pedestal in a shadowy corner. The butcher's grass, the structures and obelisk, the melted foil and bronze leaf, small Soviet flags atop each building, hoisted on gilded toothpicks. A tide of regret rippled through him, his shoulders heaving just slightly, contracting his gut, as if weeping, but he had no tears, just hurting eyes and the fact of her before him, the vague smell of lard. Despite everything, it had been finished somehow, as if he could somehow save her from suspicion.

Darcy sensed his minutes of freedom being sliced down into seconds. Then a shadow clung to the corner of his eye, a slip of a figure in a dark coat receding between pillars; dressed like a babushka but moving too fluidly, her head covered in a lavender scarf. The distinctive briskness to the footfalls as she vanished past a mosaic of St Basil's. Had she meant him to see her or had he conjured her? She'd spotted him and smelled trouble, now she was breaking away—Darcy half running towards the great double doors, out into the darkness, chasing a shadow, expecting a first quick bullet in his back. He heard the guard on his walkie-talkie but leapt ahead down the steps—let them shoot me right here in the square—with the violet scarf fading into the rush hour, down into the shadows of the ramparts. Voices from behind, he bolted through the commuters, pushing past a queue, skidding through slush underfoot, unsure what he wanted, to get away or to go with her, find her, desperate for a flash of that colour, tripping, hands in snow and up again, winded, a siren in his head or on the streets he wasn't sure—then a flash of violet inside a trolleybus, caught like a flame in a street lamp, wires up into the fading light. Darcy slid among those boarding a back door, ignored the honesty box, got a glimpse of the flat-faced agent swimming through the crowd towards him but the doors were shutting, the bell sounded and the bus lurched forward unhindered. The agent's angry puckered face left out in the dark and the colour that had caught Darcy's eye, the lavender scarf, just a blue plastic bag against the bus window. Not Fin, but a sinewy-faced old man leaning his head on it, watching Darcy with a corrugated frown. Maybe he'd led them to her after all; or maybe he'd imagined her. He stood in the aisle, breathless, a pain now deep in his chest like the dull, patchy lights of the stifled city.

Does anyone speak English? he asked. *Po-angliyski?* His voice so dry with panic he repeated himself, but the locals either ignored his plea or observed him blankly in their stale cigarette air, winter storage smells, onion breath, pushing each other as the bus turned a corner. The paralysis of fear and the mind-numbing cold, taking their own troubles home. Darcy ducked down and looked out at what looked like the Maly Theatre; he pulled the cord, forged his way roughly to the door. He jumped out into the dark afternoon, hurtled through the headlights across the sleeted lanes of Prospekt Marksa and stood alone beneath a burgundy awning. A new uneasiness welled in his chest. He didn't believe the general would let him get away.

The snow began again, gentle as feathers, as Darcy mounted the shallow stone steps and kneeled under the portico. If he'd been tailed, no cars turned into the street behind the cab, not a soul, just the night and the sounds of families at home, someone practising violin, a couple yelling at each other, a crow picking dirt where weeds poked through the snow. A figure emerged from the mist across the frozen garden, the sound of snow crunching, a man with a suitcase who entered the front door.

Darcy skiffled around the side and into the courtyard, couldn't see anyone, just a hole dug in the cement, dark as an animal trap; an old pneumatic drill leaned on a shed like a stork. Fin's window above him was dark, the shadow of her pink-checked blanket draped where her hand had been, pressed against the glass. He ducked inside the back stairwell, crept two steps at a time, saw no watcher skulking in the corridor.

His key was still in the pocket of Aurelio's coat, but the apartment was unlocked, the door not quite closed and Darcy felt suddenly afraid to enter, friends of Fin's or friends of the general's. Aware of the tremor in his arms, he edged the door open a hair. Fin's umbrella in the entry hall, her quilted coat gone from its hook, the place still warm. Either Fin had been back and left in a hurry or others had been here, ransacking, books strewn about the

rug, drawers upturned from the kitchen, utensils everywhere, the donkey painting tossed from the easel. Silence
except for the windowpanes rattling, a television downstairs. He threw Aurelio's coat over the heating pipes to
dry, stood before the open fridge, the only light. A stump
of dried-up salami and Solovyov's *Meaning of Love* with a
note paperclipped to it.

> *This wasn't supposed to happen. Forgive me.*
> *The donkey painting for you. May you be the one. Fin xx*
> *P.S. Wretchedness and Inspiration are Inseparable.*

He stared at it, unmoved. The postscript, did she
think that was some parting gift? The sort of thing she'd
paint on a peasant dress, but the dresses were gone and he
wasn't sure if forgiveness was in him. He pulled angry
chunks of salami with his teeth, crouched among books,
squinting at covers in the faded light: *The Soviet Achievement*,
Quotations from Mao Tsetung, *The Brothers Karamazov*, no
Fodor's. He rifled through his duffel bag—clothes and
drawing pads, charcoals, vitamins, a map of Prague.
Without the restaurant he only had his roll of money,
nowhere left to go. He searched busily under the couch,
tried to remember. The list of restaurants, he'd checked it
before he slept, the dog here with him, drinking milk then
ruefully climbing up on the couch beside him. The dog
and now Fodor's gone.

He stared out into the dark afternoon, separated from
everything he knew. Svetlana's apartment closed up with
metal shutters. Down below, an old woman under the
courtyard lamp, the digging beside her almost archaeolog-
ical. Darcy thought how Jobik and his Dashnaks must have
channels, sympathisers, Fin in the back of some Armenian-
owned lorry on the road to Yerevan, to a southern border,

the Caspian Sea. Darcy left here as a sacrifice.

He thought he heard movement in her bedroom, stopped chewing and listened, but all he made out was the sound of his own breathing, then footfalls. Someone in the flat above. He stared up into the shadows where the ceiling fluted, a sense of being toyed with still.

He grabbed Fin's Opinel knife from an upended drawer and quietly closed himself in her windowless room where he could turn on the light. The suet smell, lard containers, foil, art scraps, the ironing table on its side, empty wire hangers in the wardrobe, her clothes all over the floor. He felt light-headed, unclear if she'd been here last, or if the general's men had come through after, if he was being watched from minute cameras. He tested the phone line; dead, as it had been since he'd arrived. Fin's travelling clock said 4.04 pm. Time felt transitory, vanishing about him, as if his life were being stitched shut.

In the bathroom, he looked at his face in the mirror, dabbing his cheek and lip with a damp cloth. The red welt of the general's slap had swollen almost in the shape of fingers; pus scabbed damply on the burn on his neck. As he pressed the cloth against it, it stung as if hot cigarette embers still lay in his skin. He cupped his hands beneath the tap and kept drinking and drinking, the rusty taste like nectar. Then, as he quickly wiped his crotch and underarms, he noticed the book down in the corner by the lavatory, the Fodor's cover with its scattered domes of St Basil's. She'd left it for him, casual as toilet reading.

Frantically, he flipped to the section on the restaurants of Moscow, the bottom of the second page: *The Jaguaroff. Traditional Russian Cuisine. In a lane off Solyanka, on the east side of St Nicholas the Wonder Worker.* He ripped out the page and headed back into the sitting-room, reread her note. *The donkey painting for you. May you be the one.* He grabbed her canvas from where it had been flung against the wall and, in the dim light from the fridge, he lay it on the counter. The two sisters and babies in soft watercolours, the suckling donkey. He remembered Fin's story, the sister syphillitic, how only one child would survive.

Darcy watched out the taxi window, hazy car-lit air, the iced petroleum smell of the night. At a red light, he swung around, gazed into the snow-laden street behind him, the muffled beams of headlights, the poor visibility a good thing, he thought. An old man on a bicycle creeping along the gutter against the traffic, a red star on the sleeve of his coat as he passed, pigeons in a cage on the handlebars. Darcy recalled Jobik squeaking past in the cold, that night outside the jazz concert. The Pimpernel, he thought, or Papillon. Anyone could be anyone.

He glanced back up. Solyanka Ulitsa, he said, a reminder, his tone too anxious, he knew. He explored the clean-shaven back of this taxi driver's head, afraid of being picked up by him especially. Darcy felt Fin's knife in his boot, its fold-out hawk-bill blade; he'd never believed he had the potential for violence but the act of the general upon him had changed something. Could he slit a taxi driver across his Adam's apple, like Jobik could?

Darcy left the painting behind on the counter, sneaked out through the shadows and down the unlit side street, then running for blocks, panting, he found this cab all the way over on Pyatnitskaya Ulitsa. It couldn't have known he was coming. He stared out, thirsty again already. His chest so tight it felt like someone was chiselling at it, wondering if he shouldn't have chosen GUM direct from the funeral, the maze of arcades and cross-walks, up and down stairs and escalators. Darcy knew he mustn't keep searching out the back window, the silent driver's eyes in the rear-view mirror, so he looked back down at the restaurant description in his lap. He'd read it three times already. No mention of Armenians or terrorists, just a throwaway reference to *some fare from southern provinces*. He stared back out into the grizzling night, trying to keep air in his lungs, as the cab crossed the drainage canal. A tug with sidelights searched the banks and bluestone drains, cutting through the shelves of ice. The gates of the old heated pool that Fin said was once the site of St John the Divine *back when God was allowed*.

Darcy had St Nicholas the Wonder Worker circled in biro on his plastic map, described elsewhere in Fodor's as a small red-belfried church. Maybe it would be open, he could hide in there among the pews, pray for his own survival.

Sporadic lights from high metal poles shed their dim bluish sprays on the pavement. He could get out and walk among the glazed-eyed men moving home through the Kitay Gorod with their vinyl briefcases, drift among the heavyset women with their just-in-case bags, see if he was being followed.

Stoitye, he said, thrusting too many notes at the driver, abandoning the taxi mid-block. He walked fast without looking back, paused in a windblown doorway, then walked on again until he noticed the dark portal of a church, sooner than he'd imagined. He couldn't be sure the belfry was red, but a narrow cobbled lane branched off, unmarked, between two plain stone buildings. The church was locked. Darcy knocked timidly on the wood but God wasn't home, not even his servants answered, so he leaned against the door, inhaling through his scarf, his fissured lips, the wind whining under the dark cover of eaves. *You're a beautiful child of God*, said the missionary. Perhaps, thought Darcy, but a child nonetheless. And yet the need in the general's eyes made the missionary seem like a first love, innocent as the Mount Eliza days.

Darcy leaned against the door of St Nicholas, the ache in his chest and arms like a fixture, knowing if he crouched he might sit and if he sat he might never get up. He closed his eyes and waited; the sound of footsteps and tyres compressing the snow, car engines, buses. Darcy appealed to a wonder worker: Keep me. He'd spent his life sneaking around, prayed he'd become good enough at it. If he'd been set loose on purpose, to think he was on his own, he prayed he might be now—he'd been quick across the streets from the apartment, no footsteps behind him, no cars following. He'd always run faster than anyone he knew, even racked with aches and pains. He listened out into the empty shadows; if he had led them to Fin, she'd left him no choice. He walked resolutely to the alley as if it held some final promise.

The lane was dark and wet and quiet, splitting around an angled wooden building a hundred yards up. He moved along a solid wall until he saw the sign in a draped plate-glass window and old-fashioned door. НЕТ ВХОН. He knew that meant 'closed' but knocked anyway. Through the curtains he thought he saw the dull shapes of small tables, some lit with candles, and there were vague kitchen smells, yet no one appeared at the window or door. A restaurant not open to everyone.

Darcy felt weak and fuzzy in the head as he ventured on along the side, skirting past crates and piled cartons, then froze at the sight of a pocked, ferrety teenager out in the cold, clad in a stained apron with a cigarette clasped between thumb and index finger, the way Jobik smoked. He smirked at Darcy knowingly and mumbled something Darcy couldn't understand, then motioned him into a narrow-countered kitchen. The waft of cabbage and warmth felt like bottled rays of possibility.

Inside, pots of broth were set on a stove and a dish-filled sink, sepia pictures of vintage sports cars lined the walls. Jaguars! A cook in a traditional patterned vest looked up then returned to his chopping but, at the beaded archway into the dining-room, Darcy turned back and the cook stared him down, narrow hooded eyes set below an olive headband. *Mozhna?* asked Darcy. May I? He felt like someone walking in from the treeless plains of the north, emerging from moss and lichen after being mauled by bears.

The cook nodded deliberately and Darcy pulled back the beads. A dining-room with burgundy tablecloths lit only by candles in bottles, threads of dried wax draped from their necks. A boy sat alone in a chair in the corner, his old man's eyes watchful and unblinking. Fat paper dolls on the sill. Then a sharp-faced woman in a print folk dress slipped through and showed Darcy to a booth beneath a coat of arms with a double-headed jaguar.

Darcy sat, didn't yet mention Fin's name, unclear if he should. *Tabaka, kartofel, pomidor*, the woman whispered respectfully, without producing a menu. Her eyes held a quiet understanding, her grey hair thickly braided, a minute silver star around her neck and a silk shawl with salmon-coloured flowers. Kvass, she added. These were not questions. Darcy noticed her star pendant had eight points—not a Star of David but a pagan or Balkan star, an Armenian symbol maybe. Did you know I was coming? he asked.

She retreated, nodding reassuringly, but Darcy guessed she hadn't understood. Maybe she was Jobik's mother, Jobik's little brother sitting against the wall, his other brother smoking, keeping watch. Darcy's ear hummed a low refrigerator sound, the jitter still in his hands as he took off his gloves. He left his coat on in case, pulled back a corner of curtain to spy out but the boy made a tsking sound, warning him, then shook his head quickly. *Nyet.*

That boy could be dangerous, thought Darcy. He was tempted to say the name Jobik, to see the boy's reaction, but the woman returned with a jug on a wooden tray, a stern expression as she poured into a water-spotted glass. Kvass; the bread drink. Darcy took a sip and tried not to wince. She offered him a steaming brown cloth and he held it to his cheek and lip and said *Spasiba*. Then the hooded-eyed cook slid a plate before him and nodded: pressed chicken, potatoes and tomatoes, slices of ashy cheese. Darcy knew food served in minutes was a rarity here. He felt himself still as if for the first time in a week. Fin might never come but these people could help him; he pictured himself in a truck heading south to the Caspian Sea.

Darcy was eating, shovelling food but stopped dead when he heard men's voices in a small adjoining room. They entered by some other door and Darcy caught glimpses of them through a slender archway as they stood in dark suits by a mantelpiece, filled and raised vodka tumblers, then laughed as a girl with a balalaika began singing for them. *Kalinka, kalinka, kalinka.* The boy in the

chair watched Darcy as if guarding his corner, folding nap-
kins. A cracked-glass fixture in the ceiling shed light in
sections that divided his face. He smiled at Darcy and
nodded as though the men and the entertainment were
just part of the ruse. Darcy heard murmurs in the kitchen
and then Fin appeared in the doorway like a mirage. She
glanced at the men being serenaded, then at the window,
and Darcy felt his chest constricting as she gestured to him
not to move. Without make-up she looked softer but worn
down, a dullness to her eyes with no mascara, nervous,
pale and beautiful. Her face mostly hidden by a black
beanie, she wore a man's grey argyle sweater. Darcy half
stood but then didn't as she walked over; all he did was
hold onto himself as she perched on the edge of the ban-
quette. He watched her in the flickering candlelight, in a
new light, knowing why she was in this city, why she'd
called him to this winter. He'd been her faithful, gullible
pigeon. Her pigeon and her painter.

Fin acknowledged the boy in the chair, leaning now
on its back legs against the wall. The boy glowered as
though he'd been taught that foreigners were trouble.
Darcy had never seen Fin so drawn, the dye faded from
her eyebrows, the pale translucence of her skin seemed
almost ashen. She took a quick sip of the silty dregs of
Darcy's drink then, registering his bruised face in the
wavering light, she winced.

What did they do to you?

They took me from the Hotel Ukraine, he said. His
voice sounded strange even to himself, without its usual lilt.
He didn't mention the call to his mother. They held me in
Lubyanka, he said. He dabbed a paper napkin in his water
and unveiled the burn, pressed the napkin on his neck.

Who did that? she asked. She leaned in close, not the way his mother would strain to see sores as if there was nothing, but concerned, as if distressed by what she'd wrought.

Darcy examined the round stamp of blood on the napkin. The Turkish Consul-General, he said. He heard her short, almost imperceptible breath and raised his eyes. What colour had been left was blanched from Fin's cheeks, her concern focused suddenly inward. What was his name? she asked.

Consul Tugrul, said Darcy.

A small fridge nearby jump-started and Darcy jolted. A new sound hummed to accompany the one that sang in his head, but Fin didn't react.

What did you tell them? she asked.

It's what they told *me*, said Darcy. He held her gaze with a mix of dashed hopes and welling fury. You brought me into this, he said, knowingly. He reached and grabbed her sleeve and the cook appeared in the kitchen doorway. Fin turned and shook her head at him like she could handle it.

You must be important, said Darcy.

If the KGB is cooperating with Turkey, she said, you can't go with me. There's too much at stake. Where's Aurelio?

He's in trouble, said Darcy. I have to come with you. It's not just that they want Jobik. The general's a madman. In the night he tried to rape me. He said he wanted to *fuck me in pieces*. I saw what happens to the likes of me in the gulag. Darcy gripped her narrow wrist tightly, the other hand pulling her sleeve. I'm not going back there, he said.

No, said Fin. He could see the struggle in her eyes, but

she was shaking her head. I can't take you if Tugrul's with them. The KGB has never cooperated with the Turks.

It's not about that. They'll kill me. Darcy was begging now, talking so fast he could feel himself spit. I wasn't followed here, I promise, Fin, I wasn't. I ran from the apartment through the dark to Pyatnitskaya, there was no car behind me, no footsteps. I caught a taxi at a light, got out halfway down Solyanka, then I walked, backtracked, waited in the dark near the church, no one followed me up the alley.

They're the *KGB*, she said, it's not hide-and-seek...I have to go back—alone.

To Jobik? asked Darcy. He clasped her hands over his plate of food. Fin, look at me, look at my face. I'm your brother. If you don't help me, they'll kill me. You brought me here. He fell silent, his teeth clenched, as the woman with the pendant appeared with Fin's unordered food, a plate of herring and bliny, tomatoes and cheese. The woman retreated and the boy watched on from the corner like he was born reading lips, Darcy continued under his breath. They told me you drove Jobik to the Turkish consulate in Melbourne. Again he imagined the Corvair parked under elms alongside the Botanic Gardens. You borrowed my car. My mother's car.

Fin stared down at her food, poured water from the carafe, then she looked Darcy in the eye for the first time. They killed more than a million, she said. She spoke with a purpose that seemed heightened; it almost didn't sound like her.

That was *1915*, said Darcy.

It has to be recognised.

Darcy knew it wasn't that. He felt something deep

from their past, an anger that shook in his gut and pitted against the sadness in his chest—she'd been intoxicated by Jobik from the beginning, out of her depth in a way Darcy understood. A force of nature that had given her this acute, anxious radiance, the sheen of her great secret, and sex that was probably as violent as the terror she'd seen and concealed in her veins all these years.

He's a killer, said Darcy.

Fin nodded. I love him, she said, unapologetically, as if that would explain it. And in a way it did. She pulled restively at the edge of a bliny, her fingers seemed smaller with no nail polish. Like Merran loved our father, she said.

What? asked Darcy. He hated the way she called her mother Merran, as if she was some friend from high school. He watched Fin pocketing bread from the small wicker basket, thinking.

Did you know that when she slept with him, your mother was in hospital, losing that baby?

Darcy cradled his neck as it throbbed again suddenly. He knew his mother had lost a three-day-old baby, but what did this have to do with anything now? Her name was Tilda, he said, the baby's name was Tilda. That's all his mother had said. Why are you telling me this?

You always want to know the truth, said Fin, so here it is. My mother flew out from Santa Barbara to be there for yours. That's what she meant to do. But she ended up in the Frankston Hospital parking lot in the back of your father's kombi, fucking him. That's how I was conceived.

You call that love? said Darcy. He couldn't believe he knew none of this, and he saw the vengeance in Fin's now verdant eyes as she told it, as if misguided conceptions produced difficult lives, but Darcy just thought of his own mother—the cruelty of it took him slightly sideways. He pushed his fingertips in under his eyes. The burring in his ears and the balalaika woman from the other room, *malinka, malinka moia!* It felt like a kind of madness.

This is what happens in our family, Fin whispered matter-of-factly. You got the Mormon, and it fucked you up. Not the gay thing itself, but the way you do it. I got Jobik when I was only fourteen and then I got pregnant and he took me away. And then he got radical but I was in love. She broke off a piece of wax and played with it in the candle flame, moulded it. Maybe it's a thing that runs in us like a kind of greed, she said. Like a gene. She reached for a chunk of cheese from Darcy's plate. Eat, she said. You look like a heroin addict.

Darcy looked down at a forkful of the floury potato, thought of himself on the verge of having sex with her in the apartment only days ago, a thing that had brewed between them. He looked over at the wan determination in the green of Fin's eyes, her lids red with fatigue. I don't want to be like that, he said.

Like what? she asked bitterly.

Like you, he said.

Fin stood gradually, nodded slightly as if she under-stood. She pressed a telephone number into Darcy's hand, a moment's apology in those blood-grained eyes. Get to Ulli Breffny in the Australian Embassy, she said. She can help you. Darcy registered this as an admission that Fin no longer could, or would.

The cook now stood in the kitchen door, removing his headband as if that meant it was time. I need to get home, said Darcy.

Then do as I tell you, said Fin.

I already did that, he said. He stared at the candle flame, then up at the tiny crystals of ice on a visible edge of the hoar-frosted pane, the scattered scraps of their lives. The annoying sound of the balalaika woman laughing, her friends clinking glasses.

You can dial that number from here, said Fin, they'll get you home.

Darcy envisaged how Fin's life would end almost more clearly than he saw his own. It would be all of a sudden. He watched her slip out through the narrow vestibule of empty fruit cartons and stacked chairs, being judged by the odd-looking boy. A lump left in Darcy's throat, the usual sense of chaos in her wake, he wished he felt relief, or a surge of confidence. He sat there in a funnel of cold air as the cook received a ladder that was being folded down from a manhole, arms extending down from the ceiling and Fin going upwards, following the legs of the cook's checked pants, his big biker boots, climbing up into the roof. Fin's elfin feet seemed almost large in her Doc Martens, quietly ascending the rungs. The sight of her dematerialising brought back in Darcy a sense of loss that felt like childhood, a sadness that eclipsed all his fear. She'd been trained in disappearance.

May you be the one, he said.

He imagined her route across the icy rooftops, a pathway back to the thrall of Jobik.

Darcy stood, looked again at the phone number, the small distorted piece of wax she'd plied. He knew he had to find the phone, but he'd been overtaken by a kind of shock. He needed the lady with the pendant, to ask her, so he could go home, but as he reached for his daypack he caught a glimpse of shadows outside, through the filmy drapes. At first he thought it was Fin and her minder but he realised the balalaika had stopped, the two suited men were slipping away. The boy had vanished.

Darcy dashed to the kitchen but it was empty, just a pig's head hanging on hooks and cabbages, leftovers, the sink full of dishes still. He searched frantically for the phone but couldn't find one, nor a cash register. There was just an unnatural quiet. *Pazhalsta?* he asked. Please? Words met with hollowness, as though he was the only one left in the world. Out the back door there was no sign of the woman, just a grey-white mist, a panic ripping around in Darcy's chest and the soundless night. He took a quick look down the side wall for the ferret-faced boy. He was there, staring up from the snow in his discoloured apron beside the rubbish barrel, dead, a cigarette butt stamped into his forehead like a small wilted horn. A wave of cold came over Darcy, a whisper behind him with a quick icy hand that clenched about his face like a vice on his swollen cheek, tight about his lips. He screamed for Fin into nicotine fingers that twisted his sore lips up and shut, forced him down to a kneel in the slush with an arm pulled up behind him. He writhed against the muzzle of a pistol pressed into the burn on his neck, an agony that blacked him out, suffocating on a hand. On a sister lost. Aurelio.

Beyond Kapotnya, outside Moscow, Sunday, 7.45 pm

Darcy came to in the back of a car that drove slowly without lights, the pain in his head like a throttle and his vision taking on shapes, a driver, bull-necked in front of him, then a sickening feeling—the cigarette eyes that half turned to greet him from the passenger side: the Turk's narrow face and pencil moustache, lit for a second by an oncoming car. A sheet of paper over the seat, being pushed by the Turk at Darcy's face.

Today's London *Times*, he said, but it wasn't a newspaper, a page that wouldn't quite keep still in his freezing fingers, encased in Fin's damp suede mittens, all he had left of her. A pain that stabbed at his temples, a headline legible in a new sweep of approaching carlights. TURKISH ATTACHÉ SHOT IN TBILISI. A photo of a body on steps, a bloodstain on his neck. His name was Isik Yonder, said the Turk. I knew him.

Darcy squinted, trying to understand. *Two unidentified suspects on a motorcycle opened fire yesterday evening outside his official residence.* Darcy felt concussed and suddenly claustrophobic, cracked his window as the city blinked by, rows of apartment buildings lay up against factories, the sting of iced air; he wrapped his coat tightly, conjuring Fin, clasping Jobik on a stolen motorbike, her heels above the splashguard. How far is Tbilisi? he thought or said, he wasn't sure, his words barely there.

Did you know the Turkish Consul-General in Melbourne was my roommate at Oxford? said the Turk. Do you know Oxford?

Darcy shook his head. He felt as if he were drowning, collapsing into the sea. An image blazed in his mind of the rodent boy dead in the snow. The sound of the tyres whispered beneath him, and the Turk snuffed a new cigarette out in the ashtray, pulled a hand-held device from the dash and listened. He cast a sidelong glance at Darcy, but Darcy still didn't answer his question, didn't care about Oxford, if they'd been lovers at college, the consul and the consul. He blinked hard, his vision still hazy, the horror of the pistol mashed into his burn, the whoosh of the pain, and his coat and the knees of his pants wet through. He was already back on the verge of delirium. He didn't know why the Turk hadn't killed him too. If death would be better than this.

The car crept past a dark row of wooden houses, then a small ragged factory. Darcy focused on smoke coiling up from the ashtray, the Turk's cigarettes like weapons. Darcy looked out into the naked woods, the black velvet dark, thought of the son-in-law slumped in the front of the Borgward.

My friend from Oxford, said the Turk. They shot him outside his home. His wife was at the door. His children, in the garden, were playing.

Darcy wanted to cup the pain in his neck in a handful of snow. He couldn't defend any of them, Jobik and his Armenians, Fin, or the slaughters of seventy years before. Where were they taking him? He watched out as best he could: the cranes of the Southern River Terminal rose up through the night like black pterodactyls. Then Darcy turned to see out the back, the burn stinging against his collar. Your friend is with us, said the Turk. Don't worry.

Another car rolled through the dark like a shadow, no headlights either, the broad silhouette of the general. Darcy felt him staring out, right there behind him, where he'd been all along; the memory of the anise smell and animal sweat brought on a new wave of nausea and Darcy was coughing up nothing into the sleeve of Aurelio's coat. He'd done exactly as they'd hoped—Fin out there somewhere, en route to her secret Armenian bolt-hole.

Urgent spurts of Russian on the two-way and the Turk now pointing to the kerb. *Naleva*, he whispered and the driver slithered to a quiet halt. A rundown industrial zone. Silent outside, and drizzling, not even the sound of a dog. The Turk concentrating on the side mirror as the other car slid through the snow and parked in behind them.

Darcy glanced back again. Through the fan-shape of wipers, the general monitored the dark with silver binoculars and Aurelio, beside him, gazed at his own knuckles on the Lada's steering wheel, afraid to look up. A wordless mourning now lay deep in Darcy's heart. They'd been reduced to shadows, the two of them. As God made them.

The Turk wiped his window with a glove and stared through his own small field glasses, down an unlit space between buildings, towards where Darcy sensed the frozen fleece of the river must lie. He didn't look at Darcy as he spoke. I would have shot you, he said, but the General Sarfin asked me no. Not yet.

Darcy crouched in the back seat, weak but somehow defiant. The Opinel knife still there, tight against his ankle.

He examined the Turk's profile, his beaky nose and tapered neck, the wolverine smile, imagined slicing with the hawk-bill blade and ripping his smile out wide across his cheeks. What are you doing with me? he asked.

Maybe we need you. Let your sister see we have you, he said, his eyes still pressed against his binoculars. Dangle you on a stick.

Darcy reached down for the knife, just to feel it. Where is she? he asked softly. But it was the bull-necked driver who turned for the first time and Darcy, his hand down by his boot in the sights of grey crystalline eyes, felt the narrow path of his life. The same snub un-Turkish face he'd left in the crowd outside the exhibition, who'd let him believe he'd got away. His fingers stiff as branches, Darcy picked up the newspaper article fallen from the seat, handed it over. The guard who'd not stopped the trolleybus near the Ploshchad Revolyutsii.

Darcy averted his eyes, gazed out into the close black verge as if he wasn't half-paralysed with cold and fright. If there were a gunfight he'd take his chances out there—a small clump of conifers and from it another pair of eyes, glowing, the shape of a wary angular dog, wolfish, staring back. They watched each other for a moment, and Darcy thought of Laika, a stray captured down by the river, hanging in the air near the sun, exploding. Darcy could only see as far as the spindly pines, through to a factory fence where the timid dog disappeared into the immutable dark. He envisaged his own feet splayed in the blanketed gutter, his face down, silent and cold on this roadside, listening to the snow, wondering if he were dead.

He looked back again for Aurelio but the Lada was empty now, and a voice on the Turk's handset, the receiver

back up to his ear as a light flickered on in the night and
spread through the dark, up the side of a rusted industrial
building that stretched from the road, down to a low
gravel barge moored where ice had been dredged in the
river. In the shadows, a tractor with a front-end loader
axle-deep in muddy snow, a narrow, tyre-slushed track to
a small concrete quay. A cold whiff of pine mixed with the
smells in the car and Darcy's words congealed on his
tongue, an unshouted warning, as a shape appeared in the
shallow-lidded helm of the barge, a figure that rose up
then disappeared. Darcy imagined a hull full of bunks
where Armenians hid—separatists, terrorists, avengers of
distant history, Jobik waiting for Fin.

The light went off and the Turk seemed agitated,
twisting in his seat, whispering to the driver in Russian.
Darcy's heart pushed at his chest. If they stormed this
boat, he could run. No more conversation as two figures
emerged from the corrugated building, creeping through
the shadows past the loader, down towards the frozen
quay, to the barge. Darcy prayed for his moment, when
the Turk and his pale-eyed driver might forget him; they
strained out in the other direction, waiting. A fire in
Darcy's neck that spread to the base of his skull, the distant
buzz of a motor, then dim lights on the river. He eyed the
door handle to be sure it wasn't locked.

Who is this man? hissed the Turk, thrusting a pair of
field glasses into the back seat. The driver turned too, a
pistol an extension of his black, gloved hand. Darcy's
hands felt so unsteady, fumbling with the binocular strap,
then focusing. Lenses that produced a strange night vision,
purple, searching down the grainy details of the sheeted
building, the magnification almost telescopic. Fin like a

species endangered, tracked through the snow, monitored from the restaurant somehow. Darcy's eyes burned with the hazy vision of her smooth, efficient movement, climbing a rope ladder up the rusted side of the boat into what looked like mounds of gravel. She was being closed in on.

Tell me who is the man? Words spat by the Turk from the front seat. Darcy turned his attention to the one who wasn't Fin. A heavy leather jacket, jeans high and cinched tight the way all Moscow men wore jeans. The cook, Darcy mumbled, from the restaurant, but the cook had worn thick checked trousers. This man who now climbed the ladder, cigarettes bulging squarely from his rear pocket, turned for a moment to check as the building light flickered on like a signal, and Darcy caught his rutted unmistakable face through the purple, butterflied lens. The Albanian he'd shared the sleeper with on the train from Prague. Different in jeans but him, and Fin there, small beside him as he shed his torchlight over stones frosted grey, crouched down and they both disappeared. Suddenly, the shape of the barge rendered nothing, a pregnant silence and two humps of gravel, the Turk talking feverish Russian, and Darcy's realisation—Jobik's people had kept an eye on him since day one, shepherding their money belt home, and the truth of Darcy's idiocy had him staring at the seat back, retreating inside himself, the thought of himself as a fool on a train trundled like a gift bag through hell to this cold, precious moment.

He turned to the night as a great silver net of snow fell like unexpected debris and, with it, the sound of a distant motor, not the sound in his head, and *nyet, nyet* from the dashboard had the Turk still peering, anxious now, impatient. No one moved to storm the boat. The barge planted like a frozen wreck and yet lights moved out from it, over the ice. The Turk's words biting into his device. No moon on the river just spidering light in the blackness. Darcy picked up his own forgotten binoculars and his heart rose slightly. A snowmobile headed out across the river, one and then another, then nothing. The barge was just a meeting place. Fin was getting away.

Quick footsteps on the road and voices, coats moving out into the darkness, ignitions starting, a chance, thought Darcy, turning to the roadside door, but in the snow-smeared window loomed the general, eyes that danced with a hint of madness. He wrenched the door wide open. Time for you, he said, little boy *blue*.

Darcy lunged for the opposite door but the driver's arm was already a fist on the handle, another acid smile, and the Turk from the passenger side, shouting at the general: *Gde most? Gde most?* Where's the bridge?

The general dismissed the Turk with a wave of his handgun, grabbed Darcy by the coat, a glove around his neck that had a yowl of agony ratcheting up inside his head, the general's thumb like a cattle prod, a pistol in Darcy's ear. Darcy closed his eyes against him, sensed these as last breaths, pulled out into the veil of snow, the flakes that feathered his face as his own hands scrabbled up to wrest away the general's thumb, his gloved fingers gripping Darcy's voiceless throat, a mewling sound sent out to Fin out on the river ice, to Aurelio, to escape these great mauling hands. Darcy flailed the binoculars strapped to his hand like some pathetic handbag weapon, the knife out of reach, the gun jammed in his now-roaring ear, just as he'd imagined it only minutes before, shot on this road in front

of Aurelio, as remonstration, left in the frozen ditchwater
for local dogs to lick his wound. He thought if he'd had any
other life it wouldn't end like this, the Turk yelling at the
general, losing his Armenians, a glimpse of Aurelio through
the Lada's wipers, a horror caught in those rounded eyes,
a barely perceptible shake of his head and in it a plea not
to struggle. And Darcy was beyond it now, exhausted.

You thought I was to kill you? the general said,
smiling, and Darcy's knee was bashed as he was thrust into
the back seat of the Lada, the familiar tobacco smell, anise.
He held a mitten to the eruption of pain in his neck,
stunned and silent. Then he righted himself, clenched the
ear that clamoured with the bullet that hadn't been shot,
and breathed as if he'd forgotten how, looking up for
Aurelio—Aurelio who didn't dare look around, doleful
eyes caught in the rear-view mirror as the general hefted
himself around to face Darcy, his great arm on the seat
back. My son, Aurelio, he said with relish, his lips loose.
You know him?

Darcy withdrew from the yellow-toothed smile, a cautious glance from Aurelio, stiff and uncertain, then silence.

Aurelio was ballet dancer, said the general. Weren't
you, boy?

Aurelio didn't suspend an elegant arm as he'd once
done for Darcy but instead put the Lada in gear and stared
out into the rough U-turn he made.

He drove now with lights, the Turk a dark blur behind
them. Darcy, his sight blurred again, watched out through
the drumbeat rhythm of wipers, unsure if he should be
grateful. A passing clump of bare black forest. He blinked
to focus, touching his lip, the burn, as both cars ran parallel with the silvery Moskva. Shabby wooden dwellings,

the ways that wove down to the river. No lights of a skidoo. The general, two fingers pressed to an ear, listening for news from scratchy, faraway transistor voices. Aurelio's downy dancer's neck didn't turn to see him, but the general leaned slightly sideways, kept watch with accusing eyes, extending his free arm along the bench seat, the pistol at Aurelio's shoulder.

Fear snaked in Darcy's veins like a system of rivers, Aurelio's hands tight on the wheel, the general's zealot eyes, bloodshot under the rim of his black fur hat. My son, he said as if Aurelio weren't there. He never dance with Bolshoi. They only use him because he is strong, lifting ballet girls. He gestured with his big hands lofted in the air, the pistol held firm in one. But they don't like *Cubanos* at the Bolshoi, do they? *Nyet, nyet, nyet.* He pushed the gun at Aurelio's neck. Not specially the half homosex, half Cubanos.

Aurelio, mute, twitched his neck and drove on, rigid. Darcy avoided the general's flecked vulture eyes, focused on the gun, the silencer, a memory of the same at Nikolai Chuprakov's feet. Could it be the son-in-law's gun or did silencers all look the same? Darcy felt dizzied, the sardonic thrum of traffic through snow as they passed beneath what he thought was the ring road. The general so big, the seat back seemed low, his square-jowled face turned around to Darcy again. He have a dancer friend. Then he turned to Aurelio, goading. What happened to him? Sergei Beloff, was this his name? He not dance anymore. Jew boy, blue boy. He can't dance *now*. A violence in the last word, an act implied, the general sweating with wrath, or it could have been drink, and all Darcy thought of was size against frailty, being heaved at, the thought of a dancer blood-smeared against the cement. Aurelio still said nothing, just the slightest shake of his head in the rear-view mirror. Darcy saw cuts on his face.

The knife felt cold and small, folded in Darcy's mittened hand as he slid it unopened up into his coat sleeve, a soundless ribbon of panic. The general with the fingers to his transistor ear once more and another almost indiscernible shake of Aurelio's head. Had he seen the knife, sensed it? If it gouged the general's pistol arm, into whose head would he shoot the bullet? The Lada would skid through the gnawing darkness, turning over like a surfboard.

The general jerked up his pistol hand. *Lyevii*, he said, nudged at Aurelio's neck with the short black barrel, shouted gruff Russian instructions. Aurelio turned left down a dark road, turned off the lights. Darcy guessed the main road had taken them away from the river; they'd not crossed a bridge, but headed back now to where the vanishing river must be. We find your friends, said the general. We make visit. He turned to Aurelio. KGB, we know how to follow. Don't we, son? First we already follow your little boy blue to his secret restaurant.

Aurelio's silence scared Darcy. He drove like an automaton, only the shadowy parking lights of the Lada on what was now a narrow snowy track, the sound of the tyres crawling into the stillness. Dark in the car now, Darcy clasped the knife in the folds of his coat but the knife felt ineffectual. He'd need to strike the general's eye, or his ear, but the general kept waving the gun like a finger, turning. With a canny smile, he offered a zippered bag to Darcy.

The Turk, he kill for this, he said. His tongue glistened as it lay on his teeth and Darcy thought of Lubyanka, and the ferret-faced boy lying dead behind the restaurant—he knew how the Turk had killed. The burn still throbbed like the head of a spear broken off in his neck as the general's mammoth ungloved hand dangled the evidence bag over the seat like another last promise.

Did Tugrul tell you about Tbilisi? he asked. Your sister in Tbilisi? Just day before yesterday. Maybe we find her any minute. Family reunion…with fireworks.

A horrible dryness returned to Darcy's mouth, his teeth as if covered in cloth; he didn't want to know any more. The prospect of a fire on the river ice, he and Aurelio lined up with Fin and her dissident Armenians. Darcy searched the shadowy back of Aurelio's head, his shoulders still rigid, unyielding as a costumer's dummy. The general dropped the bag down in Darcy's lap. It was light, almost floated. Just paper.

I can't read, said Darcy.

Aurelio cleared his throat but the general barked at him sharply, scolding, then turned back to Darcy. It is English, he said, placing his elbow over the seat. He cocked a silver cigarette lighter, his face like a ghoul's in the fluttery flame, and Darcy thought to stab those fingers if the flame came near his face. He cagily held up the evidence bag, the thought of it burning, a decoy for Aurelio, a chance, but in the jittery light a date: *July 13, 1915. American Ambassador, Constantinople.* Typewritten, faded, beige letterhead frayed in the folds and corners. Old and authoritative.

You know this? asked the general. Is it original or forgery?

Darcy looked at the cream paper behind the plastic, the ridges of the seal. *Index Bureau*, stamped with an official seal, to Robert Lansing, US Secretary of State.

I never saw this.

A copy is left with the body of the dead Consul Turk in Tbilisi. The general a shifted personality, not the drunk transgressor but probing. This one they try to deliver to manuscript museum in Yerevan. You ever go to Yerevan?

Darcy didn't answer, felt the night crawling by, his life, the lives of dead Armenians. He wasn't even sure where Yerevan was but he was drawn to the undulating typeface. *Persecutions assuming unprecedented proportions. Uprooting, tortures and wholesale expulsions accompanied by rape, pillage and murder turning into massacre, to bring destruction and destitution on them.* Levitical-sounding words. Initials above a signature stamp. *Lawrence Andersen, United States Ambassador to Turkey.* In the margin he read *Classified.* Could it not be real? He directed his eyes to the general, who looked back at him with a predatory disdain.

You bringing this to Moscow, he said. Strapped to yourself like suicide. But you never *saw* it?

Darcy felt his own head shake, dubious and slow, as he lifted the plastic flap, the page where it creased, and knew it could have been folded, sewn into the lining of the money belt. In the pit of his stomach he believed it was true.

You very clever, said the general, or very stupid. He flicked the lighter off and muttered into a miniature speaker between fingers, men out in snow flurries still tracking Fin. Darcy heard her phone voice, the night she'd called in Melbourne, offering him a chance, sensing his suspicion, her faith in his need to escape that world, believing he'd come. And he had known even then it was stupid. Now, he cradled the old document in the dark, its red stamp embossed like the burn on his neck. If he'd been part of something, that something was over.

Aurelio stopped the car where the track dead-ended, glanced up at the rear-view mirror but Darcy couldn't make out his eyes, just the sound of the other car pulling in quietly behind them. He felt a strange surrender, a momentary transcendence of fear. Aurelio? he said softly, but Aurelio still didn't turn, it was the general who swung over the seat back, dark wild eyes and his pistol shoving at Darcy's face. You never speak with him, he said. You hearing? You do what *I* tell. Darcy reefed back from the small black barrel, his eyes so tight they burrowed deep inside him until he could feel his lips open, but he heard no shot, only words. You will walk through those trees. You will see a house. You knock on door.

Stoitye. Aurelio's muffled voice, and Darcy looked up as the general grunted, pistol-whipped his son against the driver's door, and Aurelio lay there, one arm draped over the wheel, horribly still. Darcy's instinct to run out into the darkness, out through the shadows of others, out of their cars, the Turk and the pastel-eyed henchman, men in black felt coats. The general half-turned.

Look what you do, he said, a quaver in his voice. He try to save you. But he cannot even save himself. As the general opened the door to get out, the interior light sparked on Aurelio's face and Darcy's eyes filled with a sudden revulsion—the cuts in Aurelio's cheeks like mutilations, not fresh from the pistol, but his mouth, scabby and black, sliced up his cheek on one side, sewn together by rough string stitches. Darcy understood why Aurelio hadn't turned—too proud to be seen, a mouth so wounded he didn't open it except to shout stop, to lunge at his father's pistol arm. The general regarded Aurelio, mumbled in Russian, an oath or a prayer, then closed the door.

Darcy sat inconsolably still in the blackness. Aurelio? he said, but Aurelio just hummed as if soothing himself, and Darcy began to rock as he'd done as a boy, side to side, holding his body together. Are you okay? he asked, but only heard humming. He closed his eyes tight, didn't look at Aurelio, then he turned to the window, the sight of the general peeing in the snow, in front of his men, delivering instructions. Painting a yellow dog, Fin had called it, pissing in the snow, the same name as the flowers. He yearned to reach through the dark and touch Aurelio now, trace about his eyes, the scars, but instead he just rocked and stared at his friend's silhouette, the snow as it kissed the window beside him, the murmuring of the KGB men outside, unaware. Then he heard the howl of a dog, far off, calling out through the snow, and the onslaught of something, grief, or a love that had lost its way, rested about the edges of Darcy's eyes, as if on the lip of a dam, and then he was keening, swaying like a branch, and howling softly with the dog but the door was flung open and the general's hand slapped him from it.

You listen to me, said the general, panicky, grabbing Darcy's collar, ripping it against the burn as Darcy stuffed the document inside his coat. You will walk into these woods and show your friends this paper. You will see their faces, he said. Then he said something in Russian that stopped Aurelio's hum. He reached into the front seat, ripped the fur hat from Aurelio's head as if he were a mannequin, and Darcy saw that Aurelio's head had been shaved.

Get out of this car, said the general, pushing the hat down over Darcy's beanie. The sound of the dog, like a distant calf bawling, stayed in Darcy's head as he fought being pitched like a leaf out into the night among men who stamped their feet, their breath fogging in front of them. Darcy felt strangely unbalanced, the snow wet against his face, indistinguishable from his tears. The Turk, hugging himself in the cold nearby, black eyes gleaming. The Opinel knife felt blunt as a stone as Darcy looked back at Aurelio, splayed against the car door.

The general patted the waterproof evidence bag stowed up under Darcy's coat. They will see what you have, said the general. You give it back your friends if you want. It can burn with them. The general's shrug was in his eyes. Just let them know we have it. And that we have you.

Darcy's mind closed in on itself for protection, from the cold that already seeped into his veins, from these grim men warming themselves. He would be their mascot, but of sacrifice, and he felt the strangeness of life as death approaches. Aurelio's gutted mouth plastered like membrane to Darcy's blinking eyes, the stitches; the distant dog had gone silent, just Aurelio's tune in Darcy's head, a Cuban song maybe. The general poked his pistol in Darcy's ear. Be a good boy blue, he said, shoving him forward in the wake of the powder-eyed driver.

What about Aurelio? asked Darcy, and the general ran a rough, wet-gloved finger from the corner of Darcy's mouth up the side of Darcy's cheek. It is a punishing, he said, we call it *smiling*. And a cry sank voiceless down inside Darcy. For being like you, he said, buffeting Darcy into the shapeless night.

Darcy picked his way through the black-haired pines as if walking through a bitter cold river, his coat turning to stone and death inviting as a face before him: come, it will be easier, come, like the face in the waves on Bushrangers Bay, the winter wants you to itself. He looked back but the Turk was right there behind him, nudging him on to follow the driver and his winking torchlight, KGB men swarming shadowy in their coats through the slender trunks. He looked back again just to see Aurelio, but instead caught the Turk's beady eyes from under the brim of an astrakhan hat.

Give me the document, he whispered but Darcy hugged the plastic-covered evidence against himself, as if that was all he had, evidence of Trebizond, *Thousands forced onto ships and dumped into the Black Sea, islands of innocent people.* Darcy didn't weep for them now, he was drowning himself. Give it to me, the Turk's voice through the snow, I can help you. The driver glanced back, whispered fiercely in Russian, gesturing to a following guard to keep Darcy coming, Darcy uncertain who was in charge, the Turk was summarily motioned aside. The joint operation felt like a death march, Darcy sandwiched in the dark, on through crunching undergrowth. He didn't believe there was help out here, no Armenian snipers swept down from these trees, no withered hand of God. The icy damp had already curled up in Darcy's skin as he cradled the grim inevitability, his feet brittle as frozen coral. If lust was the cause of all sorrow, what had love done, what had it done for any of them? Herded out here to die, Aurelio an *opuscheny*. Fin weaving her way to some hut in these same woods, unsuspecting. Her departure up through that restaurant roof with not even a word of goodbye, just a telephone number in Darcy's wet jacket pocket, her snowmobile lights switched out on the dark ice river. *They're the KGB…it's not hide-and-seek.*

Darcy pushed a wet coat sleeve over his face, his footing unsteady as they crossed the end of a white stone culvert, he almost collapsed, a new pistol held to his neck in the dark like a branding iron. Then, in a knot of black furs, the torch ahead turned into darkness and the driver crouched beside someone waiting in the shadows with binoculars. A clearing. A small wooden dacha not a hundred feet further, a figure through the branches in the lamplit shelter of the doorway, the new gun barrel pressed deep in Darcy's ribs to silence him. With his bare eyes Darcy knew it was Jobik, alone in the cone of lamplight, wrapped in a blanket, his thick black hair pushed back from his beaky face, waiting. The Turk looked over at Darcy, his dark face wet and weathered, his glasses fogged. He removed them angrily, cleared the lenses with his fingers, his narrow eyes, antsy, and the general with them now, from out of nowhere, short-winded. The fear in Darcy that he'd be sent out into that no-man's-land to pleasure the general's imagination. Into that painterly stillness.

Jobik was drinking from a mug, the steam from it wafting in the funnel of light, just him beneath a hanging basket made from rope and the wet sound of the snow on the leaves, the soft hail hammering like winter storms climbing in off the Tasman Sea. Darcy's mouth struck dry as a figure appeared up a path from the river. Fin, like a vision, delivered. The general's bestial smile. We follow good, no? he whispered like a friend.

The sight of Fin had an instinct well deep in Darcy, their secret call from school, *elly elly etdoo*, the warning from outside her window, but now he could barely walk, the sight of her returning, wet through as a child coming in from a rainstorm. Jobik, as he opened the door like a husband might, relieved she'd made it home. If Fin had found love, Darcy felt forgotten, like something forfeited, out here among these dripping trees and guns. His loyalty washing from him like rain as the lamp was snuffed and he looked into the spattering snow from a forest full of crouching men, waiting for their signal.

Go to the door, the general beside him now, whispering. You congratulate them on Tbilisi, he said. Showing them what you holding. Make it a ceremony.

Darcy looked up at the barbarous smile, then into the speckled dark. A door to be kicked in, planks hanging from hinges. The Turk's bared teeth, the gold in them almost visible—he seemed to know it as lunacy too. His reluctant nod still held its invitation. Darcy stared again at the general's massive face. Aurelio, as he'd known him, was gone.

You are primitive, said Darcy, and the general looked out into the night as if he knew.

Darcy turned and walked from them, no sound but himself, no barking dog now, just the rhythmic contraction of his heart as he scraped his way through dripping tree trunks, his feet on pine spindles in dark quilted snow, waiting for a shot in his back or a battle cry, in a godless zone among histories and atrocities he barely understood. He didn't hurry, he couldn't; the porch lamp wasn't there for him like it had been for Fin and if he were noisy Jobik would hear, the dogfight would begin. All of them killers, warming themselves on the blood of others. He tried to remember Aurelio's face as it had been, a last memory to hold, piecing his way through sodden branches, snow like gauze.

He wasn't sure why, but he drifted, drawn to a pine-encased window, he stood there, divided. Waiting. A gap in the blind, a simple, dimly lit kitchen, old cream cupboards and faded wooden floors, a washboard and enamel sink, the black worn through to a flea-bitten grey. A last window. He made no sound as Fin came in and pushed life into the fire with a poker, watched the embers ignite. A kettle on the rusted iron of an ancient Aga, a yellow-painted mantelpiece. She warmed herself by the flames for a moment, before she closed the stove door. Just her and Darcy, and muffled voices from the other room, the innocent chitchat of terrorists. The kettle began its whistle and she poured herself tea, black with a dash, how she liked it. She opened an iron drawer below the ash-catch at the bottom of the stove and took out a shallow tin, then sat at the end of the table, warming her hands on her cup. Darcy knew he'd not see her apartment again, but in a way he'd been happy there. Above her a cross with a carved wooden Jesus hung on the wall, shadowed behind from the light. It had given the Saviour a dark side. Fin put her tea bag on the table and watched it form a small brown puddle on the wood. And Darcy felt the restlessness behind him, preparing.

Dully, he hummed out loud and then she looked up with an artificial calm. Tilda, he said, the name of the baby his mother had lost. He held up the document but Fin never saw it, she only saw him as she ran to the next room and Darcy heard shouting inside and a rush through the woods as he flung himself down deep under the eaves of the window, alongside the house; among the wet stove wood, he lay like he was dead already as the waves crashed around him and nothing to be done save listen to the gunshots and running, someone rushing for him. Give it to me, the Turk grabbing at him then bullets splintered on the boards above, shattering the window, the Turk on all fours like a beast beside him, and then face down and glass on Darcy's legs. Darcy's face bandaged in the crusted snow, the document held like a biblical thing, his eyes tight, sinking, imagining Fin tearing through black pines, feeding herself to the frozen river. Come to Moscow, she'd said, it'll be fun, but she'd fallen in love with a savage and Darcy, drowning, reduced to a hum.

There were no more shots, just cries in the night from the direction of the river. A figure disappeared around the house into darkness and Darcy scrambled up blind among the snowy logs, so numb with cold and not even sure if he was wounded. More shouts and he kneeled. The Turk face down in the dark beside him, he didn't dare kick him to see if he was dead, just felt the document inside his own wet coat, and then he was running back through the firs, away from the hut, stumbling through the black under-brush, back towards Aurelio. More gunfire behind him, the pine branches whipping his face, and he imagined Fin somewhere down near the river, scooting across the ice, covering ground on her elbows like one of those frogs that run across water, or laid out on the edge, riddled with bul-lets, the general inspecting his kill.

Darcy felt feverish, heaving for air at the sight of the Lada, its parking-light eyes shining orange. But the general was here—he leaned against the car smoking in a black velvet overcoat, a dress coat. No shape of Aurelio in the car. Run, thought Darcy, turning back to the forest, but the general was opening the driver's side door. You will drive us back, he said, waving a pistol produced from a holster under his coat. You can trust me, he said. I take you to a nice place now.

Where's Aurelio? asked Darcy, his voice faraway.

He is better now, the general nodded, and waved the pistol. Get in.

But Darcy didn't move. What have you done? he asked.

I deal with him, send him out into the night, said the general, like I deal with Tugrul, like my men are doing with your Armenians. He fired a silenced shot into the grey-black snow near Darcy's feet. Like I can deal with you.

Darcy approached the car slowly, doubting his will to survive, if he should just turn back into the gun-yielding trees and receive the shot in the back, fall face down and be gone like the Turk, or just die of exposure on his own, out where the dogs barked. But he got in the Lada and sat where he'd last seen Aurelio, the general resting the gun against the velvet of his coat, the tinny smell of a weapon just fired. Opera on the radio. The heater. As if civilised. Darcy didn't flinch as the general reached over into his wet coat pocket for the plastic bag.

He try to take this from you, said the general. Now he is dead. He placed the document inside his own fresh coat.

Darcy fixed on the narrow track that appeared in the car lights, looking for eyes in the night, for witnesses, but there were just shadows and blackness. He changed roughly through the Lada's gears, drove where Aurelio had driven, trying to the fight the blur of tears and his imaginings—Aurelio out in the splintering night, the blood from his cuts, from his mouth, run thin.

What did you do to him? asked Darcy, his voice hardly his own.

He has been digging his own grave, the general said. Digging your graves, all of you. His calm had a shiver that ran through Darcy, a calm that filtered psychosis, and the flourish of horns and operatic voices from the radio. That

he dared listen to music. But as the general tapped his cigarette ash onto the floor he looked away, and Darcy
thought he saw the slightest shake in the leather-gloved
hand. A hand like a black claw that now rested on Darcy's
leg, smoke curling from it, and Darcy imagined acceler-
ating off into the tree trunks, their heads dashed against
glass. He tried to ingest the warm tobacco air but all he
could feel was an animal panic. Then, at the main road,
the general directed him, the pistol like a wand, back
towards the city. And now all Darcy saw in the gliding
darkness was the light that had left Aurelio's eyes. You
killed him, he said.

The general emerged from some reverie. You do not
know that, he said.

Darcy looked out at the half-lit factories, then down
at the gun, the way it was pointed at him. He is your son,
he said.

The general nodded resignedly. But he was not a man,
he said. I could not trust him. He gestured with the weapon
for Darcy to turn from the river and pointed up a narrow
street, carved between cedars, an area of compounds.

We have invitation, he said, but Darcy didn't believe
him, wondering if he could slide the car off the road and
turn it over without being killed. But he was halted by a
guard who appeared from a booth between stone
gateposts and the general leaned forward in the torchlight
to be recognised. The Lada was saluted through.

Someone wanting to meet you, said the general.

But it didn't make sense, everything short-circuiting:
Aurelio abandoned out in the night and a driveway
opening up to a pale two-storey mansion. A lantern by the
door threw a triangle of light on the walls like a Magritte

and Darcy recognised it from the photo, the garden now in winter, the stones clawed with deciduous ivy in the dark. In the general's photo Anyetta Chernenko had stood on the lawn. And Darcy in this car with the general, fresh from his Black Sea honeymoon, his new wife nowhere to be seen, untouched by his newly dead son. Talk, thought Darcy, make yourself seem human.

What do you want from me? he asked.

Just be polite, he said. She is my friend. Wanting to meet with the artist. He checked himself in the rear-view mirror, removed his hat and pushed his hand through his buzz of white hairs. Darcy stopped the Lada without the handbrake, let the tyres lodge in the slough, and he stared out in the way he'd learned when his mother was drunk, when dealing with someone irrational, but it hadn't equipped him for this. Did you never love Aurelio? he asked.

The general reached for the keys and placed them in his pocket. You do not know that either, he said, magnanimous, perverse, and with his gun he motioned Darcy into the cold and Darcy wondered fearfully what he was being spared for. He opened the door to a narrow avenue of poplars, trimmed as thin as pencils, and for a moment Darcy hoped he'd be sent in alone, to knock on the door like a soldier returned from the trenches, the lapels of his coat and the knees of his jeans wet with snow, to take refuge in a woman's face. Maybe Fin by the fire, wrapped in a mohair blanket—perhaps it was all a surprise. The panelled door opening, a tall figure silhouetted and the whippet bounding down. Darcy knelt to nuzzle its warmth against his hands and it pushed its face against him like a cat might. The general strode past and was ushered inside by the widow.

Darcy looked up at her waiting for him in the chill of the threshold, in the same evening gown and a silver fox stole, her eye shadow Elizabeth Taylor blue. Can you help me? he whispered, but she bent her head towards him puzzled, not hearing, not wanting to, as they both watched the dog lift a leg in the snow.

Thanking you again for caring him, she said softly, is very kind. She observed Darcy as if trying to take him in, but he didn't understand. Her husband was dead and she'd been out in bright colours, socialising.

Help me, he whispered, he pulled down his collar, tried to show her the burn but she glanced away, and together they watched the gossamer dog, a fine Gucci belt fashioned as its collar, and Darcy remembered the Borgward, the sadness in the son-in-law's eyes. I'm sorry, he said, but the woman shook her head, it wasn't the time, and still Darcy wanted to ask her for sanctuary but the general loomed in the doorway, tuxedo shirt and holstered gun, a Western bolo tie, his formal clothes beneath his coat all along. Come on, he said, smiling. Is cold.

Boyar, said the woman and the whippet bounded inside, but the general stayed, smiling, waiting. He swung his black-rimmed glasses by an arm of the frame, as though he were the man of the house, and the sight of it disturbed in Darcy a morbid loathing. He looked up as if seeking help, at a face in an upstairs window, an old man, wrinkled and unshaven, and for a moment their eyes met and Darcy wondered why he'd really been brought here, if there was hope in this house.

In an entry hall he removed Aurelio's black fur hat but not his coat. He noticed the general's velvet dress coat on the hallstand, hung like a pelt. The general was already in the next room, a lavish parlour, but the widow stood waiting, observing Darcy, her old-fashioned Soviet elegance like something from a silent film. She pointed humbly at the Laika painting leaning against a low bench, her whippet's slender shape atop the obelisk, *Finola Dobrolyubova* scrawled across the lower right-hand corner in black. Darcy looked up, disconcerted.

Your dog, he said tentatively, acknowledging the canvas.

She smiled shyly as if she knew. *Your* painting, she said, as if she also knew it wasn't Fin's, and Darcy searched her eyes for something, recognition or deliverance, the way he trusted women.

I arrange it for her, the general interrupted from the adjoining parlour, and through the archway, past her, Darcy could see him standing by a fireplace, and as the widow now joined him, Darcy felt the need to protect her, to hurt him. He remembered her appearing in Lubyanka, through the grate in the interview room, but he couldn't tell what she'd been told, how much she knew. He checked down a narrow corridor, searching for exits, but a maid in a black dress and white apron stood there, holding a tray, observing him from the shadows with dark cynical eyes. She watched as if she was the one who knew things, the old man from upstairs now sheltered behind her in a doorway, a craggy face, a valet or apparition.

Darcy stood in a kind of stunned abeyance, like something dragged in from the night, uninvited in his sodden coat, too grimy to enter and join the couple as they chatted by the fire, the whippet curling comfortably into a shallow wicker basket at their feet. Darcy took in the room as if the furniture might warm him, anchor his longing for beauty, a pair of floral sofas, a low table. Silk flowers, irises and hyacinth. And art. A Hockney swimming pool on one wall and a Rothko, mournful and abstract. Replicas, probably, but Darcy didn't know; he looked at his own canvas, the image of the stray found by the river replicated from the dog in the other room. The general leaned in towards Anyetta Chernenko, their heads close together, bald and caramel blonde, he was telling a story with words Darcy recognised—*Dashnak, Jobik, Nikolai, Garabed,* Armenia— seducing or using her. The general's eye fixed on Darcy like a bear might eye a fish that flopped about on shore.

Tell her about Aurelio, said Darcy, but his voice was so raspy no one heard except the maid, who surfaced unexpectedly, as though on cue, and offered Darcy herring on bread and a tumbler of vodka poured from a jug. Darcy drank then ate voraciously, wanting another, more, but she glided into the main room, the general accepting drinks with Anyetta Chernenko as if Darcy had not been at his wedding to somebody else, or been pressed against the cement wall in Lubyanka, and now things undreamed of, unhinged, bodies mounting up in the woods, by the river. Then he heard his name, the general calling *Darcy*, as if they were friends, and Darcy looked over. You can be showering, said the general. My friend says you can be shower here. How you are so dirty? The drink raised in the general's hand.

Darcy felt a wave of nausea, the promise of *clean you up* suddenly reverberating, had him sweaty again, *clean you up pretty…like a real Polish boy*. Next time. But why here? The general issuing orders to the maid in Russian, Anyetta Chernenko looking on, bemused, and Darcy taking another vodka from the maid's tray, chugging it,

and the shiver of it ran through him, familiar; afraid that's
what the general wanted: him loosened, clean, spared to be
cut like Aurelio, or worse.

The general sitting on the sofa in the parlour, consoling Anyetta Chernenko, holding her to him in front of
the fire, and it looked like she was weeping. He eyed Darcy
through strands of her hair and the maid, waiting for
Darcy to put his glass back on the tray, emitted a grunt of
annoyance, as if she didn't care for what she saw. As if she
were Nikolai Chuprakov's maid.

She ushered Darcy down the corridor, the old man in
a doorway, his rugged poet's face, and Darcy remembered
the roll of notes in the hem of his coat. These people might
help him, he thought, as he wrestled for the money deep
in the hole through a pocket. He found himself in a bathroom with plum-coloured carpet, the maid gesturing to a
towel and a shower, and Darcy showed the roll of roubles,
offered them in the flat of his hand. *Pazhalsta*, said Darcy,
please, he will kill me, and the maid glared at the fat little
wad of money, wanting but not understanding, her
button-like eyes full of fear. Help me, he pleaded, but she
retreated, afraid.

He grabbed the green jug of vodka from her tray as she
slithered out the door and he drank and felt himself unravelling, his pledge broken again when he knew he needed
clarity most, the buzz about his face like a quiet sponge and
the sound of a key as it turned the bolt; she'd locked him in.
He searched frantically for an exit, found only a vent and a
too-tiny window, a long wrought-iron dresser with a silver
shaver and a wooden-handled brush, two small framed
drawings from covers of *Vanity Fair*. A candy-striped tooth-
brush dry in a mug. Nikolai Chuprakov's?

Darcy caught sight of himself in the mirror above the sink, his face bruised purple and strafed with mud, lines where dimples had been. He took a swill of vodka as if that would help him think, washed dirt from his face, the water steaming hot straight from the tap, scabs on his lip and cheek tender. In his face he saw Fin, lying dead out on the ice. Wishing he had the whole bottle to upend in his mouth, something caught his eye in the mirror's reflection; by the toilet was a niche with a black phone. He left the taps running, turned on the shower to add to the noise, and fumbled in his coat for Fin's slip of paper, a wet folded piece with ink that had run, but numbers. He crouched on the toilet and dialled hastily, listened to the beeps, the most-tapped phone in Moscow or, if he was lucky, the least. He stared at the bolted door with his chest pounding like there were animals fucking inside it and listened, the pungent smell of dread that he now knew lived in his sweat. The shower water smacked the tiles.

Hello? A woman, well-spoken, accented.

Darcy knotted his eyes in supplication. Ulli Breffny? Hysteria in his whisper.

I'm listening, she said.

My name is Darcy Bright. I am in the house of Anyetta Chernenko. I am in danger.

You must get to the embassy, she said. I will be here. The gates will open for you. She paused for a moment.

General Sarfin is killing people.

We cannot come there, she said. You must get yourself here. She hung up and Darcy couldn't breathe enough to cry but he peed and didn't know what else to do so he knocked on the door for the maid and prayed that the old man might help him but it was the general who answered.

You talking with someone?

Darcy stood petrified, unsteady. No, he said. Myself.

The general undid his holster belt and placed it on the vanity, the pistol clipped inside it. You think we don't hear you, he said, you think we don't know where you are? He grabbed Darcy, vice-like, by the upper arm, ripped a brass-covered button from Aurelio's coat and thrust it up at Darcy's eye like some gold signet. This is device, the general said through the steam, blood vessels bulging at the black rims of his glasses.

Darcy arched up with the pain, the general's thumb dug deep in his bicep, but Darcy didn't struggle, he felt for the knife in his pocket with his free hand, the general shaking him savagely. We track you like this every day. Aurelio did give you this coat. You think he did not know? You think he love you so much? He turned Darcy around, wrenching him from the coat but the knife had already unfolded, the rumble again in Darcy's head. I clean you up, the general hissed, I clean you, jerking the coat sleeves off Darcy from behind but Darcy bent his arms up, struggled now, the knife cold in his palm. He let the sleeves fly free, his arms unthreading and turned, the general losing his balance, his glasses falling through the thick white air and Darcy reached through it, quick as a diving bird he swung across the general's face, as the general slipped on the tiles, lurching back with a stifled wail, big hands all over his bloodied face, he kicked and slid as his great head made a hollow sound against the lip of the iron bath, hitting, and Darcy's head went deaf as the general's hands flopped down like slabs and Darcy lunged and stabbed through the vapour, went for his eyes through the blood on the flesh of the general's bloated face, plunging the

blade deep, until he retched vodka at the sight of what
gushed from the eyes to the salivating lips, the surge of
dark red onto the wide bristled chin, onto the white ruf-
fles of the shirt. Darcy could neither speak nor hear nor
think, his mind glazed; blood on the knife, the knife still
in his hand, he knew he had to rinse it, fold it back into
itself, blood on his hands as he grabbed the holster from
the counter, the jug knocked over, smashed on the floor, a
river of vodka clear through the curtain of steam towards
blood that coursed from the spigots of the general's
hacked-up eyes, the body still not moving. Darcy felt his
chest constricting, everything upside down, reaching, as
if into the pelt of an injured, stunned animal, its heart still
pumping, he searched the pockets of the general's tuxedo.
Repulsed by the blood-infested face, the mouth laid open,
accusing, he had to turn away, the tremor in his own body,
in his hand as he felt for the Lada's keys, the pistol in his
free hand, the keys in his fingers as the general's arm
twitched.

Darcy jumped up as if swept outside his consciousness, the fact of what lay there, half-alive or dying, the fact
of a gun in his own hand, and, bathed in steam and the
drum of the pouring water, Aurelio's coat behind him, a
black lake on the floor, the brass button that had been listening all along, floating like a tiny crucible. Darcy found
himself out in the dark abandoned corridor. The gun in a
hand that didn't feel like his hand, his blood-smudged fingers turning the key in the door, locking the general in.
Darcy stood there in a hallway silent but for the whippet
skulking in the shadows as if sent down to check, the dull
thrum of the shower. As Darcy pocketed the key he began
to shake, a trembling rippling through him, and he knew

only violent people should be violent. Darcy knew he had to keep moving, that if he'd stabbed a man in the eye, he could use a gun. The echo in his head of the general's hollow contact with the bath, skull on iron, the stolen car keys and knife now stuffed in the pocket of his denim jacket, his vision seemed altered as he searched for a servant's entrance out into the cold black coatless nothing, but the corridor ended so he moved towards the entry hall, rubbing the blood on his pants, the dog by his side licking up playfully as he walked.

In the entry hall stood the widow by the Laika picture, not hiding but standing, pale and stricken, the old man by her side. They were expecting the general. Darcy held the gun in the air like a quivering grenade but the old man had no weapon, and Darcy saw his face in the light for the first time. Nikolai Chuprakov, older, the same mournful dark eyes, Nikolai Chuprakov's father. I'm so sorry, said Darcy, he slipped the general's dress coat from the hallstand, soft as mink, and he was crying as the old man opened the door for him as if he somehow understood.

Darcy stumbled down through the narrow poplars, shouted no at the following dog and heard the widow call its name. He pushed its felt snout from the car door, set the gun on the passenger seat. He slammed the door and closed his eyes for an elevated second as he turned the cold ignition and it started, the rattle of the engine, the crunch of tyres reversing. He glanced back and saw the maid standing under the eaves like a shadow and prayed she'd not called for help, that they somehow believed he was Nikolai Chuprakov's lover, and forgave him.

The snow fell in a sudden sheet as he drove through the columned entrance, from a place with a climate of its own, and the last thing he saw in the rear-view mirror was the whippet, perched like a statue in the lantern light behind him, the old man and widow gone. Now he felt engulfed in darkness, the taste in his mouth almost sulfuric; perhaps they'd have helped him, hidden him, but why? He couldn't trust a look in an old man's eyes.

He'd sneaked cars down driveways since he was nine, but then he'd felt an exhilaration, now he gripped the wheel to stop his own shaking, jumped through a gear and switched on the lights to blind the sentry who raised his hand. Through the snow and the thrash of the wipers, Darcy was the general with the general's gun, leaving for the night, but then he saw the guard in the mirror, outside his box in the blanketed street, and Darcy accelerated.

Darcy started ripping buttons from the general's coat, throwing them out into the snow, with no horrid exhilaration, just disgust; and Darcy couldn't know if he'd ever forgive himself but the shaking wasn't stopping and he didn't turn back to search for Aurelio, or for evidence of Fin. He drove on towards the city.

A siren, but it was a train, the gates of a level crossing lowered quickly before him. He looked back at a van behind him, prayed it wasn't police, imprisoning him, he gazed ahead into the hoot and rattle, the blur of endless hammers and sickles emblazoned on carriages, symbols of cutting and bludgeoning, in rhythm. He touched the burn on his neck, scabbed now, and he tore at it, the pain like a tranquiliser, ripping the crusted edge as a whoosh of windswept snow blasted the car from the last carriage passing and he stared at oncoming cars at the crossing—two green sedans in tandem, militiamen, and as he jolted the Lada over the tracks, Svetlana turned from the second car and caught him there, and as they passed they watched each other but Svetlana's eyes said nothing to him but *go*. And he wished he could tell her to look for Aurelio but the city was somewhere ahead, the river to his left, and he wove through the night, his vision blurred with fear and vodka.

He dabbed his neck with the collar of the coat with fingers already tainted with blood, and thought of axes pounding through the bathroom door, searching for spare keys, the widow calling her father, the head of Special Forces. He thought he saw the beacons of the Siminov Monastery above him, lights that hit the pistol on the seat, his fingerprints all over it, his eyes that stung like nettles, straining as far as they could; he twitched and slowed at a claxon sound, an ambulance blaring, coming towards him, but he pressed the Lada forward, passing cars that pulled over, a snow plough, a military truck, if he could just keep the river to his left, but he felt as if the road was veering away. The outlines of buildings clustering, closing in, he wondered if he could find the metro station at Taganskaya, abandon the car, but he knew how to get to Kropotkinskaya by road—follow the river to the Chayka Pool—the weather so thick, his head aching, he dabbed his neck and pressed his elbow against the velvet coat and sensed the slide of plastic, the sacred telegram, how the Turk had almost reached him, crouched and then been felled. Darcy pictured KGB men, done with the Armenians, waiting for him at the embassy gates.

He looked over at the gun, uncertain how to shoot it, then up at a stoplight that burned red and the gun flew from the seat to the floor as he braked and his heart rose up, the car was sliding, bunting a black metal barrier. He swung into the skid so the Lada caught traction and Darcy turned left; then he saw what he knew was the lustreless sweep of the river. Out behind him everything refracted, camouflaged in snow, but there was the embankment approaching, the high sloping stones, and his hopes high with it. He couldn't yet see the lit panorama of the Kremlin, but he knew where he was, the unyielding stone towers, the Armoury Palace and the endless facade of the walls and cathedrals, all of them above him, places with names he remembered. The Ivan the Great belltower and the Presidium.

In the wake of a bus he looked up at the school-age eyes peering scattershot out a back window, children in a winter like this, and he didn't feel Russian, crushed by loss and steeled by it, he felt desperately alone. He reached down for the gun but grasped cigarettes. Aurelio's. But there would be no Aurelio. There would be stray dogs in winter, a general congealing in steam. There would be shaven-headed boys being raped in the gulags or cast out into snow.

He turned at the swimming pool onto Kropotkin-skaya Prospekt, but a car turned behind him, and all he could do was stare in the rear-view mirror as he slowed for number thirteen. The other car crept past and no obvious convoy of KGB vehicles waited, yet the quiet felt suspicious, the guard hut lonely as an outhouse in the gut-tering light. He reached down for the pistol and rested it in his lap, under his new coat, pulling in beside the sentry box, and he felt how easy it would be to use a gun, after cutting at eyes with a knife—you could turn a gun on yourself if you had to.

No one inside the gates, in the snow-blurred shadows, the pitch-dark mansion. A torch shining in the window and Darcy held the roll of notes from his pocket and closed his eyes as he wound the window down into the light on his face and the sleet that spat on his cheeks—the blunt, oval face and same spare chin that denied him the last time. Darcy handed over what remained of the roll of money and looked straight ahead.

Ulli Breffny, he said, clasping the wheel so his hands didn't tremble, willing himself through, letting go and holding on. Another car passing, the guard picking up a receiver concealed under the counter and phoning, mumbling in Russian, a call he hadn't made last time, and Darcy felt the gun in his lap, about to point it up, to be sure it was the right call and then, ahead of him, the iron-barred entrance began its drag through the slush, and a pair of rusted arms lifted like they were about to embrace; Darcy drove in almost convulsively, more wary still than elated, faint, as he held for the sound of the creaking gates to lock him in, the hinges like a child screaming.

Darcy looked up in disbelief, craned his head to see if anyone waited, if a striding figure would emerge to welcome him, but the butter-coloured mansion sat in an unnatural dark. Then he saw a woman at the top of a low-lit set of stairs, coiffed like an air hostess, her head covered in a plastic rain scarf. She walked down the slick narrow steps and Darcy watched her, hardly dared breathe or swallow. As she approached, he pocketed the pistol and opened his window, quelling his instinct to rush.

I'm Ulli de Breffny, she said through the snow. A *de* before the Breffny, a strawberry-blondeness to her hair, eyebrows carefully pencilled, and Darcy felt his spirit returning. Darcy Bright, he said. He fumbled his collar up over the bloodied sore and tried to get out but his legs seemed weak beneath him like he'd been crippled. He wanted to drape himself over her for safety, but she was formal, touching his shoulder as if she understood. She shepherded him to the stairway with a certain urgency. Darcy looked over at her. Thank you, he said. Is this still Soviet soil?

Yes and no, she said, as they entered a faint spray of light from the canopied doorway. Technically no. And Darcy staved off tears of exhaustion, his fingers shaky as flames.

Ulli de Breffny slipped the rain scarf from her head. In from the cold, she said, aware of her joke, but Darcy couldn't see it as funny. He glanced through the glistening snow behind him, the night that had let him go; these people who'd given him passage, the old man like an angel out of nowhere, Svetlana. And now he was inside, in a small austere reception room. A place that no longer seemed possible. An Australian flag on the wall, metal desk and office chairs, a plain teak table with a silver tea service. A holding pen perhaps, for quarantine, debriefing. The gun shoved deep in his coat as this woman double-bolted the iron-clad door and they both looked down at Darcy's wet Blundstone boots on the dry taupe carpet.

He stared up at her beseechingly. Can I speak to the ambassador? he asked.

She draped her scarf on the back of a chair and motioned him to sit. I'm his envoy tonight, she said, pouring tea into a gold-lipped cup, her English impeccable but not Australian. She passed Darcy the cup on a saucer, a plate of homemade lemon squares and lamingtons. She smiled reassuringly. She hadn't patted him down.

But who are you really? he asked.

I am originally Finnish, she said, pouring her own tea. The dull pink of her lipstick, a woman who still traded on her looks. She leaned back on the desk. I liaise with the Soviets, she added with a quiet authority, as if that might suffice. Also, she said, I'm the wife of the Australian cultural attaché. And Darcy knew she was a spook.

Darcy watched as she leaned against the desk, assessing his scraped-up face, the way he shook, as if trying to judge what he'd been through. As he drank tea, the cup quivered at his lips, and the liquid burned down inside him. He noticed the Southern Cross on the flag, listened for activity but the building seemed oddly silent; he'd still not seen an actual Australian. He cleared his throat. You know Fin? he asked.

Ulli de Breffny made a slight face as if she might not run in quite the same circles. I met her only once. My husband was responsible for her grant to come here and paint. He was very taken with her portfolio.

They were mine, he said.

She nodded. We know that now, she said. Then we got a message from her. About you.

Darcy looked down at the tea leaves in his cup. What did she say?

Ulli de Breffny sipped her own tea but still didn't sit. That you were in over your head; that you were an innocent.

Darcy felt the shape of the pistol against his ribs. Can you find out if she's alive? he asked.

We can try, she said. We know there's been an incident.

Darcy felt a rush of anger. An incident? He clasped his hands around the tea cup to retain his composure. He needed to be practical. He remembered his map inside his denim jacket, his body layered with damp pockets. He unfolded the map and held it up, pointed to where he'd seen her last, down the river past the Danilov Monastery and the Church of the Ascension, but he suddenly wasn't sure of directions. He couldn't find the Southern River Terminal, only the weight of what he'd witnessed, what he'd just done, unravelling within him. You don't know what I've seen, he said, but she told him they were doing what they could, that it was difficult here. Darcy looked up at Ulli de Breffny sensing his bewilderment, and he wasn't sure if anyone would ever understand.

You know what she was doing here, said Ulli de Breffny, don't you?

Darcy nodded. I learned, he said, I learned in Lubyanka. He thought it might make an impression but she merely inclined her head.

Essentially, she said, she's a fugitive. She spoke as if Darcy might need reminding.

She's my sister, he said, and Ulli de Breffny stared down at the map, at Darcy's clenched hands. Then she acknowledged a green folder on the desk behind her. A string around it, a row of numbers printed.

We never told them that, she said. We thought it might protect you.

What? he asked. Told them what?

That she's your sister.

They knew, he said. Again he felt the gun, wished her'd thrown it out into the snow.

I know who you are, she said. I saw a copy of the photo they took of you in Prague. I don't judge you, she added, touched her fine-edged hair, and as Darcy closed his eyes, he felt it seeding inside him, the fact that one of the hands in his lap had gouged a knife into a Soviet general's eyes.

Ulli de Breffny placed her tea on the desk. Foreign Affairs got calls from your mother, she said.

The mention of his mother, the thought of her trying, had Darcy battling a new wave of tears.

Apparently, she was very upset, saying how you telephoned and told her you might disappear. She kept saying your name and then the name Sarfin.

Darcy looked up with a kind of glazed wonder. Do you know who Sarfin is? he asked.

An associate of Gorbachev, she said. He works inside the KGB, and outside. She knew all about him. She broke off the corner of a biscuit and held it out in the air.

Darcy closed his eyes tightly. His son, Aurelio, became my friend here, he said. He has disappeared. I think he might be dead. The general cut his face up, he said, as punishment.

Darcy could tell by the way she shifted against the desk that this was a thing she hadn't known. We're doing all we can, she said sincerely, but Darcy watched her, trying to gauge the scope of her authority—there was nothing she could do, not about Aurelio, not about Fin, and now the phone beside her was ringing. Ulli de Breffny glanced at her watch before she answered. She listened, not speaking, then she responded in measured Russian. The only word Darcy recognised was *Sarfin*. She replaced the receiver and went to a small window, looked down at the Lada. A man called Tugrul has been shot, she said. The Turkish Consul-General.

As she turned, Darcy peeled his collar to reveal the blood on his neck. I knew him, he said. I was there. He could feel himself rocking, wanting to confess before others arrived, but Ulli de Breffny didn't pick up her tea. She was thinking.

Did you really not know you smuggled a stolen document? she asked. You travelled with a time bomb.

Darcy's breath hung quietly in his lungs. No, he said. I didn't. Not then.

Do you know where the document might be now?

Darcy was silent and the woman's face softened. What do you want, Darcy Bright?

I want to go home, he said.

Then you should tell me, she said. And I will see what we can do.

Darcy found himself seeing, in a way he'd forgotten, a chasm of hope placed in the air like a next breath. He removed the damp plastic envelope from his pocket, watched Ulli de Breffny examine the telegram. She allowed an odd pursed mouth. One more thing, she said. Why is it you have the car? She waited, almost smiling, as if inviting him.

Darcy stared into his emptied cup. You said you could only help if I got myself here, he said, careful with each of the words. General Sarfin didn't kill me. He wanted me. He tried in Lubyanka. To rape me. He would have been raping me now.

Ulli de Breffny shifted along the desk, flattening her skirt. But you were in the house of the General Secretary's daughter.

He wanted me clean, said Darcy. That's what he said. He told me he'd split me in two. Darcy nodded, afraid he was telling too much. He's on the floor of Anyetta Chernenko's bathroom. I put a knife in his eye. Darcy didn't produce the gun but he pulled the stained knife from the velvety coat and placed it on the low table beside him. It's his car, he said.

Ulli de Breffny was clearly unsettled. She stood and, taking the folder and the evidence bag, left the room. Darcy could hear her on another phone, but the words were just murmurs and he had a sudden desire to wash himself now, see if he could stop the shivering, the noises in his head. He took off the coat, cautiously, as if the general still lurked in its folds, and removed the gun, the shining silver, unsure who lived or who died. He laid the coat hurriedly over the gun in his hand as Ulli de Breffny returned. We will need to get you out of Moscow, she said.

Darcy looked over at her pale lipstick, the intent in her eyes. She was more official now, laying out a possibility. You will need a passport, she said. And we will need to change your name. But we have to get you out before this becomes a major incident. The Soviets may suppress this but they will want you silenced. She went back to her window, stared down at the general's car. I don't understand how you are alive, she said.

Darcy looked down at the coat draped over his arm, covering the gun and the hand that had sliced up the face of Gorbachev's friend and touched Aurelio's cheek. He unveiled the pistol and stood, offered it to her, his palm splayed open, trembling.

Whose is it? she asked.

General Sarfin's, he said. It was used to shoot Consul Tugrul and Nikolai Chuprakov. And maybe Aurelio Sarfin.

And your hands have been all over it, she said. She held out a cloth napkin and Darcy slid the gun onto it as if performing some ritual exchange, the velvet coat still hanging over his forearm. She wrapped it in the napkin and weighed it in her palm. She seemed somehow impressed with him.

I want to ask you a personal question, she said gently. Why did you really come to Moscow?

Darcy thought of the urgent tone in Fin's voice when she called the first time, when she'd said she needed him here, a chance to be far from home, where he might avoid the new disease. He didn't know what winter meant then. He raised his eyes to respond, searched the face of this immaculate woman, looked at her as if he really knew. I came to see my sister, he said, and to paint. It had been true back then, mostly. The word *paint* seemed to resonate.

Ulli de Breffny turned and looked back out her window, the gun in one hand, the telegram in the other. Only in a world without evil are the naïve devoid of guilt, she said.

The Aeroflot 747 taxied. Darcy peered out nervously, past abandoned cranes like rusted mantises, old jets waiting for Lufthansa parts. The control tower thrust up through the earth like an ancient corrugated rocket. Almost as he'd envisioned it, yet not—the hum had fixed itself as a low note in his right ear, his hands were shaking, but he had a dressing on his neck and he'd showered, eaten, he was warm. He clutched his new blue passport and airline ticket, fearing still he'd not be allowed to leave the ground. He examined the passport, the coat of arms and a sober photo, pieces of Fin in his face. His new name was War-wick Rawson, it seemed obvious as a made-up name, a reinvention, but it wasn't Dobrolyubova. And it struck him now, deep in his core and his psyche, that he was leaving without her. He'd never known her, not really, and he'd never get to know Aurelio; there were only the pangs of longing and mistrust, a love that lay too close to destruction and a small colour photo, wrinkled now, of Aurelio as a boy.

Ulli de Breffny had held onto the telegram from Con-stantinople, the missive of death marches across Anatolia. *Whole villages of peasants herded into the sea.* Words that still felt like the truth. She told Darcy about a commis-sion on Armenia meeting in Geneva in June, assured him that she could arrange for delivery, and as the jet taxied to the runway, Darcy imagined the document traded for secrets, his brushes with history, and again he prayed for the moment the wheels would lift from the earth.

As the plane commenced its clatter down the runway, trembling in its overheads, Darcy held onto the seat arms and his ticket receipt shook in his lap. Aeroflot from Moscow to New Delhi, a Qantas connection through Singapore and back to Tullamarine. Twenty-nine hours, no evidence of any price or payment; the ticket and passport arranged overnight.

Ulli de Breffny had heard the general might end up blind in at least one eye and then she almost smiled. Armenians, she said, were found dead near their dacha, three shot and one found frozen. The woman, she heard, was fast and light, had tried to skim across the river ice but disappeared. Darcy sensed he was being humoured with the possibility, but all he felt was emptied. As Ulli de Breffny bade him goodbye, she assured him he'd be officially notified. She shook Darcy's unsteady hand and held it warmly, met his eyes. Our arms are wide, she said, and he wasn't sure if it was more than a form of embrace, if it clothed an invitation, or merely a warning that he'd be within their reach. He didn't ask whose arms they were, he was just grateful to be boarding a plane.

As the plane rattled up through steep slides of vertical mist, Darcy didn't search for a glimpse of the Kremlin, the gold-domed churches, or the oxbows of the river. They were all enshrouded in a caul of fog. The city enveloped itself in its greyness like the culture had, concealing itself from itself, just listening. He imagined his mother's frenetic telephone calls to Foreign Affairs, her barking whisky voice. Moisture streamed across the cold oval window and it reminded him of tears. That he'd left Australia without even telling her. He pressed his face against the icy glass and thought of the frosted window of the train that he'd come in on, the money belt against him. He'd never been truly innocent, not since the missionary and maybe not even then, and now he'd blinded a man who only deserved to live disfigured, but Darcy knew he'd also scarred himself.

Down to the right, a shelf of snow moved, an iceberg separating. It must have been a kilometre long, or perhaps it was just in the shifting of clouds, but he felt the fissure within him, the separation of past. He remembered the time he lay with Fin in the gully as a boy, looking up at the sun, and then he remembered Aurelio, only days ago, handsome, walking ahead through the snow to the dacha. He gazed out into the ballet of clouds as if there might be a song to be learned but the aftertaste felt bitter now. He felt changed, like a soldier returning from war to pretend things weren't all twisted, heading south and east to India, cloud mountains concealing the endless steppe.

Ulli de Breffny had bought him a pencil and sketch pad from the airport shop and now he felt the pencil in his hand, its CCCP insignia, the hands he'd scrubbed for twenty minutes. He didn't draw, he wrote: *What do you want now, Darcy Bright?*

He began carving shapes on the paper. He craved to feel pure again, like the juggling boy, to paint for the pleasure of others, not to skulk in parks and putrid places, not to use sex to medicate memories. For some reason, he thought about butterflies, making love without facing each other, but without agenda or intrigue. Fin once told him that butterflies carried the souls of the dead. He imagined her now, floating up on thistledown wings; but it had been far from butterfly season. His hands shook unevenly and he tried not to think of her dead in the snow, or Aurelio, or the general, a blade in his eye like some horrendous miracle.

He tried to find a new space in his mind, an opening. *I want to be able to love*, he wrote haltingly, *differently*. But a love of a kind unknown to him seemed far off, someone who might wake up at his side and speak of simple things, be honest. Darcy looked back out through the streaming rivulets, above the cloud reefs, where painterly light skipped along the crests of cirrus. The footprints of this winter would trudge deep around inside him, wake him up on summer nights, but he could no longer lose himself. He could return to the College of Fine Arts with a new name, paint in watercolours—he'd paint a fierce young woman, running across the river ice, a small girl alone on a gravel drive wearing an African print dress, a dark-eyed boy on the steps with his mother in Havana, a colourful dress of her own, a juggling boy, rare butterflies, dawn. He'd paint eyes full of blood. Outside, sky and earth joined as patterned wings, and Darcy felt hinged there between them, between a boundless, deathless infinity and the transient mortality below.

☆

With howling of a dog frost-bitten,
The moon will freeze on iron heels,
And stuffed like liar's jaws with lava
Of breathless ice each mouth congeals.

Boris Pasternak, from *Winter Skies*,
translated by Eugene M. Kayden

Acknowledgments

In the U.S., to Marion Rosenberg for reading and reading and for her unwavering support from day one. To my Los Angeles writing posse: particularly Janet Fitch, Rita Williams, Julianne Cohen, and Josh Miller for their ongoing input and guidance, and to Mark Sarvas for his friendship and literary know-how. To Jane Smiley for her encouragement, wisdom and humour, and to Les Plesko, who helped me find a voice. To Elaine Markson for embracing this book with such unflinching enthusiasm and to my friends at MacAdam/Cage—Julie Burton, Melanie Mitchell, Dorothy Smith and Scott Allen, as well as Kate Nitze and Khristina Wenzinger for their meticulous edit, and my profound appreciation to David Poindexter for his contagious commitment to literary fiction. Also, my sincerest gratitude to Don Hunt, Lisalee Wells and all the folks at Fulbright for their enduring support.

In France, to Madame Simone Brunau and the Cité International des Arts where this story first found its legs; to Penelope and Jobic Le Masson at the Red Wheelbarrow for a home away from home; to Marie Gaulis, George Walker Torres, Clayton Burkhart and Christel Paris for being there; and to Jenelle Sanna and Greg Simpson and their lovely house in Barbizon.

In Australia, to the legacy and indelible memory of my mother Judy, to my father Derry and to all who help on the farm at Tooradin, to my dear sister Sally and brother Peter, his wife Peta, and to Tristan, Josephine and Tim at Jeetho. To my aunt Margaret Street, Clare Gray and the burnished Hugo inspiration, and also to Jane Turner for her friendship and for inviting me to Moscow in 1984. My deep gratitude to the Literature Fund of the Australia Council and the Nancy Keesing Fellowship, to Jane Palfreyman at Allen & Unwin, who saw this book for what it might become, to Barbara Mobbs who wasn't afraid to represent it, and to Ali Lavau and Alexandra Nahlous for their loving and insightful edit.

Lastly, to my friend Caz Love for her counsel, spirit and art, and to James Hunter, Jean Wingis, Peter Paige, Jane Nunez, Marta Ross and all those who help me find my way—you know who you are.

About the Author

David Francis is an Australian lawyer and former international equestrian who lives in Los Angeles. He is the author of the acclaimed novel *The Great Inland Sea*, which was published in seven countries. David received the Australia Council Literature Fund Fellowship to the Cité Internationale des Arts in Paris in 2002.

11/08

Fines 10¢ Per Day